A Mile in
Her Shoes

From the same author:

An Hour Too Soon?
ISBN: 978 18487 63883
(Watch the book trailer online.)

For more information regarding the author please visit:
www.christophersantos.net

A Mile in Her Shoes

CHRISTOPHER SANTOS

Matador
9 Priory Business Park,
Wistow Road,
Kibworth Beauchamp
Leicester LE8 0RX, UK
Tel: (+44) 116 279 2299
Fax: (+44) 116 279 2277
Email: books@troubador.co.uk
Web: www.troubador.co.uk/matador

ISBN 978 1780880 563

British Library Cataloguing in Publication Data.
A catalogue record for this book is available from the British Library.

Typeset in 11pt Palatino by Troubador Publishing Ltd, Leicester, UK

Matador is an imprint of Troubador Publishing Ltd

Printed and bound in the UK by TJ International, Padstow, Cornwall

CHAPTER ONE

June 1998:

*T*hat Sunday morning there was just the one space left in the church car park. The driver of the white BMW had begun to reverse towards it when an orange Volkswagen Beetle clattered swiftly in to claim the space, a manoeuvre that was met with a blaring of the BMW's horn.

The driver of the Beetle got out and smiled victoriously to himself as he heard a woman's irate, middle-class voice exclaim:

"Manners maketh the man!"

Jack Fearnley locked his car door without replying.

Anna de Courtney was forced to park her BMW in a side street and now, later than usual, she walked purposefully towards the Narthex of Our Lady of Sorrows Catholic Church. On entering she nodded to one of the Brothers before instinctively moving to the metal display stand that she had erected for the charitable organisation LATE, of which she was Chairman. Anna pursed her lips disapprovingly as she saw some of the leaflets in disarray, and deftly rearranged them to her liking. Then, taking the church newsletter from the stand and with her missal and hymn book in her hand she glided forward to dabble her fingers in the Holy water, and with eyes and head lowered moved with stately grace up the centre aisle of the church.

Anna expected to sit in the same pew every Sunday. This morning, however, a frown creased her brow as she saw it was already occupied. She had to move one pew back and genuflected before stepping sideways to take her seat, knelt down on the leather hassock and recited her usual prayer. It was a moment of peace; she crossed herself before focusing her eyes upon the altar.

The candles there flickered as she sat back. Recently she had not been sleeping at all well. Unpleasant nightmares had invaded her mind and sometimes she was frightened to go to sleep, unsure of what hideousness the next dream would conjure up. Slowly she withdrew her mother's Rosary from the pocket of her navy blue silk jacket and her long, white, elegant fingers with their bright red-tipped nails fingered the beads. The congregation rose to sing the first hymn while the priest and servers walked down the centre aisle. The smell of incense hovered and the Mass commenced. Anna crossed herself again before bowing her head slightly to join in the murmuring of the Penitential Rite.

The words tumbled from her tongue. She steered her mind to dwell on all that she did for others. Was it recompense? Had she washed her soul clean? Would she ever? If only she could tell someone of the terrible secret that lurked in her memory, unburden herself. Perhaps that would make it easier – but who want to listen and, more importantly, whom could she trust?

Now she watched as Father Matthews raised his hands and bestowed the blessing. Was it only yesterday that she had made her usual Saturday morning visit to Confession? To kneel in the silence of the church. Allowing the Rosary to slip through her fingers.

Sometimes she would remember a line of the poem her mother used to recite:

"...*Each bead a thought, each thought a prayer...*" Anna had forgotten the rest of the words. The thought of what she should say in her Confession had started to worry her. There was so little she wished to say and yet so much she had done. Sin was such an ugly word, wasn't it? And what did it really mean? Had she sinned? She closed her eyes, not wishing to think of the answer.

She had talked in a vague way to Sister Joseph about the merits of the Confession. Sister had tried to be helpful and presented her with a small booklet. In it she learned that Confession usually amounted to no more than mentioning the uncharitable acts that even a good Christian couldn't avoid.

But Anna knew only too well what the ultimate sin was. She thought again of yesterday's visit to the confessional. She sat before Father Mathews in the small cramped room. It wasn't the confessional of old – it now resembled more of a counselling session. She would recite her diluted shopping list of faults and inadequacies. Again she failed to recall the one event that was constantly on her mind.

She ran her tongue lightly over her lips, her attention drawn to the occupants in the pew in front; it looked to her like a mother and daughter. She turned away, wanting to ignore them as Anna heard the choir sing the Gloria so joyously. Her voice swelled to join in the words. Inexplicably, her attention was drawn again to the occupants in the pew in front. One carefully dressed upright female, with glasses beneath fringed dark hair who would occasionally turn and smile down at the frail figure, with the stoop of old age, in a flowery patterned dress and white cardigan. Anna saw the wispy white hair and the care-worn hand that shakily held the missal. Why did they have to sit in front of her, she thought petulantly. Anna felt a moment of tension and then her voice swelled again to join in the words the choir sang.

Involuntarily her eyes travelled again to the occupants as she heard the old lady's missal drop to the floor, despite its slight weight it seemed too much for the feeble hands. The companion gently retrieved it and then placed an arm beneath the cardigan elbow. Anna heard the concern in the whispered question from the younger woman:

"Are you all right, mother?"

An affirmative nod of the white head.

Anna closed her eyes; she did not wish to listen to them and fixed her eyes on the priest. Her mind was unable to concentrate; it resembled a leaf blowing in the wind.

They sat after the Gospel and then, during the Homily, Anna thought of the unexpectedly hot June they had experienced. The long days of sun had not helped the garden. It had not been mowed since the gardener had been taken ill during the middle of May. It now needed a great deal of attention: the edges trimmed, and more plants put in. Perhaps she should attempt some gardening? Apparently it was therapeutic! But there was never any time. No, that was wrong, she did have the time, but she surreptitiously glanced down at her well manicured hands; gardening would mean broken nails and dirt. No, it was not for her! Suddenly her thoughts were shattered by the noise of another book dropping; she turned round, irritated, and recognised the bad mannered young man who had stolen her car park space sitting across the aisle.

Jack Fearnley was taken aback by the sternest of stares from the beautiful woman who was now frowning at the disturbance of her peace. He felt his heart jump: he knew in a blinding flash that she was the most sexually appealing woman he had ever seen.

He swallowed and managed to raise his eyebrows, half-apologetic and half-mocking, as he gave a faint smile. He saw her frown deepen and then an eyebrow rose ever so slightly as she caught her lower lip between her teeth. He was mesmerised as her eyes met his, ever so briefly – but in that second his world stood still. His heart thumped as he sat transfixed by her long black eye lashes and the high-winged raven brows. Her carefully made-up face and the luxurious long hair. And her clothes: an expensive blue jacket, a long white summer pleated pattern skirt and blue, open toed, high-heeled shoes. For the woman across the aisle suddenly evoked all Jack's secret fantasies, in which an unobtainable, sophisticated, older woman would look at him and their eyes would fuse in a flare of immediate intimacy. He would dare to attempt the beginning of a smile. Her eyes would hold a secret message and her mouth would stretch, as if against her will, into a smile; a faint smile, but a smile redolent with promise.

Jack turned away and lowered his eyes, as he accepted an inner conviction that he had known her, seen her in his dreams. She had been next to him in his bed. He cast a surreptitious glance; yes, she is quite beautiful, he thought. Her eyes averted from his and returned to her missal. He stared at her for a moment longer, unable to pull his eyes away.

In that instant he knew what all the poets had been saying throughout the ages. 'The fleeting glance that made instant wanting'; he felt his heart thumping against his chest. He knew now how Romeo must have felt when he first saw Juliet. Jack drew his brows together and tried to gather his scattered thoughts as the words of the Homily were said to his unresponsive ears. His large frame could barely sit comfortably within the restrictions of the pew. He rested his boots on the kneeler, conscious that they looked well-worn. They reminded him of his days of freedom. They looked scruffy now. Perhaps he too looked scruffy: his jeans were clean but well worn, as was his denim shirt. At twenty-five he was good-looking, with thick dark hair long enough to rest on the collar of his shirt – but brushed back at the side to reveal one gold earring – sideburns, and a straggly moustache and beard. He clasped his hands loosely over his knees and stared at the altar. Once, long ago, he had been an altar boy, swinging the incense or holding the books.

5

It had been quite some time since he had been to Mass; when he'd left home for University he had also left his church-going days. He had returned spasmodically to the church when he moved in to live with his girlfriend, twenty-three year old Mary. Then suddenly their relationship started to get serious and there was the mention of marriage.

He yawned, and wished he could stretch out his legs. In a few months hence his life would change forever. He was going to settle down, his wandering and lusting days would finally be drawn to a close. Mary. He smiled inwardly as he saw her now in his mind's eye. But his gaze was drawn again to the woman across the aisle and his mind did somersaults as his imagination set her into his fantasy.

Jack vaguely heard the words of the Homily, but his mind drifted back to his future. Was marriage coming too soon? Did he want to enter the all-absorbing world of commerce? Sometimes he wondered if accountancy was the career for him. His period of work experience in a city accountancy office had proved one of the most boring times of his life.

He heard the Sanctus Bell and joined the congregation to stand. He'd done well to keep single for so long and even better not to get a girl pregnant! Mary was someone every mother would want for a daughter-in-law and he was looking forward to being married to her. No doubt he would become respectable and ambitious. How tedious and dull it all sounded!

He'd had his brief moment of freedom: a year off at the end of his degree course. It had, he admitted, changed his perceptions on life. It had been Mary, who, after he had made one of his flip remarks, had goaded him into it. It had been a sobering six months. The orphanage in Romania where every child fought for life. Shell-shocked children scrabbling amongst the debris, not only of their homes, but of their lives. It had all filled him with a sense of guilt at the money he had wasted on luxuries, money that would have kept those people from starving. He remembered a girl, aged fifteen or sixteen, thin, with matchstick legs and burning eyes in a skull-like face. Her hand outstretched for food. The young priest saying Mass in a burnt out church to a congregation who miraculously still believed. It had made him realise the value of life. He had gone out a boy and returned a man with a secret that he was not keen on sharing.

Mary had accepted that there had been a wild streak in him. She felt she had now tamed it. He had never got into the drugs scene, never even felt a temptation to puff on a cannabis weed, nor to snort some white powder that would give you brilliant dreams but at the same time rot the inside of your nose, not to mention your brain. No, he was beer man, worried only about the beer-gut that had yet to materialise.

The Mass continued. He looked again at the woman across the aisle. Confused by his lustful thoughts, he gave her another small, sideways glance, but she did not reciprocate.

She was not young, that was true enough!

He saw her hands clasped as they stood to sing the Lord's Prayer. She had long, white slender fingers with rose-tipped nails; he made himself imagine these same fingers running through his hair and over his body.

He surveyed her as she stood singing with fervour. She had a good figure, a classic profile.

How old, forty?

Alone?

Divorced?

Maybe even single?

Never!

As if conscious of his scrutiny she turned briefly and met his eyes again. Surely she was not embarrassed? But she was! The congregation were offering each other the sign of peace. He had forgotten this handshaking bit.

"Peace be with you!" He turned and shook hands with those behind. And then on impulse he took what seemed a long step across the aisle and held his hand out to her. She turned with a startled expression in her eyes. "Peace be with you," he mumbled, drawing his mouth back into a crooked half smile that furrowed his cheek.

She raised her eyes once more to meet his; they were serious but they did not linger long as the eyelids blotted out the windows to her soul. Her mouth relaxed into the beginning of a smile as she murmured reluctantly, "…And with you." Her voice was light and her fingers warm and tender as they touched his.

It was there, the fantasy, an instantaneous magic. He saw her draw her tongue over her lips, but she would not meet his eyes. For a brief moment he felt an affinity, a need. No, a longing, just to know this woman, and to know her intimately. He was overcome by this immediate imagined contact, despite its brevity. He could not explain the acute sensation, or put it into rational thought. Quite simply: if this woman asked he would give up everything to be with her.

He suddenly realised he was still holding her hand and felt her tug it away. He returned to his pew. Had she felt the emotion of the moment? he wondered. His heart was racing and he felt the sweat now on the palms of his hands. He brushed a finger across his moustache as he watched the priest break the host.

Slowly, as if drawn by an invisible string, he turned his head to see her face. It was serious and intent. He knew she was beautiful and he wondered what she would look like if the long black hair now drawn back into a long plait were allowed its freedom. In his dreams she had long black hair that covered them both when they made love. He bowed his head. He was engaged! Thoughts of another woman had to be cast aside, and yet he could not help but turn his face again to observe her. She was not one of the silly, giggly girls he had known; she was not even like Mary. He breathed in – an older woman! He would have to make love to his fantasy woman before he got married. Obsession, the image, had been in his mind a long time, and now across the aisle was reality. He gave her another sideways glance. Was she a bored married woman? This was ridiculous; he tried to bring his thoughts back to prayers, to God and the reason he was here.

But he couldn't.

The last hymn, and he watched the procession move slowly back down the aisle and then he knelt for the final prayer as he waited for her to leave. She seemed to pray for a long time and his knees started to ache in the confined space. Finally, she rose and he watched her genuflect as she left her pew; he waited a few seconds before he too got up, seeing he was almost the last to leave. He hovered, and on impulse went and lit a candle and dropped a one pound coin in the metal collection tin. Then he walked out, putting his fingertips into the Holy water where a minute ago she had dabbled hers. He saw her smile and nod to people as she walked out and the sunlight caught her outline and he gasped again at her beauty.

Father Mathews, a small squat priest with a balding head was shaking hands with members of his congregation. His open toed sandals covering sock-covered feet contrasted with the opulence of his vestments. Jack watched as the Father greeted his mysterious woman effulgently as they stood outside the Narthex whilst he hovered pretending to read the notices.

The sunlight made her shade her eyes with a hand as she talked. A faint breeze wafted strands of her long hair across her face and then she laughed as he too moved out into the sunshine, casually hovering until Father Mathews glanced to beckon him to join them.

"Jack!"

He ambled across. "Good morning, Father," he said laconically.

"It is nice to see you back at Mass." There was a faint note of censure in the priest's voice, but the blue eyes were kind.

"Sorry, Father!" Words of old as he shrugged his shoulders, conscious that she too was standing silently witnessing, and he half-turned to acknowledge her presence. He could sense her knowingly near. Did she feel it too? He was never tongue-tied and prided himself that he had a silver voice that that could cajole, flatter and win any woman.

"Jack, let me introduce you to Mrs Anna de Courtney." There was an obsequious note in the voice. Jack straightened his shoulders and let his eyes meet hers. The laughter had gone and had been replaced with an intent, serious expression as his hand took hers. This time the handshake was firm and brief and he inclined his head in a mock bow.

"Mrs de Courtney," he acknowledged.

"Ah, the ill mannered young man who took my parking space!" she replied haughtily.

He felt his confidence ebb away and she continued in an accent that Jack could only describe as snobbish.

"And also the source of the noise across the aisle." Her eyes swiftly sped over his untidy appearance.

He wished he could reply, and the beautiful Mrs de Courtney, but that was in his dreams, now he could only mutter as he met her cold stare.

"I'm sorry for the all the noise, I'm too tall for those pews!" he continued.

There was a pause; she raised her eyebrows a fraction, almost provocatively, but not quite. Then he felt her hostility, her coldness and was momentarily chilled by the disdainful glance she now threw in his direction as she continued, determined now to have the final word.

"One doesn't normally cross the aisle to extol the virtue of Peace!"

He felt his lips move into an uncontrollable grin.

"Depends what you cross the aisle for, Ma'am."

A faint look of embarrassment swept over her face. She chose to ignore the remark and opened her handbag to retrieve her sunglasses and place them on her nose, to shade her eyes more from his inquisitive stare than from the sun.

"...And Jack is going to be married in...?" Father Mathews interjected, unaware of the change in the atmosphere as he smiled once more in Jack's direction.

"A few months, Father," Jack replied, annoyed that his personal business had been mentioned.

"So you have the summer to prepare... and how is Mary?"

"Enjoying her last moments of freedom!"

They were suddenly conscious of Mrs de Courtney moving away and Father Mathews held his hand out and took her arm.

"Well now, Jack, you may be able to help Mrs de Courtney," Father Mathews continued briskly, "She is in need of a gardener... I'd say urgently in need of a gardener." Father Mathews clasped his hands together and looked from one to the other.

Suddenly Jack felt an urge to laugh; it was a need he could supply. Then he coughed, aware of her disapproval at the priest's interference. He felt her withdrawal like a curtain distancing her from the conversation. He knew then she was a private person, self-contained and that added to the challenge. Father Mathews seemed oblivious or he chose to ignore her disapproval as he continued.

"I know you are doing gardening work this summer. Mrs de Courtney may be interested in your services. He did help clear the grass round the graves last year. He may even help this year, eh, Jack?" he smiled.

Jack nodded.

"Good, good; and now, Anna, I'll leave you to see how you can make use of this young man's services."

Jack smiled at the incongruous comment from the priest and watched as the Father nodded and moved across to another group.

There was an awkward pause as Jack and Anna stood staring at each other. Instinctively Jack knew she had not taken to him. Well, he thought, I'll not make it easy for her. He rubbed his hand across his moustache, wishing she would act as he imagined a beautiful woman with a beautiful name would act. It was there, he felt it, a hidden sensuality that she was used to keeping well masked. He saw the faint but distant and slightly superior smile on her lips. The intrigue of a perfume that lingered, a challenge from a beautiful woman to be noticed. Yet why didn't this woman start to lighten up? Her face was serious and her body language very defensive.

"So you need a gardener?" He put the question to her without interest. "Give me a try!" He gave her an engaging grin and he could see from the flash of annoyance in her eyes that his innuendo was not lost on her. But there was no response as he continued. "I'm honest, Father has at least vouched for that."

"Mmmm," there was doubt in her voice, as she surveyed him from behind her dark shades. He wasn't really what she wished for in a gardener. She envisaged an older man, someone who looked as you expected a gardener to look, experienced and servile. She couldn't imagine this young man taking orders or being servile. But she had to admit gardeners were hard to get, and one who came recommended by the priest was surely acceptable.

He saw the hesitation in her eyes, and felt like saying *piss off* but he couldn't, he wanted to get to know her. This was a challenge. The conquest of Mrs de Courtney? It sounded like a film. He waited patiently, unsmiling but attentive, until eventually she said.

"You say you have some experience?"

"Graves!" he laughed but there was no returning laugh and he felt sorry for her, so uptight and determined to be correct. He continued, "Yes, I've a fair knowledge of gardening and what's required."

"Well," she said with reluctance, "I will give it some thought. You have a phone number where I can contact you?" He frowned.

"Write your name and phone number down, and I may call you."

Jack wrote his phone number down on the piece of paper she had offered him, murmuring, "I do get booked up." He handed her the paper, taking in exchange the neatly printed visiting card she gave him.

"Let me walk you to your car," he said and she hesitated for a moment, then started to walk slowly out of the car park, her high heeled shoes making a crisp clicking sound beside him.

"Where are you parked?" he asked.

"I should have been where your car is," she said in a matter of fact tone.

"I'm sorry I took your space," he said apologetically. "If I'd realised the car belonged to you I'd have let you have it…" He hoped he sounded contrite.

Anna turned sharply and he knew from her expression she did not know how to deal with his light hearted compliment and chose to ignore the apology.

They approached the white upmarket BMW. It bore, he noticed, a quite distinctive registration number. Then he saw her take out her remote control and heard the thud as the doors unlocked automatically. She moved towards the driver's door. He quickened his pace and placed a hand on the door handle to open it for her as she approached; she got in with an elegance few women could have bettered.

He waited until she was seated before saying, "Safe journey!"

He paused for a reply before closing the door but Mrs de Courtney barely smiled, acknowledging his subtle innuendo, but saying nothing.

He stood quite still and watched closely as she drove away.

CHAPTER TWO

*J*ack pushed open the gate and walked down the path to the green front door of the small semi-detached house he shared with his mother and sister. He glanced up at the flaking paint on the window frames and knew that before the wedding he was going to have to give it all a quick repaint. He had a self satisfied smile on his face as he strutted into the small narrow hallway, past the thread-bare carpeted stairs, the crucifix on the wall and the rack of coats that led straight into the back kitchen. He saw his mother, Rose, plump and homely, dressed in her usual baggy slacks and overshirt, prematurely grey hair pushed back from her flushed face, eyes peering through large spectacles. Rose stood in front of the open oven, basting the leg of lamb for their Sunday lunch. Since his father had died three years previously it had been a ritual to have her brother George, a widower, round every Sunday.

Jack nodded to his mother and sister, who were immersed in the preparation of the meal. He wanted no part in it – cooking was for women – and smiled, knowing that Mary would not approve of his sexist outlook. He picked up the *News of the World* , went to the fridge to fetch out two cans of lager and took them into the small dining room. He edged his way through the clutter of self-assembly furniture to throw himself on to the comfortable, worn out old sofa.

"You look pleased with yourself," George, a thin gaunt man, a retired railway worker whose wife's death had left him embittered, gave a cursory glance at Jack from over the top of the free local newspaper. Jack thumped the can of lager on the table beside him and sat down, ripping the ring-pull and taking a long gulp from the can before he too picked up the paper and turned to the sports page.

"Put those papers down," Rose said crossly as she and Becky, Jack's attractive nineteen year old sister, came into the room carrying two plates of meat, potatoes and vegetables.

Becky was a slim girl with short blonde hair, who worked in the local library. She had an engaging people watching personality so she missed nothing. Becky had never looked for the high life: a small house, a loyal husband and two children would suit her fine. She had taken the death of her father especially hard, but had immersed herself in domestic matters: a hard worker and loyal to the family, Becky would take great pleasure in winding Jack up for she was of the opinion that he took parts of his life too seriously and his attention would more often than not become fixated on a particular subject – until he got tired of it. *A typical male* is how Becky would often affectionately refer to her brother.

Reluctantly Jack folded the paper as he and George exchanged comments on the current state of English football, with some sensible interruptions from Becky.

"Can't you talk of anything else?" Rose snapped. "I spend all morning preparing a meal…"

"Sorry, Mum," Jack grinned and then said, casually, "I have been offered some gardening work." He looked up at his sister. "Someone by the name of Mrs de Courtney!" he said smugly.

Becky took the card from him and scrutinised it. "So?"

"She's soooo beautiful!" said Jack with a careless shrug.

"Who's beautiful?" George glanced up.

"This woman Jack's met... he never changes... poor Mary!" Becky replied.

"What do you mean, poor Mary?" Jack said, "she's nothing to fear... I'm marrying her aren't I?"

"This Anna de Courtney, you know she's a Magistrate – and married as well!" Becky raised her eyebrows, "You working for a Magistrate, what next?" she threw her head back and laughed.

Jack reached forward and grabbed the card. "So what if she's a Magistrate?" he muttered defensively.

"You going to tell Mary?" Becky goaded him.

Jack ignored the remark.

"When do you start then?" George asked.

"She's going to phone me," Jack enthused; he sat down at the table and took a long drink from his can.

"I bet she doesn't!" Becky interjected.

"What's this then?" Rose asked, entering the room with two more plates and a jug of gravy. "Here, take these before I spill something." She sat down, reached for the mint sauce and splashed some over the slices of lamb on her plate.

"Jack's going to do some gardening for the beautiful Mrs de Courtney, that's Mrs de Courtney, JP!" George said as he stuffed a large quantity of food into his mouth so gravy dribbled down his chin.

"Her name's Anna, once you've been introduced," Jack replied.

"Mrs Anna de Courtney?" Rose's voice was sharp. "Not the Chairman of LATE?"

Jack shrugged, "Could be!"

"Let's see it," Rose gesticulated for the card to be passed to her and peered at the printed name. "Oh that's her all right. She's got long black hair?"

"Oh and she's be-you-tiffle!" Becky said, with more than a hint of sarcasm.

"Yes, she is," Jack said defensively, "she's slim, thirties perhaps!" he said as he shook the pepper pot over his meal.

There was a loud laugh as Rose said, "Oh yes that's her, very well dressed and well known in the voluntary field… a real committee go-getter. But she's never thirty."

"Why are women so bitchy about age?" George asked without looking up from his plate.

"Perhaps because we're not taken in with a pretty face and a slim waistline…" Rose snapped as she piled another dollop of mashed potatoes onto George's emptying plate.

"So you know her?" Jack said, interest in his eyes.

"Of course I know her," Rose managed to say between mouthfuls of food. "I am one of her volunteers. I help at the day club. Anna de Courtney is our exalted Chairman. She's…" Rose paused and bit her lip, conscious that Jack was hanging on to her every word. "Well, she's very pleased with herself," and then, as an after-thought, "She seems dedicated enough."

"Well it's good that someone cares…" Jack frowned. "Too many people don't these days."

"Oh, her services come…" Rose paused with a confident smile, "…at a price!"

"Meaning?" Becky cut in.

"Well," and it was clear Rose intended to relish what she was about to disclose. "I heard that when the printers of the new office letterheads had missed the JP off her name she had the entire stock scrapped and re-ordered. Now, what do you make of that?" She gave a significant sniff and sat back.

"She sounds very small minded," Becky purred.

Jack worked steadily through his dinner.

Anna placed her missal on the hall table and stood listening to the silence, realising how quiet the house was.

She stood in the hall, her ears pricked, but she knew there would be no sound. Her eyes moved in the direction of the dark recess at the far end of the hall, beyond which lay the room. Now the solid oak door shut out all light, for it was rarely left open. The room and its despicable secret remained hidden.

Sometimes she would see her pedigree British Shorthair cat called Hector sitting in the hall gazing at the door as if he could see the events beyond it – but he would never venture into the room, even when the cleaning ladies had accidentally left it open.

Now as if drawn against her will, Anna found herself walking slowly to the door. Gently she turned the ever present key in the lock; it moved back noiselessly. She eased the knob and slowly pushed open the door.

The room was in semi-darkness, illuminated only by a thin shaft of light escaping from a gap in the curtains. Anna felt her heart beating as she edged her way to stand beside the bed. Her fingers trailed over the quilted cover, then up to the pillow. She stood staring down as her mind played its old tricks again with her memory.

Her eyes glanced up to the crucifix over the bed, illuminated by the thin crack of sunlight. The agony and suffering of the white figure with the blood dripping from the nails and the crown of thorns seemed suddenly more poignant. She shuddered, turned away and walked across to open another door. The white tiles of the shower shone back into the room. Nothing had changed, but then why should it?

Closing the shower room door Anna turned and stood in the centre of the room. Despite the heat of the day the room was chill. She saw the chest of drawers, the wardrobe, the pictures and on the bedside table the well-worn missal. Many thoughts entered her mind. Thoughts that she did not wish to remember. Unwanted images crept insidiously into her consciousness. She had known it all along. She had committed a crime against all her beliefs. A crime that could send her spiralling down into

Hell. Such a crime that mere Confession could never wash the muddy stains from her soul. Stains that would besmirch her for ever.

Those final days of agonising torture of what to do. The unthinkable dilemma in the middle of which she had found herself. To carry on as before, with all the disruption and emotional hurt inflicted on both of them – or to put an end to it – once and for all. Her father had come into her thoughts many times over that week. What would he have done in the face of such a heart-breaking decision? Could he have coped? Would he have coped? How could he have coped? Silly questions. So few answers.

Anna's family had been closeted away from the everyday occurrences; when the children came home from school and her husband Charles from work all they saw was a neat, tidy house, a mother and wife who was in control, perfectly dressed and ready to listen and discuss all their problems. The dinner always ready to be served. Only the daily nurse and Anna knew what really happened during the day. The nurse, Helen, was a tower of strength but even that, in the end, had not been enough.

Their last day together had seen Anna sitting on the bed and talking and talking and talking until she could talk no more. There was not one word or response from the silent figure. Anna had related their life together, the memories, the holidays, the disappointments. Their roles were now reversed; Anna was the talker and occupier of the bed was the child. A child who fidgeted with the bed clothes and who had a limited attention span. Tears made their familiar journey down Anna's face whilst her mother lay impassively as school friends, birthday parties and Christmases were all related in agonising detail.

The family had been away that day: Charles and Steven at some rugby match in Edinburgh and Kate spending a weekend with friends in Southampton. Had it been subconsciously planned?

The events of Saturday, the 12th of April, 1997, would remain with Anna until she died. It would be a secret she would have to take with her to the grave. She had made a vow to herself that she would never tell a soul what had gone on in that room.

It was six o'clock in the morning when she had left her bedroom and walked down the stairs to stand in the hallway. Every footstep seemed to take longer than usual. Like a thief in the night Anna crept into the room. A room that once had been light and airy; her mother's sewing room of years long gone. Now as she opened the door the familiar overpowering stench of urine greeted her. No matter how many times the room was cleaned and disinfected, the smell lingered.

The room was lit by a small low-voltage light. The figure in the bed was gently snoring. With tears in her eyes and her whole body shaking Anna walked across to the small table, picked up her mother's rosary and placed it beside the pillow.

"Oh Mum," she said, "I always thought I would cope, but I can't any longer." Anna moved to the corner chair and picked up the spare pillow. Now, standing over the bed, she stared down at the shrivelled mask of a face, the hair white and the eyes closed. This time the figure was quiescent; it no longer reminded Anna of a trapped animal. Moments of doubt assailed her. She went to place the pillow back on the chair. She doubted her ability to cope with the situation. How could she bring herself to carry out her private promise? With her face white and sweat gathering on her brow, Anna turned once more to the frail figure in the bed. Was this really her mother? No! It was a shell, a dirty, moaning, stinking shell. Her mother's spirit had gone, flown back to its maker. Anna had been left to care for what remained, on her own.

With tears streaming down her face, and her whole body

convulsing with fear, she burbled in between mouthfuls of air;
"Please forgive me, Mum."

Anna had not noticed Hector sitting in the doorway, his
orange eyes faithfully following Anna's every move. With the
pillow firmly in her hand she placed it silently over the
breathing face. There was an immediate reaction. The figure
tensed and the thin white pathetic hands fluttered momentarily
like a trapped bird. Then, quite soon, they ceased. All became
quiet again.

Anna stared aghast at the still form. To her surprise there
had been no real sound, no protest, no fight-back. It was only
then did Anna realise how loose a grip her mother had had on
life. Ten seconds was all it had taken. Ten seconds to wipe out
ninety years of living. Ten seconds to kill her mother.

Anna turned slowly to see Hector whose eyes were now
glancing beyond her towards the window, as if he saw
something she could not. Her heart jumped as she spun round
to see what – or who – it was. She froze, her heart beating
nineteen to the dozen. But all was still. There was nothing to
see. And gradually her pulse steadied. Only after she had
waited anxiously for several minutes did she relax.

Surreptitiously she wiped a tear from her eye. Even now,
over a year later, the memory would haunt her and she would
often ask herself whether she had done enough when her
mother had been alive. Had she treated her with the respect she
had deserved? Anna knew the answer to that only too well.

Anna closed her mind to all these unwanted thoughts and
remembered the absurdity of the morning's Mass. She could
see his face surreptitiously glancing in her direction and then
the touch of his hand that had held hers for a little too long in
the Peace. His sudden youthful diffidence at their meeting with
Father Mathews when he could not meet her eyes. Did that
gardener really think a small spark existed? Did he know that
behind this beautifully made up facade was a soul crumbling

away on its foundations? Secrets. Everybody had them, didn't they?

Closing the door to her mother's room and walking towards the kitchen she now realised that, whatever she thought of Jack Fearnley, the house did need a gardener. Perhaps she should have engaged him there and then instead of her usual prevarication. Yes, she would telephone Jack and arrange for him to come tomorrow afternoon.

Only now, when she felt shivers running through her body, did Anna wish that her family were not away. She wanted to cook them all Sunday dinner.

Once, years ago, Anna had complained about Sunday dinner: so much preparation for such a quick meal. That was long ago when they were a family sitting round the table. Her husband, Charles, carving, and Steven and Kate and of course her mother.

She heard the faint meow and felt the silky fur rubbing against her ankle.

"Oh Hector!" she bent down to pick up the cat. "Are you hungry?" she buried her face into the soft grey fur and the deep orange eyes stared unblinkingly at her as a contented purr rumbled on.

"Come on." She placed Hector down on the kitchen floor and picked up his bowl and filled it with his favourite food. He followed her into the utility room, tail up high.

Then on to the patio to place food outside Seth's kennel, to pat him and watch as the dog's tail swept back and forth. Finally she sat in the conservatory. She fumbled with the *Sunday Times*, but found herself unable to read, her mind mish-mashing through that extraordinary encounter with Jack Fearnley.

Did she really want him as a gardener? she asked herself again.

Anna glanced out to the garden. Sometimes, in the summer,

she would invite committee friends round and would do a croquet evening on the lawn. But the garden usually reminded her of her mother. She knew how proud her mother had been at the large, beautifully kept lawns and the immaculately laid out flower beds. And of course when she was growing up; the garden was her safe haven, with her mother's watchful eyes not far away.

Anna brought her thoughts back to the present. Sometimes, if it was very hot, she and Charles would invite friends to bring their swimsuits round and they would use the pool. Friends: well, they had no real friends, only business acquaintances and some of the voluntary workers. She put her paper down, realising it was over a year since she'd given a party.

The grass was looking dry, but she didn't wish for rain, not yet. She got up and walked through to the sitting room and on into the hall, then on impulse into the study. It had been her father's favourite room and now it was Charles's. They had not changed it since her father died. She went across to the solid desk, running her fingers over the worn leather swivel chair before sitting in it, and swinging round to see the bookcases full of his books. The room reeked of his maleness, but that was an irony. Oh, they were all the right sorts of books, leather bound volumes bought for effect, as were the three original oil paintings of race horses.

She put the glasses that hung round her neck on the end of her nose as she glanced down to the written notes that she prepared each week. Her list of things to be done: sometimes accomplished other times only half done.

She picked up the phone and, taking the piece of paper from her pocket, dialled Jack's number. She waited impatiently as the phone rang on and on until finally a female's voice answered, asking her to 'hold on'. Anna heard voices yelling in the background and wondered why people in small houses always seemed to have to shout. When Jack finally picked up the receiver her voice was, she knew, slightly brusque as she asked him to come round the following afternoon.

That Monday morning Anna dressed and made up with care; she felt it was important as a Magistrate to be seen to be playing the role. Now she drove confidently to the Civic Hall in a neighbouring town. She had had to give serious consideration to whether she should accept the invitation to the talk: the irony of the subject matter was not lost on her. But as Chairman of LATE, a position she told people she took very seriously, it seemed incumbent upon her to accept.

Anna parked her car just outside the hall and meticulously placed her anti-theft device across the steering wheel. Then with a swift, subtle glance in the vanity mirror she alighted, straightened her skirt and adjusted the LATE identification badge which she always wore on such occasions. Then she walked purposefully across the car park and up the concrete steps to the entrance.

As she paused by the desk to register and collect her name tag she had a good look round to see who else was there, and was able to nod and smile to a number of known faces. Then she walked half-way down the centre aisle and chose a seat mid-way along the row.

Doctor Patricia Ray, the Chairman for the discussion, was a stout middle-aged woman with mottled grey hair and a rusty, outdoor complexion. Dressed in a tight sleeveless blouse and an unsuitable summer skirt, she stood gazing down from the platform to the audience below, rubbing her hands together in a nervous gesture. Having taken a last look at the clock she banged on the table with the side of her fist. Eventually the noise subsided.

"It is pleasing to see so many of you here," Doctor Ray beamed sweetly round the hall. She continued: "Today we are having a talk about two aspects of getting old. Both controversial, neither pleasant. But sadly both exist." The Doctor paused and coughed and then, as if frightened of the words, mumbled them quickly: "*Euthanasia*...is the subject of our talk this morning and we will try and cover all aspects." She stopped again and turned to hold a hand out to indicate the lady sitting beside her. "So please will you welcome Mrs Jane Compton, from NAG, the National Ageing Group. Mrs Compton has an insight into the problems we are all going to face as we grow old in today's society, and the problems of those who care for the elderly. As well as her busy life as Chairman of NAG, she is the wife of a gynaecologist and the mother of four children; she is also a carer who looks after her own mother, who sadly suffers from dementia."

The Doctor paused and smiled round the audience. "Mrs Compton."

There was enthusiastic clapping as a willowy figure dressed conservatively in a well-cut and obviously expensive lightweight trouser suit stood up to replace the Chairman.

There was a faint murmur from the body of the hall as Mrs Compton walked confidently to the table and placed a slim black briefcase down before snapping open the clasps. She then withdrew her notes, neatly hand-written on lined paper and arranged them methodically in front of her before taking off her wrist watch. Anna gave a sigh of relief, knowing the speaker was accomplished and would speak to a set time. Anna had long since realised that most people have a limited capacity for absorbing information. Mrs Compton smiled down at the upturned faces as she slowly adjusted the microphone to suit her height.

"Thank you, Doctor Ray, for your introduction.," Her left hand adjusted her spectacles before she continued. "I am Chairman of NAG, an organisation that is concerned with ageing and the elderly, their needs and the needs of those who care for them. We will all, God willing, grow old healthily. I am sure we all pray that we will have our faculties, because if we do not, and if we should become burdensome, we may well be... *put down*..." She held her hand up at the dissension in the hall. "Sounds dreadful, doesn't it? Is there a nicer way of saying it?" She reached forward and picked up a glass of water and took a quick sip. "I am particularly concerned about the ever growing idea that we are slowly being conditioned into dismissing the life of the aged, the infirm and handicapped as having *no value*. Euthanasia, like abortion, is the taking of a life that is not ours to take. There are, of course, many who do not hold with the Christian ethics, but for those of us who do, we have to learn to accept our own suffering and the suffering of our loved ones. *We cannot, must not and should not play God.*"

Mrs Compton spoke authoritatively, barely glancing at her notes, her voice clear and her words concise.

Anna listened to the words flowing so competently. The destruction of life, abortion and euthanasia, these had all once been causes dear to her own heart. At the end of forty minutes Mrs Compton glanced at the clock. "I think I we have had enough for today on this particular topic. I understand that we will now have a coffee break: please return in twenty minutes, when I will outline the frightening topic of abuse of the elderly. In twenty minutes, then; thank you."

"You are always so convincing," said Doctor Ray as she rose slowly from the table. "I wonder if there are any circumstances that might change attitudes?" she mused quietly.

"Convictions are convictions," Mrs Compton said brusquely as she gathered her notes together before taking a folder from her briefcase and placing them inside. As she snapped the lid shut she sighed. "I hope I covered everything." A frown furrowed her brow as she took her spectacles off and blinked as she allowed them to dangle round her neck from a gold chain.

Doctor Ray accompanied Mrs Compton down the steps

from the platform and along the aisle to where morning coffee was being served.

"Anna," Doctor Ray called, "Do come and meet Mrs Compton." She gave a gushing smile as Anna approached.

"Anna chairs LATE, a similar organisation to NAG." Patricia smiled from one to the other. "All concerned with the elderly. Your mother suffered from dementia, didn't she Anna?"

Anna ran a tongue over her lips and managed a bleak nod. It was still difficult for her to accept that outsiders knew of her mother's condition for she had once been such a well known and respected member of the local community, had given many coffee mornings to raise money for charity and was always on hand to help people in need. It was distressing to think of this once strong woman wilting away in the prison of her mind. "Yes, it is not easy for the sufferers of those who watch them."

"Perhaps our organisations are really a safeguard for our own old age," Mrs Compton said, holding out her hand. "Your mother died peacefully, I hope?"

Anna gritted her teeth and forced out the lie as naturally as she could. "Thankfully, yes." She helped herself to a *Rich Tea* biscuit. "It was a most interesting talk."

"I've heard a great deal about LATE and the effortless work you all do there," Mrs Compton replied.

Anna gave a faint self-deprecating smile. "I just wish I could help more people." She turned back to Mrs Compton.

The three of them were joined by other participants and after they had finished coffee they walked together back towards the platform.

"Abuse of the elderly, is fact not fiction," announced Mrs Compton as she continued with the second part of her talk. "Let me show you what I mean." She reached down to the table and opened up a folder and extracted a photograph. "This photograph depicts an old lady in a wheelchair. She is cared for by her now middle-aged bachelor son. He is devoted to his mother. Unfortunately, she irritates him and when he's had a drink, well..."

Slowly Mrs Compton held the photograph up. "The marks on the back of the hand are cigarette burns." There was a pause as a wave of horror sped through the audience. Anna sat, her eyes glazed over and she constantly turned her wedding ring round and round on her finger. She suddenly became self-conscious; were the rest of the audience looking at her? Was Mrs Compton specifically addressing her remarks to her? Suddenly Anna felt all eyes were upon her – did they know of her secret?

Mrs Compton continued. "The woman's black eye was the result of a blow to the head... the purple marks on the arm are pressure marks, someone had held her *very roughly*. Her backside is covered in bruises, and she had a broken arm when they located her." She sighed, "There are no words to describe the sheer cruelty often inflicted on the elderly by a member of their own family.

"But whilst you shudder in horror you have to also remember the burden of pressure looking after an aged or infirm relative can bring to bear on other members of the family. They may have little or no support, feel isolated, be stressed out and yet society expects them to be on hand to care. But *everybody* has a breaking point."

Mrs Compton continued to instance more cases of cruelty and showed more photographs.

Feeling the heat of the hall overwhelm her Anna could not listen any more. She quietly gathered up her handbag and with a nod of apology to Doctor Ray and Mrs Compton she slipped out of the side entrance of the hall to stand for a moment on the steps to take in deep breaths of fresh air.

As Anna drove the twenty minute drive to her house, she decided to divert to the park on the outskirts of the village.

Here, the junior football team played, people walked their dogs and fed the ducks on the pond. It belonged to the community and Anna would sometimes walk round the green with Seth. She would often nod and chat to people she knew.

Anna parked her car and locked it. She just wanted to be on her own to think but instinctively she knew where she was going. Realising she was dressed somewhat inappropriately for walking across a park, she headed for the main path. It was not long before she came across a metal bench painted in black and brown. She stood hovering, her eyes going to the brass plate that had been fixed on to the middle of the back.

Anna did not need to read the inscription, for she knew it off by heart. Nevertheless her eyes scanned the words:

Rest here with the spirit of 90 year old, Elizabeth Jennifer Jenkins, who walked these fields as a child.

Slowly Anna put her hand over her face and started to cry, a short muffled sob that concealed a great heartache.

Half an hour later Anna turned the car into the avenue. It was so peaceful and the trees were now bedecked in their verdant summer green. She opened the window of the car to breathe in the freshness of the day.

She sighed as, turning the car to draw up alongside the tall wooden gates, she waited for them to slowly open. With vandalism now rapidly creeping from the town into the country electric gates were a necessity.

Anna loved the house, it had always been part of her life. It never ceased to give her a sense of well-being as she drove up the long gravel driveway flanked with flowering shrubs and small flower beds. The house always gave off a sense of tranquillity and a feeling of peace as she pulled her car up to the porch of the small mansion. The house had been built as the result of her father's ambition to own a gentleman's residence; and so it was.

"Imposing, practical and expensive, befitting my position

as Chairman of a bank," he had said all those years ago, with the smug smile of a self-made man. He had dabbled on the stock-market shortly after the war and made a substantial sum on overseas development.

The family was small: she was a lonely child, yet her mother had lived in the village all her life and had finally fulfilled her ambition to live on the avenue. Her father had spared no expense and no modesty with the house, as he had told everyone. Only the best was good enough. It was his temple: *Kinellan House*.

It had been so good all those years ago when she had been a child. The house had been alive with people. Lit up like a beacon of prosperity, with expensive cars lining the driveway. Her mother had always liked to entertain and was a good hostess. She had taught Anna a lot about surviving and adapting to a way of life.

They had sent Anna to a respectable convent school, where she boarded for a few years and which she had left with manners, etiquette and confidence.

Anna was lucky; she had not needed to work for longer than three years; there had been no shortage of money and marriage had come sooner than she had anticipated. For quite suddenly, at the age of eighteen, her father had died and her world had spun into turmoil. Her father's will had been uncompromising in its request. Anna would inherit the remainder of his estate when her mother died. The provision was that the mother should remain in the house for her lifetime.

The will had been crystal clear. *"Mrs Elizabeth Jenkins must not be placed into a nursing home should she suffer from any illness that affects her mentally and physically. She must be cared for in Kinellan House – the home she loves."*

Provided this was adhered to Anna would, on the death of her mother, inherit the house and a considerable amount of money.

Then Anna had met Charles, mature, steadfast, a respectable businessman, through an introduction from the priest. Their courtship had been short, no highs, no lows. Charles had no family and he agreed to her request they live with her mother in the house after they married; it made economical sense to him. Charles, like her father, dealt in finance, which resulted in him travelling frequently to the Far East.

Charles's money had provided the capital to effect a modernisation of the house, for which old Mrs Jenkins would not release the funds for. A substantial extension and an outdoor pool were added. Within three and a half years of marriage they had two children, Kate followed swiftly by Steven.

Anna still enjoyed the air of possessing the house, although in the back of her mind she realised it was still her mother's home. She would often admire the paintings her father had chosen with such care. She remembered how satisfied he had been when the small brass covered overhead lights had been placed above each of the paintings, which had certainly grown in value by now. The ornaments and the silverware. Trophies he had received for golf. He should have had a knighthood; perhaps he would have achieved that in time.

Now Anna accepted her life had changed and she was stranded in a backwater of inactivity, using voluntary work to blot out a problem in her marriage.

Kate and Steven had attended the local Catholic schools. Anna had not wanted them to be educated in single-sex schools, she wanted a normal, balanced education for them. Soon she would be left alone with Charles and the complications that would bring.

Anna opened the car door and stood for a moment on the gravel drive before walking across to open the front door.

It wouldn't be long before that gardener would arrive.

An hour later Anna heard the intercom from the gate buzzing and picked up the receiver.

"Yes?"

"Jack Fearnley."

She could hear the youthfulness in his voice. She did not reply but merely pressed the button for the gates to open. She got up slowly and stood in the bay window, watching in horror as the battered orange VW Beetle puffed and huffed its way to finally stop with a wheeze and groan outside her front door. Not the sort of car that usually came up her driveway – unless it was one of the children's friends, but that was different. He should have a van with *Gardening Services* written on the side, so people would know why he was calling. She hoped none of the neighbours had seen it, and then hated herself for her need to conform to be so middle-class. She sighed and wished life was not so complicated.

As Jack emerged from the driving seat Anna somehow didn't really feel like interviewing this young man. Her initial encounter with him had been embarrassing and his stare had been unnerving. She had to admit nobody had ever stared at her in that way before, or not that she'd noticed. Eyes that said…, she shook her head, she was imagining it! Swiftly now she patted her hair to ensure it was tied back at the nape of her neck and affixed the clasp. She placed her glasses more firmly on the bridge of her nose, not really needing them, but knowing they would give her a shield from his too prying eyes.

She saw him slam the car door hard making the vehicle rock back and forth. He rubbed his hands together and then ran them through his hair, trying to smooth it down; she wondered if he was nervous or apprehensive, but she thought not, remembering the intensity of his gaze and the way he had held her hand at Mass.

CHAPTER THREE

*J*ack felt out of place as he stood there on the immaculate gravel drive. It was a new experience, for he had always believed that he was quite at home anywhere. He had casually mentioned to his mates over a lunchtime pint that he had this gardening job on offer at a house on snob's hill, as the locals called it; they had mocked as they read the address on the visiting card.

As he'd driven down the leafy avenue he'd paused to peer through the gates at all the luxurious houses; he knew it would be years, if ever, before he'd be able move into such surroundings.

'Kinellan House', it said on the small brass plate on one of the gateposts. The house, red bricked with Virginia creeper burgeoning towards the white, shutter-framed windows upstairs, lay at the end of the curved driveway. He saw the large gardens, the high copper beech hedge, the tall oak trees, the summer house and the wall with the rambling roses. He guided the car slowly up to the porch and now he stood uncertain as to how to approach this situation. Where was the husband? Did she have any children?

Perhaps he should have found a rear entrance; it seemed incongruous to be standing here in his worn jeans next to his clapped out car. Did he really want to see her again?

Yes, he certainly did!

He went to the front door, pulled at the brass handle and heard the jangle echo round inside the house. He had her in his mind's eye. Would she stand before him cool and sophisticated, her long hair wafting gently round her face? Would her eyes gaze into his? Would she remember him holding her hand just a fraction too long? He waited and wondered who would open the door. He rested his boot against the boot scraper and wondered what her reaction would be. Embarrassed? No, she wouldn't be – probably cold and distant though.

He heard footsteps and knew they pattered over an uncarpeted floor. He drew his mouth into a set smile and pushed his hair back from his eyes. He had thought of the immediate attraction he'd felt; he couldn't explain it, he only knew when he touched her hand he had wanted her like he had wanted no other woman. Not even Mary.

The front door opened.

"Mrs de Courtney...." He had hoped his voice was rightly pitched, his smile easy and his eyes full of sophisticated amusement, but he knew that as his eyes scanned her face he felt a sudden and immediate sense of being let down. His vision had crumbled; this wasn't the beautiful, sophisticated lady he'd seen at Mass the previous day. He stared at her, remembering suddenly his sister's words: *beauty is only skin deep*. Was this the same person? His eyes swept over her face. Gone was the sophistication, the delicate make-up, the beautiful clothes; now she suddenly looked ordinary – well almost. The dark hair had been pulled austerely back to the nape of her neck and the eyes were hidden behind dark-framed glasses. She seemed to be a different person and he wondered just what he had imagined he'd seen in her – but there was something, just something about her that attracted him. He shook his head, conscious he was staring at her.

She was taken aback by his silence and unnerved by his stare.

"Jack, isn't it?" She tried to make her own voice lightly superior as she raised her eyebrows.

"Hi!" he held his hand out, his composure regained; but she ignored the gesture and he at once felt irritated.

There was no friendliness in her eyes as they swept over him and he decided that she was someone who liked to be in charge. He had not flustered her or even made her embarrassed; she was treating him for what he was – her gardener. He felt a faint twinge of annoyance that she was de-personalising him. Reluctantly she held her hand out in a half-hearted greeting; he took it, clasping it lightly, but the magic had gone. She had a bunch of keys in her hand as she started to pull open the front door. Then the sudden shrill clangour of a telephone echoed through the house. She frowned and glanced at him – it had to be Charles, or even one of the children.

"Oh, I must answer that. Could we leave this until tomorrow?"

He felt a surge of annoyance. "You did ask me to come…" he muttered.

"I'm sorry, but it just isn't convenient… I have to answer it."

"I'll wait, then."

There was a look of hesitation on her face. "I would prefer it if you'd return tomorrow," she stuttered. "If that is not convenient, well, it's up to you." She was dismissing him as she would any tradesman.

"I don't know," he sounded childishly irritated seeing her shrug her shoulders.

"Please, yourself!" Her tone was dismissive. She started to close the door, retreating behind it, forcing him to take a step back. She appeared briefly through the remaining gap: "Tomorrow evening would be best," she muttered hastily, and closed the door firmly before he had time to answer.

Outside, he kicked at the gravel and wished he could tell

her to forget him as a gardener, but he couldn't. He was the fly to her spider. As he walked back to his car he saw the lights go on in one of the downstairs rooms; he stopped and watched as she picked up the telephone receiver, removing her glasses as she spoke. He watched her nod and speak briefly, but she did not laugh. She was staring ahead and he knew the conversation was not a happy one: still no laughter and her body language was taut. He felt her misery and saw an unexpected vulnerability as she shook her head; her hand reached across to the side of the window and closed the blinds. He was shut out.

Then his resolve returned: he'd try again tomorrow. His anger evaporated, and he got back into his car, started the clattering engine, and sped back down the drive, skidding gravel at each gear change.

Anna felt a pang of guilt as she glanced out of the side window, before closing the blinds on the main window. Her attention was diverted as she heard the faint petulance in Charles voice.

She sounded contrite as she listened to the happenings of his business world.

"You want me to fax... what?"

He droned on while she made frantic notes.

Anna sighed in exasperation and replaced the receiver. She reached down, opened his desk drawer and looked through the files for the one he had indicated. That found, she placed it on the desk. She could send it tomorrow, it was much too complicated for her to concentrate on right this minute.

Jack was irritated at his wasted visit. Who the hell did that woman think she was? He got out of the car and slammed the door shut and stalked down the short path to his home.

"You're in a fine temper, what's happened?" Rose asked, surveying his angry face.

37

"Do you want chapter and verse on everything I do?" he snapped.

"There is no need to be rude..." her tone matched his and he saw a flash of hurt in her eyes.

"Oh go to hell." He ran up the stairs into his room, slamming the door and making the whole house shake. Jack needed to be on his own, to analyse his thoughts; how was he going to handle this? Now, listening to music on his CD-player, he opened the bedroom window, lit a cigarette and went through the events of the evening. He desperately wanted to get to know Anna - she was intruding into his thoughts in a way he had not thought possible. Ever since that morning in church he longed to be with her. He had calmed down now, realising his mother didn't merit such a childish display of anger. Petulance, Mary would call it. He felt ashamed now of the remarks he'd made to Rose. They had a good relationship and she didn't deserve to get the sharp edge of his tongue for no proper reason.

He stubbed the cigarette out, walked downstairs and opened the living room door. She did not look up; he stood shame-faced.

"Can I make you a cup of tea?" he asked, offering an olive branch.

There was a pause, for they seldom quarrelled and when they did neither sulked nor held recriminations.

"Oh go on then," she said in exasperation. "I suppose you're missing Mary?"

"Yes," he lied, as he left the room.

Anna waited until the chimes from the grandfather clock had ceased: she had to check on the room. It had been her nightly ritual for the past four months – getting up in the middle of the night to make sure all was well. The house was still: she stood on the landing waiting, a shaft of moonlight enveloping the hallway, giving it a ghostly light. She drew the folds of her thin night-dress more closely round her body. With her hand resting on the familiar banister she moved silently down the staircase to stand on the lower step. Without realising she had moved forward towards the door, she felt the smooth round knob of the handle in her hand. She blinked and then felt the handle silently turn at her touch.

The door opened and she stood still, her eyes flickering round the room; in the semi-darkness she could visualise each object of furniture. The curtains were half-closed and through the lace the moonlight cast a moving pattern on the ceiling, bathing the room in a gentle glow. There was no movement from her mother in the iron bedstead in the corner of the room, but then Anna didn't think there would be.

Now she padded across to the bedside table and gazed down at the still form beneath the blanket. Suddenly her nostrils picked up the familiar and unpleasant odour of human excrement and urine. With an exasperated gesture she peeled back the bedclothes to reveal a thin figure lying in a puddle of sodden faeces. Anna felt physically sick, but more, she felt angry. She tore the bedcovers back from her mother and marched across to the bathroom and in the darkness took down the plastic apron, and tied her long hair back before putting on the rubber gloves.

"Get up!" She cried and went over to the bed. Her voice was harsh and she could see her mother's mouth wide in a gaping scream as her hands tugged at her mother's arms as she dragged her from the bed and, ignoring the gasps of terror, she marched her to the bathroom and threw her down into the darkness like a rag doll. Then, storming across to the bed she ripped off the sheets and stared down at the dark stained rubber sheeting; taking a floorcloth from a bucket under the bed she wiped it cursorily. Next she moved over to the chest of drawers in the corner of the room and took out a batch of un-ironed bed linen. Swiftly she remade the bed and returned to the bathroom to be confronted by an emaciated body, wrapped in a filthy night-dress, crouched on the floor whimpering. The face skull-like with yellow skin stretched back so the mouth seemed to be permanently grimacing.

"You make me tired," Anna said and turned on the taps of the wash basin and threw a sponge into the hot water. She bent down and dragged her mother up, propping her between the two toilet rails. "Hold on," she snapped "while I clean you up," but even as she spoke the figure started to whimper like a frightened dog.

"It's no use crying, I'm the one that should be doing that..." Anna removed the night-clothes. She could not look at the skeletal form, as she peeled back the thin buttocks and shuddering with nausea she washed away the mush of excrement from around the anus.

Once that had been achieved she reached up to the shelf above the toilet and took down clean nightwear, which she put on the now shuddering, teeth chattering figure. Then, taking the thin arm she guided the trembling form back to the bed.

Anna came to with a jerk. She glanced round the bedroom. All was quiet and she sat up in bed shivering. It had been another of the horrific scenes that played in her sleep nearly every night. If only she could confess, perhaps that would purge her soul of the terrible deed she had committed. As it was, her conscience wouldn't let her sleep; tending to her mother had involved the utmost degradation for them both. Why should human beings have to tolerate such a filthy environment, when a restful death was the only outcome? She closed her eyes blotting out the memory before drifting back to sleep.

Anna awoke the next morning accepting she was tired and irritable. It had been another stressful night of little sleep. Nightmares; she was tired of them and despite having the cooling fan on all night in the bedroom she had been hot and restless. She wondered, not for the first time, why she could not have pleasant dreams about her mother? The sleeping pill which she now took let her doze in brief snatches, but she would toss and turn as the memories crowded in. She wished there were someone to hold her who at least understood and would listen to the thoughts that continually pounded inside her head.

It had turned out to be a frustrating morning. She had read through her mail in the kitchen and jotted down the dates of meetings she would attend. After she had made numerous phone calls the Vice-chair of LATE had called round for morning coffee. They did not always get on and sometimes she wished Mavis would resign. Mavis had been on the committee far too long, and now at seventy-seven she was becoming more of a burden than help. Looking back was not progress. They had sat chatting about future programmes. Anna had been glad when Mavis had left just before midday and had watched her laboriously attempting to turn her small car around in the driveway only to run into and almost ruin a bush.

Anna had eventually felt compelled to offer to guide her out.

In the afternoon Anna had sat by the pool and now after a light lunch she was sitting at Charles's desk searching through the instructions for the fax machine. She had attempted many times to fax the papers through to a number in Hong Kong but all of them had proved abortive – she did not know how to operate the fax machine and the instructions made no sense. Technology was not for her.

Jack was late, he knew that. It had not been a good day. His car was giving him problems and he had arrived home too late to eat. He only had time to shower and change. It was not a good start to impress the impressive Mrs de Courtney. Arriving at her house at past eight o' clock in the evening was no time to go touting for business.

"Start, you bastard!" he yelled and laughed inwardly, remembering a similar scene from the television series, *Fawlty Towers*. He turned the ignition key again and the engine spluttered into life. It was too late to view the garden, but he didn't have a phone number. She was of course, ex-directory, and he had no means by which he could contact her. He thought it was odd that her visiting card omitted the most important item of information – her phone number – and his mother did not have it either, for Anna never gave personal information to her volunteers.

The imposing wooden gates to Kinellan House were open. He wondered what his reception would be as he glanced down at his watch. He was very late.

He stopped the car and looked round and then slowly got out and walked to the front door. He heard the bell chiming. There was a long wait before the door slowly opened. Anna frowned, she looked irritated and he started his apology.

"Look... my car," but she dismissed that with a wave of her hand.

"Yes, yes... I know all about cars that do not start..." He heard the asperity in her voice and was about to utter another few words of sorrow but she shook her head.

"I know it's late," he interjected, "but I'd like to see round the garden, get an idea of how much work you need," he said, as they both stood hovering in the porch. She ran a hand across her forehead in what looked like a nervous mannerism and he saw the lines of tension round her eyes. "Can I walk round myself?" he asked.

The door remained half-open, "I suppose you could," it opened a little more and he saw now the worry, and anxiety in her eyes.

"Are you okay?" he asked.

"Of course I am all right," she snapped.

"Sorry," he wasn't sure why he felt it necessary to apologise and then as he was about to turn away the door opened again.

"Can you use a fax machine?" Her voice was abrupt and he glanced up at her in surprise, but she did not meet his eyes. Seeing his moment of hesitation she said quickly. "Oh, it doesn't matter."

"Is it broken?"

"No, anyhow, I shouldn't ask you, but…" her voice was now unsure.

"You need help?"

"I need someone to fax a letter for me," she sighed. "It's to my husband, Charles," her voice was flat, and she stopped and held her hands out in a helpless gesture, and he waited for her to continue. "He's away and he asked me to fax some information through to him." She shrugged her shoulders. "He is not the most patient of men. He gave me instructions as to what to do, but of course, I've not been able to make it work." She heard the unexpected sound of a woman unable to cope. "I sound stupid…!" she admitted.

"No…" but he did not sound convincing. She was not a woman, he sensed, who usually asked for help, especially from a stranger and a gardener at that! He felt amusement come into his eyes that did not go unnoticed.

"Do you know anything about fax machines?" she asked again and flushed seeing the humour in his eyes.

He could see she was annoyed, annoyed at her incompetence and he waited a moment too long before replying. "I know a little!"

"Can you or can't you operate a fax machine?" there was no disguising her irritation.

He nodded and smiled. "I don't think it's," he was about to say, too difficult, but stopped, not wishing to imply she was stupid… but she cut him short.

"Yes, I must be stupid, Charles would probably agree with you." Her voice was cutting.

He was tempted to walk away; tonight she had an acid tongue, no humour, yet he wondered why he was so attracted to her.

"Let me have a try!" he volunteered.

Anna hesitated for a fraction of a second and then held the front door open and ushered him into the hallway. Jack felt the nearness of her body and knew his heart had started to beat as he caught the scent of her perfume. He heard the squeak of his old training shoes on the highly polished wooden floor as he scanned the hall; it was bigger than his Mum's front room. A grandfather clock ticked solemnly in one corner. There was a small table and chair, flower arrangements and ornaments. The walls were covered in pictures.

"Please follow me!" Anna instructed as she pushed open the door to the study.

He saw more paintings out of the corner of his eye as he followed Anna to the impressive desk where she was now sitting, fumbling in a drawer to produce a folder of papers and fax transmission reports.

"Okay, what's the number you've to fax?"

She scrabbled round the desk, "Here."

"And the document you want to send?"

She handed him four closely typed A4 sheets.

"Take one and place it face down like this," he instructed her. "Then dial the number." He waited until she completed the task.

"Now press Start."

They both waited and listened as the machined bleeped a long number, the distant phone answered and then whistled; paper slid into the machine and out again.

"Let's read the transmission report. Status reads *correct*. Fax sent." Jack was glad he had been able to prove she was more competent than she thought she was. "That makes up for me stealing your car park space on Sunday," he commented with a faint smile.

Anna had no option but to return his smile; a weak one, but the corners of her mouth were no longer dourly lowered.

He wandered across the study to look at a spectacular painting of the race horse *Red Rum* and then down to a small glass display which seemed to house a piece of old radio machinery. He looked at the metal-plate inscription: *In honor of the German radio pioneer Heinrich Hertz.*

"You've been very kind." How stiff and formal she sounded. She tidied the paper away and locked them in one of the desk drawers.

"Your husband is interested in horse racing?" he said as he moved across to peer at another picture.

She gave him a cursory glance as she placed the key of the drawer on the desk, "My father was, my husband is into amateur radio!" she replied in a monosyllabic tone.

"And you?" he moved away and looked round the study, fingering two of the golfing trophies before he turned to see her shake her head.

"I'm not into sport. Steven, my son is totally absorbed in football, cricket, and snooker."

"And your husband?" he asked, standing looking at a framed photograph of the family.

"No!" she said, "he is not into sport at all." There was a flicker in her eyes that he could not evaluate and she indicated she did not wish to pursue the subject. She glanced out of the window, "It's getting dusk; we had better leave your tour of the garden until another time." She saw the flicker of disappointment in his eyes. "Tomorrow morning, could you come then?"

He shrugged, "I've a job on at ten, I could pop across at say nine and have a look at what needs doing, if that's all right?"

Jack was standing with a disgruntled expression on his face, so Anna was immediately reminded of Steven. His hands were dug deep into the pockets of his jeans. "Well, I hope it'll be convenient in the morning…"

Anna stared at him as he continued.

"I have come out twice already… I mean…"

"You want paying for your time, is that it?" she asked bluntly.

"No, but I thought the offer of a drink wouldn't go amiss." He gave her an under the eyelid look and waited.

She was taken aback at what she considered to be brashness.

"I think not, Jack," her voice was tardy as she stared at him, about to suggest they forget about the gardening and dismiss him when, as if sensing her disquiet Jack said,

"Look, you've got a patio, perhaps we could sit out, I can see a bit of the garden, have an idea of the size… you know!" He was persuasive and now Anna hesitated, unsure as to whether to accept or not.

"It's late," she eventually said.

"Mrs de Courtney, it's only a quarter-past nine," he shrugged his shoulders. "Look, I'm wasting your time… I would appreciate a glass of water… it's a hot and thirsty night!"

Anna met his eyes and shook her head slightly at his sheer cheek. She sighed in resignation. "A beer, Jack… in the kitchen, follow me."

He gave an open grin. "A beer would be just fine," he acknowledged, following her out of the study, across the hallway and into the large modern kitchen. It was so clean and tidy it reminded him of a show house. How Mary would love it, although she wasn't domesticated and could hardly cook, yet this had to be every woman's dream. He spied a grey cat as he watched Anna go to the huge cabinet fridge. She asked him to chose one.

He glanced at the selection and settled for an American *Budweiser* and without waiting for a glass he ripped open the ring can.

"I'll get you a glass."

"It's okay. Aren't you having one?"

He saw her hesitate about to shake her head. Then she changed her mind and reached to the cupboard to the side of the fridge and took out a wineglass and back to the fridge for a bottle of white wine which she placed on the breakfast bar. Then, opening a drawer she took out the corkscrew and handed it and the bottle to Jack.

"Would you?" It was not a request but more of a statement.

She watched him peel back the foil and then carefully insert the corkscrew to turn it gently but firmly before placing it between his knees to extract the cork. He took the paper towel she handed him and wiped the rim and then poured her out a glass of wine.

They stood awkwardly together at the breakfast bar. Anna taking small sips from the glass and Jack conscious of his loud gulps. He wanted a cigarette but knew it was probably a *No Smoking* house. He walked across to the large picture window and glanced out, seeing the shimmer of the water in the swimming pool reflect in the first glint of moonlight. He noticed the patio and deck area with the wooden poolside furniture.

"Can we sit out?" he asked.

Anna hesitated and then, admitting it was hardly relaxing standing in the kitchen trying to make unnecessary conversation with her gardener, retorted, "Yes, it'll give you the general layout of the garden." She turned and walked down a small passageway to the back door. She stopped and switched on the patio lights, and Jack saw the discreet orange glow illuminate the poolside area.

47

He walked out and sniffed the warm night air and then placed his can of beer onto the wooden table and arranged one of the chairs for Anna. He held her glass of wine until she sat down.

"Have you been to Arizona?" he asked as he settled himself into his seat.

Anna shook her head.

"You get these sort of nights out there."

"You went on holiday?" Anna asked without interest.

He stretched his legs out, as he leaned back. In the distance he could hear the drone of insects as the first fingers of night were appearing. He closed his eyes as he remembered his time spent in America.

"I went out there to visit a friend who was at Leeds Uni with me. The whole trip was really spectacular – we went to the Grand Canyon; fabulous!"

They lapsed into silence once more. Surreptitiously Anna glanced at her wristwatch, a gesture that was not lost on Jack. He could sense her lack of ease, her body language told him she was tense and her glass of wine remained untouched on the patio table.

"You do a lot of voluntary work?" he said tentatively trying to prolong the evening. She stared at him and then gave a brief nod and he knew she did not wish to converse. He persisted and with reluctance she replied tersely.

"I chair a committee…" she expanded as briefly as possible.

"That's good," he said.

Her eyes were sharp as she tried to hear a patronising inflection in his voice, but there was none.

"And you?" again it was a question asked without any real interest in the voice. He reached into the pocket of his shirt and withdrew a packet of cigarettes and lit one. Anna frowned and sniffed audibly at the smoke.

"Do you mind?" he asked as an after thought.

She was about to say Yes but instead heard herself saying. "No."

He stared up at the sky contrasting the peace, safety and the comfort of the English summer with that of a ramshackle refuge in a war-torn country as the guns rattled their anger in the distance and the group of frightened homeless, hungry people wailed their fears. Involuntarily he shuddered for the images often came to haunt him in the night. The smell of death and the hopelessness of life.

Anna glanced across seeing with surprise the reflective expression on his face as he slowly recalled the moment to her. She heard the pain in his voice and could visualise his nightmare. She was surprised at the depth of feeling he had conveyed to her and she reassessed him in her mind. He was not as shallow as she had thought.

They sat, each locked in silent thought until Jack picked up his can and drained the remainder of his beer.

"You barbecue?" he asked after awhile.

"I leave that to my husband," she replied and he saw a frown crease her forehead.

"Your family are away?"

"Yes," but she did not elaborate.

"It doesn't worry you being here alone?" he asked.

"No, should it?"

"I suppose not," He thought of Rose and Becky; neither liked to remain in the house alone overnight. "You are obviously competent, like Mary." He paused, "My fiancée, she's travelling abroad with a girlfriend."

There was another pause and Jack knew she was willing him to go. He picked up the can and pretended to take another gulp, and sat holding it in his hands.

"You must miss Mary?" he heard Anna say.

"We'll have each other for the rest of our lives, God willing," he leaned forward and Anna heard the serious note in his voice.

"You believe in marriage?" There was surprise and for the first time a glimmer of interest.

"Yes!" he admitted. "We've lived together, but it's time we wed… at least Mary and her family think so!" He paused and then added quietly, "And so do I, really."

Jack watched as Anna picked up her glass of wine and took a sip before saying. "I did Catholic marriage guidance some years ago; sadly not everyone takes the vows of marriage as a life long commitment."

"Mary is sensible and Irish with a hell of a temper."

Anna found herself smiling as she said, "Does she have red hair?"

"Like a furnace, and green eyes," he laughed but stopped suddenly, not wishing to bring Mary so intimately into the conversation

Jack saw the cat stealthily approaching; its round owl-like eyes stared up at him, and then with one calculated spring it was on his lap. Jack could hear the cat's loud purr as it slowly settled down and arched his neck and demanded a tickle.

Anna watched in surprise; Hector seldom encouraged affection from visitors. Choosy and very discerning, he would usually walk past disdainfully. She saw Jack stroke the cat.

"What's it called?" he asked.

"Hector!"

Jack smiled and Anna did as well. She was now more relaxed, sitting back in her chair, her legs crossed, glass in her hand. He continued to stroke the purring cat. It was now Anna who spoke first.

"And this is a period of separation for you both, is it?" she asked raising her eyebrows.

"Preparation, Mary says," he replied seeing the scepticism in Anna's eyes. He grinned and with a shrug said, "I'll not ask what she's done and I'll not tell her what I've done. When we are married my life will be an open book. Mary says these are our days of grace… memories before marriage."

"You mean secrets?"

"Well, doesn't everyone have secrets?" he replied thoughtfully, surprised at her question. "But no, Mary is a very honest person… we know each other pretty well!"

"I hope you do," Anna replied quietly, "secrets are sometimes difficult to live with," she said seriously and then added on a lighter note. "And what did you call them; your 'days of grace'! Will those days remain a secret forever?"

"Probably… depends what I do!" then he shook his head. "I'll probably never tell Mary…" He continued to stroke Hector.

"And what do you hope your days of grace will bring?" she asked with an air of disapproval.

"To spend a period of time with a beautiful woman. Mary is well, just Mary: we know each other, you know, unspoken words and all that." He gave a wry smile.

And all that, she envied them, their bond, their trust and their love but couldn't resist saying, "Won't that be a betrayal of Mary?"

"It will only be days of grace, Mrs de Courtney, I will in the end marry Mary."

"Mr Fearnley, I fear you are an out-dated commodity!" He heard the bantering tone in her voice.

"How's that?"

"A romantic in a materialistic, commercially minded world."

He gave a sheepish grin. "I guess I am, Mrs de Courtney."

There was a silence and he could see her face silhouetted against the setting sun etching the unmistakable lines of sadness. He wanted to reach out and take her hands in his and bring them to his lips. He wanted to make her throw back her head and laugh. He wanted, more than anything, to take her to bed.

"Do you have anyone in mind?" she asked now turning to face him.

He frowned.

"For your days of grace?" she raised her eyebrows.

"Oh yes," he said very quietly, "But I don't think she'd be agreeable."

"You have asked her?"

"No, but I will!"

"And Mary?" she asked, "Does she know she has a rival?"

He shook his head. "No, it's not a rival in that sense."

"You mean you want an affair?" Anna heard herself say and realised that the conversation was resembling a marriage guidance session. Someone always wanting the unattainable.

"That's an out-dated word, and it implies a commitment when there can be none." Then seeing her expression continued, "I can see you don't approve."

"No, I don't. This careless attitude to promiscuity... it used to be known as adultery. But then I am staid in my views." She stopped and bit her lip. Was she preaching?

He stared at her. "I wouldn't call you staid, Mrs de Courtney..." He lifted a now restless Hector from his lap and placed him carefully on the ground.

"I am forty-four. I have been married for twenty-four years, I have a grown up son and a grown up daughter." She stopped and frowned, why on earth was she telling him all this? She drew her lips back in a half smile as he replied.

"Women never admit to their age so you are an exception to start with," he reached into the pocket of his shirt and produced his packet of cigarettes and placed another one between his teeth as he searched for a match. She watched him from beneath lowered lids.

"So," he said as he blew out a jet stream of smoke, "Does being forty-four make you old?"

She opened her eyes wide and stared at him, nobody had ever spoken to her in such a manner before and she felt a moments irritation at his too familiar attitude and answered stiffly. "I have principles," she cringed inwardly, but had to continue. "I suppose these are old fashioned traits now… today it is all sex scandals and selling your uninteresting story to the newspapers."

He could see from the expression in her eyes that she did not approve.

"Sex is now predominant over love, you only have to look at television, people don't even know each other before they are throwing themselves into bed." She lowered her eyes, "I find it quite distasteful."

"It's liberation."

"Is that it? And this girl who is to be the object of what, your philandering, is she to be a sex symbol?" there was a note of censure in Anna's tone.

"Well, Mrs de Courtney," and the way he said her surname gave it an intimacy so she frowned. "I didn't say she was a girl, but we'll have to wait and see, won't we?"

Suddenly Anna was conscious of a wave of tiredness that swept over her. She rubbed her eyes and yawned. "I am sorry, it has been a very trying day."

He turned and raised his eyebrows but she did not elaborate as she stood up and he knew he was being dismissed.

CHAPTER FOUR

*J*ack watched as the gates were closed slowly behind him. He would be Mrs de Courtney's gardener... and a lot more besides. She was the answer to his days of grace... for there would be no commitment on either side. He smiled for he could imagine her panting beneath him in bed. Wakening in the morning and finding her beside him; this beautiful woman. In a euphoric mood he drove straight to his local pub; he needed a drink.

Parking the car he walked confidently into the bar, it was crowded with the regulars, who glanced up and acknowledged his presence. He was noted for his easy-going manner and for buying his round. Standing at the bar he rested one foot on the brass foot rail and nodded to the young girl serving.

"Usual," he said giving Melissa, the barmaid, a friendly smile. He remained at the bar, a pint of lager now in front of him.

"Put up another one," he said as he heard the jokes and laughter and knew his friend Gordon, a tall angular figure with short black hair, a brightly patterned sleeveless pullover and large spectacles was approaching.

They spent a few minutes in idle conversation.

"So how you getting on with Alison?" Jack said, as he took a sip from his second pint.

"God, you know she works in the local hairdresser's. I went

in for a trim, felt a right berk with all those woman round me. She gave me a lousy haircut and I ended up giving her a tenner tip…"

"A tenner, you mean you bribed her to go out with you?" Jack shook his head in disbelief.

"Yeah and what a bloody hellish evening it was, too." Gordon took another gulp at his beer, "Silly cow could only talk about paintings and sculpture all night long…"

"What you want is a beautiful, older married woman with no complications!" Jack said smugly. "You can't lose."

"You and an older woman? Never!" Gordon replied with incredulity, for Jack had always liked to be seen with a young attractive girl on his arm. "And what about Mary?" he said as an afterthought.

"I haven't married Mary yet, have I?" Jack replied in a matter of fact tone, "When I do it'll be a different story; I won't cheat on her!"

"Yeah, but an *older* woman…" Gordon shook his head in a faint gesture of despair.

"Think what you like, you know what they say about mature wine…"

"Yeah, it comes out of an old bottle!" Gordon laughed.

Anna wakened with a headache. It had been a long time since she had felt so bored; her life really was quite empty. She had taken a six-month vacation from the Bench, but was due to return soon. Being a magistrate had been a status symbol, chairing the Bench, listening and evaluating, but now, she had lost the will to sit in judgement on others. She wanted to back away from committees, decisions, and just reflect on where she, as a person, was going.

Her thoughts switched to Charles. He had been very good to her mother; not once did he complain about sharing his life with her. But then he had found another outlet to satisfy his needs. She closed her eyes; even now she could not think of it.

But Anna was perceptive, indeed she would be a silly woman if she couldn't admit things were not really as they should be between her and Charles. They had had little in common in the beginning but when the children had come that had bound them in a general interest. Somehow when the children had been young she hadn't noticed that she and Charles were not really compatible. And yet they had coped with the trauma, hidden it out of sight, it was rarely mentioned.

Now that the children had grown up she and Charles were almost strangers. They each had their own interests, and were joined only by name, not even love and certainly not by sex. Had her need for religion and good works become a sublimation for lack of love? She had once known all the answers, she gave them out to people in her counselling sessions. But self-realisation, self-knowledge and self-admission, they were different when it came to accepting them within yourself, and much more difficult to know what to do about it.

Charles was not happy discussing problems.

"Psychological clap-trap!" he would say in a dismissive tone whenever she tried to talk on an emotional level. So they never talked, not about feelings, and certainly not about sex or the lack of it. He could not even look at love-scenes on the television.

"All this heaving and panting," he would snap and there would a look of embarrassment on his face as he picked up the paper and pretended to read, or he might just leave the room. Occasionally he would simply switch channels.

It offended her, the lack of inhibition that television portrayed, but it also made her, in the deep caverns of her mind, know she had never really experienced such wilfulness.

Suddenly the twenty years difference in their ages seems like an unbridgeable gap; their needs were totally different. Work was all he wished, retirement was a word they did not discuss, even at sixty-four he insisted that retirement could be postponed until he was seventy. Then she would only be fifty. Recently she had worried about his retirement. Perhaps he would remain working forever; she hoped so. They were comfortably off, but what would they do... money was not the enemy, time was... too much time for Charles with too little to do except, well, she still couldn't think of that facet of his character.

Did she want to go into old age with Charles? What a dreadful image that conjured up. What had provoked her sudden restlessness? Deep within she knew it was realisation of her age. Would she become a burden like her mother?

The usual routine of getting up weighed heavily on her mind and she spent longer in morning prayer than normal, the rosary running through her fingers, her mind trying to concentrate on the prayer. It seemed all asking and little thanking.

Days of grace: the phrase had run through her head all night. She wondered who Jack would spend them with? She remembered holding Jack's hand at Mass. He held hers far too long. Her eyes meeting his, so briefly... an imagined attraction. She couldn't possibly be attracted to a young man she did not know; she was obviously too old for him.... It was incomprehensible. She stopped, what was she thinking of? Had she been too informal last night? Why did she offer him a drink? Had he read more into it?

With a feeling of dissatisfaction she clambered out of bed and replaced her rosary beads in the leather case. She stood looking out across the expanse of lawn, which the scorching sun was turning a patchy brown. It was going to be another hot day. She showered and dressed with her usual care and then went down stairs, to murmur her usual greetings to Hector as he sidled round her ankles. Finally he got his way and she bent down and picked him up to give him his morning cuddle.

Then with morning ritual she went out and walked down the driveway to the closed gates and opened the mail box set into the brick posts, another of Charles' security ideas. It had proved to be excellent in dry warm weather but hazardous when one had to trudge out in the cold frosty mornings. She opened the gates before scooping out the morning paper: the headlines read of a possible drought if the weather didn't change. She laughed inwardly; Britain was so ill-prepared for hot weather – and cold weather for that matter. There was an assortment of envelopes and cards and she walked back to the house. The postcard was bright and showed clear blue/greeny water of the Great Barrier Reef. She recognised Steven's handwriting: *Hi Mum, beats England!*

It certainly did and she felt a tinge of envy. The blue envelope contained a letter from her cousin suggesting a luncheon, two large buff envelopes contained minutes and agendas of meetings; the rest of the mail was for Charles. She looked at the large brown manila envelope addressed to the PO Box that Charles had set-up. It had been redirected to the house; it was probably one of Charles's catalogues. She shuddered and closed her eyes, not wishing to think of the contents. Her life seemed to be all problems: first her mother and now Charles – although his problem was hardly new but it disgusted her nevertheless.

Back in the house, she placed his post in the tray on the right hand side of his desk; orderly and methodically she would open them later and glance to see if there was anything needing to be paid or discussed when he phoned. Except of course the large manila envelope – that would have to remain unopened.

She took Seth for his morning run in the back fields and returned to make her usual breakfast of fresh orange juice, black coffee and wholemeal toast.

Anna had just finished when she heard the slam of a car

door. Slowly she got up and adjusting her glasses walked to peer through the small hall window: Jack was standing on the driveway, yawning as he stretched his arms above his head. This time he had managed to arrive on time.

He could smell the summer freshness of a new day and waited in anticipation now for her to open the door.

"Hi!" he smiled a nice easy crinkling-of-the-face smile and held his hand out to take hers.

Jack was dressed in his usual jeans, trainers and denim shirt and he seemed to tower over he. She wished he would cut his hair shorter, trim the straggly beard and moustache.

"I will get my *FiloFax*," she murmured leaving him momentarily on the doorstep. "Now, I will make notes of what I wish done and ask for your input." Her voice was brusque and business-like as she stood beside him and gently pulled the front door closed.

"Okay, so let's have a look round at what needs doing… got a busy day ahead."

"I thought you would be starting this morning?" she said tartly.

"Sorry… I just want to look round, I'll come tomorrow, Wednesday… okay?" He held his hands out in gesture of understanding. "I've an old lady wanting her hedge cut; and she wants it done yesterday!"

Anna felt let down and wondered why she had expecting him to start today; she heard her voice cold and impersonal. "Tomorrow… it's not really convenient, we did arrange that you would look round today," she sighed in an exasperated manner. "It isn't a very good beginning, is it?"

He was surprised by her tone, for he had imagined the beginning of an ease in her attitude last night as they'd talked. "No, but the delay's not my fault…" his reply was abrupt.

"Oh really and how do you make that out?" she asked cuttingly. "I suppose it is mine."

"Well…" he bantered, "You did alter the arrangements."

She frowned and he could tell from the toss of her head that he had irritated her so she snapped, like a terrier at his heels.

"We altered the arrangement to this morning you will recall."

"You want to sack me?" Now he grinned at the absurdity of the situation, and watched as she slowly shook her head.

"Oh don't be so stupid… you young people you cannot take any criticism at all."

"Not if it isn't warranted," he protested.

"I just ask that you be reliable… time-keeping is important to me."

"Well, it's not one of my strong points, as Mary would emphasise. I do try, but somehow…"

"Well try when you come to me." Her voice was still sharp.

"Sure will, Ma'am," and he touched his forelock. "Mary gets pretty exasperated with me. Gets pretty boring being reliable," he said jokingly as he followed her round the garden, "I mean this is the sort of day you want to be doing something exciting," she heard the undercurrent of enthusiasm and excitement in his voice. "You know: going mad, living life to the full!"

Anna laughed inwardly; it was a long time since she had done anything remotely exciting let alone mad. "I would say it was an excellent day for doing the garden," she replied practically, knowing she sounded flat and unenthusiastic.

"I suppose you would…" he muttered.

"Are you being impertinent?" She turned and took off her glasses to give him a hard stare. He saw the flash of anger in her violet eyes and realised he was not making a very good impression.

"No, I'm sorry I didn't mean it to sound like that. You are a very serious person, I probably seem trite…"

"I don't follow you?"

"Well…" he paused, "You really don't seem to laugh much…" As soon as he uttered the words he wished he could retract them for her eyes had glazed over in a frosty expression.

She replaced her glasses. Serious? Yes! She supposed she was. "I was under the impression I was employing you to be my gardener, not my analyst."

"It was merely an observation… I didn't mean to…"

"Offend me, oh you haven't done that. You have merely irritated me with your impertinence." There was no doubting her annoyance as she stopped and looked at him.

He wanted to say take off those damned glasses, unloosen your hair and yourself. Instead he said, "I apologise… it was rude."

She gave him a brief glance unsure how to answer. Instead she gently shook her head. "Well having dissected my character we will hear your views on the work required in the garden." Anna moved in the direction of the swimming pool.

"Do you swim?" he asked seeing the blue water, shimmering and inviting.

"Seldom." Her voice remained cold.

"Just the weather for a poolside party!"

She did not reply and in the background he heard a dog barking.

"Your dog?" he asked trying to make conversation, but she merely nodded.

She appeared far more formal now than she had the night before and he sensed she wished to show she was again in charge. He watched as she pocketed the keys to the front door and then gesticulated for him to follow her as she walked down the gravel pathway. She offered no comment and he could think of nothing appropriate to say. He saw the large conservatory and the mass of flowering plants.

He noted that the lawn had dried out, and he wondered why the sprinkler was not operating.

She saw him stop and followed his glance. Then he bent down and felt the grass. "It's totally dry," he muttered, feeling the need to break the overpowering silence.

Anna was heavy going. Jack was used to women who were at least sociable.

"We do have sprinklers." She continued down the pathway, until they came to a more secluded area, here Jack saw a garden shed and greenhouse. "Mower and tools," she informed him and walked to the shed door and fumbled with the key. But he sensed her mind was not on gardening.

"Needs some oil," he leaned across and gave the key a sharp twist and then moved back to allow her to open the door. He peered in: two lawn mowers and an array of tools. In a corner he saw two sprinklers.

"Look, I'll connect those now if you like," he suggested and she hesitated but then nodded and stepped back as he bent down and dragged them out. "Where's the water?"

Anna wrinkled her brow and brought the forefinger of her right hand up to her lip. "Oh, by the greenhouse," she pointed and he walked down the pathway and saw the tap and the water trough. She watched as he picked up one of the sprinklers and connected it seeing his hands tanned and strong, with short cut nails.

"There you are!" he felt a sense of satisfaction as he saw the sprinkler distribute its stream of water across the brownish grass. "If you could switch if off this evening and move it to the flower bed for the night."

As they were walking around the path, Anna looked up at one of the overhanging branches of a nearby tree and asked Jack if he could cut it.

"Have you a ladder?" he asked.

"Oh," she hesitated again, "I think there is one in the garage, we don't keep it outside in case of burglars..."

"Can I check?" he said.

She nodded and they walked towards the triple garage and Anna pointed towards the side door and handed him the key. "Should be along one of the walls."

Jack slid the key into the lock and opened the door and felt round to finally locate the light switch. Pressing the switch the garage was illuminated and he saw a large Mercedes and at the far end a small Morris Traveller. He then noticed the ladders.

Leaving the garage he switched off the lights, locked the door behind him and once outside handed Anna back the keys.

"Your husband likes classic cars?"

Anna gave him a blank stare.

"The Morris Traveller?" for a moment she seemed confused and then said quickly,

"Yes, yes, he does."

They wandered slowly round the remainder of the garden and she was surprised at his knowledge as he named the plants and trees. Father Mathews had been correct, Jack was not at all stupid and she watched as he bent down and felt the petals of a rose, his hands sensitively touching it before he named it.

"You should be a horticulturist," she commented as they stood admiring the rose bed. Anna gave him the ghost of a smile and he returned it with a grin and a faint shaking of his head. He stopped and leaned against the trunk of a silver birch.

His eyes roamed round the garden saying, "No, that's not for me. Dad was with the university as their Horticultural Officer," and he laughed. "Today's name for Head Gardener, no," he saw her frown, "I'm not putting him down, it was his expression, he didn't like pretence... a great guy for realism."

Anna met his eyes and saw the sadness in them as they walked back to the front of the house.

"He died a couple of years ago... knocked me out for a while, couldn't get my head round it." There was a trace of bitterness in his voice. "I just wish he'd been alive to see me get my degree." He stopped and turned away, wondering what had prompted him to talk about his father, a private subject that he kept closed and he continued. "My hourly rate is six pounds," his voice was business like as they approached the front of the house.

"Thank you," Anna said as she stood pen poised and daily organiser open. "I have marked down the areas you note need attention. Let us say three mornings a week?" she cut in. "If it needs more we can come to an arrangement. I will pay you each week by cheque. You mentioned tomorrow, Wednesday?" She glanced up and waited pen poised.

"I'll come tomorrow perhaps we can arrange my next visit then."

"I would prefer to sort it all out now, that way we both know our commitments." She scribbled once more on the page. "Tomorrow then?"

"Yes, I'll make tomorrow and change my schedule and next week come Tuesday, Thursday and Saturday morning if that's okay!"

The interview was finished; it had taken no more than half an hour.

"Till tomorrow, then…," said Anna dismissively. As she turned her pen slipped to the ground. Instinctively they both stooped to retrieve it.

"Well, now," said Jack with a grin, "if this was a movie we'd have fallen into an embrace there."

There was a cold silence as Anna delved for a suitable reply. "Very amusing, Jack, but with my lack of humour I would not find it remotely funny!" Anna analysed.

"Touché!" he replied giving Anna a disarming smile.

Jack felt elated as he spun the car away from the drive. In his rear view mirror he could see Anna walking back into the house. He would see her again tomorrow. His mind started fantasising and before he realised it he was drawing up outside his own home. He was about to get out of the car when he saw his mother slamming the front door shut. Dressed in her usual attire of blue anorak and blue skirt she purposefully walked to the car with a flustered expression on her face.

Grabbing the door handle she flung the car door open. "Jack, Jack... I am terribly late," she gasped. "Could you take please me to Allan House?"

He could see the beads of perspiration on her brow and wondered why she could not go anywhere without wearing her blue anorak.

"Are you late for LATE?" and he leaned across to make sure the door was firmly closed.

He waited until she had finally straightened her skirt and settled herself down in the passenger seat, noting as he released the handbrake how much surplus weight she seemed to carry. This was such a contrast to Anna who he could never imagine becoming even slightly plump. Women were odd, he thought; his Mum should take herself in hand. Perhaps go on a diet and stick to it. Learn from people like Anna how to dress and talk. He wondered if Mary would ever become sloppy in appearance. Even if she had children he hoped Mary would keep a dignified figure. Didn't women realise what a turn-off they could become when they became overweight? All he could think of was Anna and how lucky her husband was. She was in her forties and still looked stunning; why couldn't other women be the same?

"I am in an awful hurry," Rose cut through his thoughts as he dawdled the car passed the parked vehicles on their narrow road.

"Will the boss tell you off?" he asked curiously.

"And who would that be?" Rose replied.

"I thought Anna de Courtney was in charge," he said as he manoeuvred the car round the roundabout.

Rose gave him a sideways glance. "No one is *the boss* as you call it," she replied quickly.

"Oh, I didn't realise," he said with a grin, "I was with her this morning,"

"Really!" Rose replied without much interest.

"I've got the job of her new gardener!" He could not keep the self-satisfaction out of his voice. Rose turned sharply for he looked like a cat that had taken the cream.

"Well, she's a stickler for time-keeping, remember that!"

"She's very nice..." Jack countered.

"Oh being nice means nothing when there are forms to fill in, people to feed and transport to arrange," Rose replied tersely.

"You don't like her do you?" he accused.

"I don't dislike her, I sometimes find her, oh nothing..." Rose did not wish to continue, she did not really know Anna that well.

"For God's sake, she's a lovely person," Jack snapped back.

"Oh you men; a pretty smile, long hair, lots of curves and you're all putty in their hands."

Jack laughed as he negotiated the traffic.

"I think Mrs de Courtney is always thinking of others," he replied earnestly as he slowly stopped to allow traffic to flow past before he turned into the small car park at Allan House.

"Here you are," he announced as he parked in the bay reserved for the LATE Chairman; he noted the look of disapproval on his mother's face.

"Your Chairman is a personal friend of mine."

"You're getting too big for your boots," Rose said as she alighted from the car.

"I'll see you in," he offered, not wishing to miss the opportunity of looking at Anna's domain.

"There's no need..." Rose started to say, but Jack was already out of the car and reluctantly she walked across the car park and held the entrance door open for him. He followed behind, seeing as he did the framed photographs on the walls of the sparsely furnished entrance hall, which had been turned into a waiting room; the chairs looked very uncomfortable. He peered at the photograph entitled: *The Board of Trustees* seeing a group of middle-aged men and women and in the midst Anna. He grinned; he peered at her more closely. Anna was formally dressed and looking somewhat ill at ease as she stood in a tight fitting short skirt, high heels, a spade in her hand, about to plant a tree. She was next to a man he assumed was the Mayor. He could almost feel her discomfort as he moved to another photograph. This time Anna was smiling and obviously enjoying greeting some dignitary. There was a group photograph, Anna at a golf tournament, Anna at a coffee morning; it looked as though Anna was here there and everywhere.

"She gets about," he admitted.

"Probably get an MBE," Rose said sceptically, nudging him towards the glass front door where a dark haired receptionist with a grumpy expression sat yawning behind a desk. With that he said goodbye and left.

CHAPTER FIVE

*O*ver breakfast Anna glanced at the kitchen clock. Jack was already ten minutes late. She had left the gates open for him but now wondered if this man could be on time for anything.

"Good morning," he called as he passed the kitchen window. She blinked for she had not heard his car come up the drive. She noted his sawn off jeans, tattered tee shirt and baseball cap. "Going to be hot," he acknowledged. "Car wouldn't start, got the bus."

She glanced pointedly at the kitchen clock. "We did say nine," she said haughtily.

"Blame the bus driver," he replied, and disappeared out the back to start work.

It was an hour later that Anna told Jack she was going out for a meeting but would be back before he left.

He heard the voice at his elbow and glanced up to see Anna silhouetted against the sun. Her silk blouse clung tightly to her breasts, and her light summer skirt held a vague outline of her long slim legs. He was immediately struck by the sensuality of her appearance; gone was the austere person of yesterday, today she was desirable with her dark hair loosely wafting round her face, her make-up appealing, her eyes mysteriously encased in sun glasses. He saw her smile and felt his heart miss a beat as he gulped and managed a strangled. "Okay!"

"Here are the keys of the greenhouse and shed."

He stood now watching her walk across the lawn and wondering – no hoping – she was conscious of his lustful gaze.

The finance meeting had taken longer than Anna had anticipated as she and the Finance Trustee went over the budget plans. It was obvious that too little was coming in and too much was being spent. If they were not prudent then the part-time salaried staff would be looking at two redundancies. Not a task that Anna relished, but one she would carry out if necessary.

It was not impulse that made Anna drive to visit her mother's grave. It was a necessity, a need to constantly absolve her conscience. She made her usual detour to the village florist's and purchased a colourful selection and a bottle of water from the general store. Now with the flowers on the rear seat of her car she drove steadily towards the church. The car park was empty; she stopped alongside the thick beech tree hedge beyond which lay the graveyard. Slowly she pushed open the iron gate that led into the cemetery. The surrounding monastery building, now sadly depleted of Brothers, reminded Anna, as she walked head bent along the weed-strewn pathway, of her Catholic background. She saw the tarnished halos with angel's sightless eyes. Row upon row of headstones of people long forgotten, buried beneath stone crosses, with empty vases or withered remains of plants. Whenever she had a moment to spare she often came to visit her parents grave.

The memory of her mother's funeral would come crowding into her consciousness. She remembered the words of John Henry Newman's famous hymn: *Lead, Kindly Night*.

That cold, miserable April day when after the funeral service she had walked behind what looked like a tea-trolley on which her mother's coffin was precariously perched. After what seemed like a harrowing last journey for her mother they finally reached the green tinged gawping mouth of the waiting grave. Her mother's coffin was lowered gently down to rest above her father's.

"She is home at last," someone had fatuously murmured and Anna had cried then, long tear jerking sobs of remorse. She had felt Charles's comforting arm round her shoulders.

Now she stood looking down at the black marble headstone with the bright gold lettering. She read the memorial message: *in memory of two beloved parents*. She felt the tears coursing down her cheeks and managed to whisper the well worn phrase that came automatically to her lips every time she visited the grave, "Forgive me." She gulped over the words.

The cemetery was a constant reminder of her own mortality, and she bent down and removed the withered flowers from the vase, taking them to the empty bin, returning to refill the vase with water from the bottle. Then she unwrapped the newly purchased flowers and carefully arranged them in the vase. It was a ritual, a need to show people that here lay someone who was cared for, someone who was loved and cherished. Twice a year she would come and wash the headstone so the names were never dulled. Now she bent her head and brought out her mother's rosary and the beads slipped over her fingers with practised skill and her lips whispered the prayers for the dead ears of her mother and as penance to her living God.

The guilt lay heavy on her heart. She crossed herself and then turned to walk slowly back to her car.

Anna arrived back at the house at midday. She had intended going out to see how Jack was getting on, but another phone call and arrangements for meetings seemed to take up another slice of her time. Then glancing up she was surprised to see it was almost one o'clock. She filled the kettle and went over to the window. Across the lawn Jack was naked to the waist, glistening in the sunlight as he stopped and pushed his hat away from his brow, mopping it with his handkerchief. She hesitated, then opened the back door and called out.

"I'm making some coffee," she heard herself say and then gave a rueful smile.

He looked round, paused to stare at her for a second, then grinned and waved a hand to accept her invitation. She pushed opened the kitchen door and heard his training shoes again squeak on the highly polished floor.

"Go in, I'll just give Seth a biscuit." She gesticulated to one of the kitchen stools; he sat down and stared round the expensive kitchen equipment. A faint meow made him glance down at Hector who stared up at him.

"Hello, Hector." He knelt down and the cat allowed him to stroke the silky fur as it purred contentedly.

Anna was standing in the doorway.

Jack stood up, "I love cats." Placing his hands in the pockets of his jeans he leaned against the wall as he watched her go to a cupboard and take out a cafetiere and a tin of coffee. He watched as she moved gracefully across the kitchen and filled the kettle, plugging it in and switching on. Then she returned to the cafetiere, taking the plunger out, opening the tin of coffee and spooning in two level measures.

"I never make instant coffee," she said, conscious of his gaze, "the family say I am stupid, but I happen to like ground coffee; I grind the beans myself every morning." She stopped, it sounded so banal.

"Well I guess if a job's worth doing... Mary manages with a spoonful of instant," he said, his eyes following her every movement.

Anna placed the two china mugs down on the breakfast bar, a bowl of sugar and a jug of milk. His usual cup was a thick mug for Mary wasn't given to china; cooking and domesticity bored her, she was career minded.

"You know Father Mathews well?" Anna did not look up as she depressed the plunger in the cafeteria and then poured out the steaming black liquid.

"I did the church accounts last year and no doubt I'll do them this year too."

"Your mother must be proud of you."

"I hope Dad would be. He thought accountants were... I don't know, the real professionals. He just wanted me to be one."

"And you did it for him?"

He stared out of the window, her directness took him unawares, he was used to people pussyfooting round questions and he wasn't sure he liked this approach. It made him face up to facts he didn't always want to acknowledge.

"Help yourself to milk and sugar." Anna placed the china mug of coffee on the breakfast bar and he reached across and dug clumsily into the soft brown granules, spilling them on the table as he transferred the spoon to his cup.

Anna blinked as she remembered how her mother seemed to have had the ability to knock over everything in sight, from table lamps that crashed to the floor, to cups full of liquid and papers arranged in chronological order. Anna had spent more time on her knees mopping up and tidying up than she did at Mass. And the wine, the glass of red wine, over the expensive Chinese lounge carpet... and her mother's distress.

Automatically she reached for the cloth and mopped the spilt sugar up.

"Sorry," he muttered. To cover his embarrassment he grabbed the cup, looping his middle finger into the handle and took a swift gulp. It was blisteringly hot and he felt its raw impact on his lips and tongue. It was also fairly tasteless; nothing actually wrong with it, but flavoursome it wasn't.

She watched as he gasped and replaced it swiftly back onto the breakfast bar; he had been about to swear, but remembered in time.

"You enjoyed Uni… university?" she asked.

"Oh yes." He engaged with her question and started to speak quickly. At first it was just a monologue of his life at the university, his chosen career and his face lit up when he mentioned Mary and Anna wished someone would talk about her in that way.

Anna listened as he went on to relate life with Mary and the forthcoming marriage. Then Anna suddenly asked, "Have you started your days of grace?"

He stared at her; it was the first reference she had made to the conversation they'd had, the first chink into her less formal self.

"With the most beautiful woman I have ever seen!" he replied.

She had asked the question lightly, somehow not expecting his reply; she frowned, knowing she felt a disappointment, almost as though he had let her down… What had she expected his answer to be? She didn't know.

"You've met someone already?"

"I have."

She turned away, wishing to hide a feeling she had never experienced before, and one she would not admit to now: jealousy.

She heard herself asking if he had known the girl long and watched as he'd laughed and shaken his head so a long lock of dark hair fell across his face. He pushed it back.

He wanted to go across and put his arms round her, hold her close and whisper, 'Anna, it's you, you I want to spend my days of grace with'. But it was not the time to say such words – well, not yet.

"Jack," she glanced up at the clock, "coffee time is over!"

He rose from the stool with reluctance.

"Thanks," he picked up his cup and took it across to the draining board. "Dishwasher?" he pointed below.

She nodded.

"Mary wants one, but I say it's a luxury we can't afford, not yet… So it'll have to be rubber gloves and a bowl." He opened the back door and walked onto the patio to gaze longingly at the pool.

"Does anyone ever use that?" he asked as he looked across into the blue depths of the pool - imagining them swimming naked together.

"Oh yes, of course. My husband will swim, and we have a sauna…" she pointed to the small log cabin behind a screen of trees. "Changing room and shower attached."

It was an hour later when she glanced up from the lounger she had set up on the patio to relax while she read through some correspondence.

She saw Jack walking across the lawn, noticing now his tall slim figure, momentarily comparing him with Charles's figure, who was getting paunchier and old, his skin no longer firm but always so white… and Jack bronzed and young.

"It could do with a clean," Jack said walking to the edge of the pool and surveying it. "I could do it for you this evening if you'd like."

Anna had joined Jack at the pool shook her head. "No one is using it at the moment. Charles will see to is when he returns."

She saw the sweep of disappointment in Jack's eyes as she was about to return to the kitchen.

"I was going to offer to clean it this evening in return for a swim!" he said.

Anna frowned and hesitated and she saw the appeal in his eyes.

"Unless you're going out," he concluded.

It was a get-out clause, she realised and was about to reiterate her No and shrugged her shoulders.

"Well come early. I've my dinner to get ready. I may be going out."

Jack felt the flush of victory: it was a step forward in his pursuit of Anna. Now he asked tentatively.

"Perhaps you'd like to do a barbecue. I could always set it up for you."

She stopped by the rear door and turned to stare at him. He saw her eyes narrow as the sunlight danced over the patio.

"I don't think so, I don't enjoy barbecuing alone," she said dismissively.

He ran his hand over his moustache and then with a wide grin said. "You could invite me," he waited, not really expecting an answer and knowing full well he was pushing his luck to the maximum.

"I hardly think so!" Anna said and then saw the amusement in his eyes. She remembered the previous evening when she had admitted that Jack's company had broken the monotony of being on her own. The prospect of another evening dining alone suddenly seemed less attractive now. She thought of Charles... she was always putting her family first, and yet did they put her first? She very much doubted it.

"If you care to come early and clean the pool, have your swim and set up the barbecue..." she did not complete the sentence for he was nodding his head in agreement.

Anna had stood that evening in the back bedroom window looking down as Jack had dived into the pool and executed a perfect crawl up and down. He did about a dozen, effortlessly fast laps, the water swirling past him, and then got out at the deep end in a single, easy thrust of his arms. As he stood there dripping, his thin trunks clinging to his manhood, his well defined muscles and easy smile. Yes, she thought, Jack is very attractive.

He cleaned the pool, dragging the vacuum brush over the bottom, taking care not to miss anything, and skimming the surface with the longhandled net. She had anticipated he would make a quick sloppy job, but he had been thorough. Then he'd changed into knee length shorts and a sleeveless vest and had started setting the barbecue up; Anna felt a sudden lightness of heart. She walked into her bedroom and changed into a light summer skirt and sleeveless top and brushed her hair so it shone like ebony.

"Hi!" he said as she approached carrying the mosquito flares and placing them round the table.

"The trouble with paradise was always the serpent..."

He stared at her obliquely.

"Flies and mosquitoes... I always get bitten!" she explained and then complimented him on the pool.

"Would you like to swim while I get this going?" he asked.

"Oh, I don't want to get my hair wet," Anna replied before adding, "I've some steak and a salad in the fridge, I'll get it." She saw his look of approval.

Food: it had always been a problem with her mother and as she stared at the fridge she remembered small incidents that had irritated her.

"No, Anna, I don't like that...!" her mother's voice would echo round the kitchen.

The sandwiches she had taken time to prepare would be pushed away.

"Oh, soup. Yes, Anna, a nice bowl of soup," and she would see the smile of anticipation on her mother's face.

"Or a sandwich..." Suddenly she could hear her mother's voice again contradicting herself.

"Oh do make up your mind!" Anna would snap at her with regularity.

"It's cold Anna... the soup is cold!" The voice was plaintiff.

Anna now sat, sipping her glass of wine and trying to blot out her mother's face as she stared at the flare that had been lit. Jack, she was pleased to see, was coping admirably with the barbecue. "You are very accomplished," she said as she poured herself another glass.

"My friend's parents in Arizona had frequent outdoor parties. Well, they have the weather, don't they?" he looked up at her and smiled, "I learned all the barbecuing secrets over there… they used to do a beautiful smoked turkey, revolving on a spit… it was really…" he put his finger to his mouth and indicated a kiss of approval.

He smiled and the evening sun froze the moment as her eyes met his. She closed hers, it was a dream, this wasn't Anna sitting by the pool whilst her gardener cooked her a barbecue. It was another person, someone who wanted some light relief from the thoughts and images that constantly pounded away in her head. He was an easy companion and her initial disquiet about him left.

"I think we can eat now," he said taking two dining plates from the side table. It was all properly cooked and they sat down to steak, tomatoes and mushrooms with a side salad. She waited and watched as he picked up his knife and fork and felt a surge of relief when he held the knife correctly.

They chatted amicably and Anna realised there was a pleasant intimacy growing between them, like friends… almost old friends, she thought.

"That was good…" he sat back with a feeling of contentment. "I'll take you for a *McDonald's* next time."

"Next time!"

"Well there is going to be a next time… isn't there?"

"You sound as if you are asking me out on a date!" there was hidden laughter in her voice. She got up and collected the plates. "Ice cream and fruit?" she asked.

"Fine!"

Dusk was falling and he wished he was staying the night with her; they had eaten, talked and laughed, and now the dishes had been stacked in the dishwasher.

"Next time, I'll bring some music. Do you dance, Mrs de Courtney?"

"It has been a long time since I danced regularly." She replied and he imagined he heard a wistful note in her voice as she added. "It was before I married…"

"I think you did a lot of things before you married?"

She gave him a sharp glance. "Meaning!"

"Oh, I think you relaxed and laughed and had fun. Now you do good works." He smiled gently to take the sting from his words.

"Perhaps you are right," she acknowledged as she stood up, and Jack knew it was time to leave.

"It's been a really good day," he said as he prepared to walk to the bus stop. "Thank you!" He stared down at her and she felt his breath on her cheek. The atmosphere was charged as she backed away.

He turned round. "Thank you," he called, "for my first day of grace!"

There was a sudden flush on her cheeks and a great thumping in her chest, and she was glad that Jack was disappearing down the drive.

Anna couldn't help feeling a declaration of intent had been made. It had taken her by surprise, or had it? The thought of sacking him came into her confused thoughts. Did she like the idea or not?

Jack arrived at Kinellan House on time the next morning, he felt that some progress had been made the previous night and was ready to suggest they had a day out together.

Anna was nowhere to be seen as he entered the garden and he took out the key to the shed from his jeans pocket. He moved the sprinklers and tidied round some of the flowerbeds, weeding and trimming and edging. He stopped and wiped the beads of sweat off his brow; it was another scorcher. Taking out his packet of cigarettes, he lit one and glanced at his watch. The morning had sped away and he was surprised that Anna had not put in an appearance; he was ready for her to make him some coffee.

He walked slowly down the end of the garden and looked over to the pool; a garden umbrella had been opened and a lounger placed beneath it. A pair of long, slim, quite naked legs were stretched out on the lounger, but the raised back hid the rest of her from him. As he moved closer he saw the figure of Anna reclining there, clad in a very colourful, and very smart, bathing suit. It was also very revealing; and what it revealed was truly stunning.

He felt his heart start to race, for her attire was so out of character with the Anna he knew.

As he approached she looked up and her mouth drew back in a smile; her eyes were encased behind sunglasses and he wished he could see if they contained an invitation.

"Good morning, Jack," Anna said, wondering if she had been wise to sunbathe with him around. Automatically she reached across for the towel revealing as she did the valley between her breasts. She saw his eyes roam across her body and there was no mistaking his thoughts.

"Have you had a swim?" he asked for something to say as he tried to avert his eyes.

She turned and removed her dark glasses. "Not yet, I just thought I'd take advantage of the sun." She gestured for him to sit on the chair opposite.

"Help yourself to a drink, non alcoholic I'm afraid!" She indicated the glass jug of juice with its half-melted ice cubes. He could not avert his eyes from her body as he started to pour himself a glass of orange, spilling it onto the table. She saw his discomfiture and felt a strange sense of power; here was a man young enough to be her son, apparently lusting after her.

"Just what I need," he muttered as he gulped down half a glassful in one go. "And you!"

"Half a glass, please"

They talked for a few minutes, but he felt uncomfortable unsure where to place his eyes, unsure too of why she was dressed so provocatively. Was she sending out a signal to him and if she was – what was it?

He got up, saying, "I've a lawn to mow."

Anna also stood up and draped a towel round her shoulders.

"I'll burn if I remain out too long," she said as she walked with him along the pathway to the front entrance.

"Thanks for the drink," he murmured with a grin.

"Oh , my pleasure…" she replied in a light tone.

He stared at her and then, mistaking her innuendo, leaned forward and kissed her on her cheek. Immediately, her hand swung out and caught his cheek a hearty slap, and he knew he had made a mistake. He backed away as her voice came over cold and disdainful.

"I think you had better leave, Jack."

He spluttered an apology but Anna had turned and was walking back to the house.

He was unsure if she approved of his kiss or not. Was she just playing hard to get? Should he go after her?

After thinking about it he decided discretion was the better part of valour. He did leave - but not until he'd mowed the lawn.

Jack returned home knowing he had made a serious misjudgement. He had misread the signals. But had he or was it that she was merely confused? He went up to his room and stood by the window, angry for his stupidity.

It was later that day as they sat round the dining table finishing off the evening meal.

"You're quiet!" Becky said as she peered at him. "Lady de Courtney sacked you?"

"Oh shut up," Jack snapped back. "No, she hasn't sacked me if you must know."

Rose poured out three mugs of tea saying, "She's probably

asked him to help out at the church barbecue... there's a meeting tonight to get more volunteers."

"Oh is that it!" Becky said, "Our Jack is a volunteer... for what I wonder!"

"She mentioned it today... I forget when I'm suppose to be there... the church hall... isn't it?" Jack lied.

"That's right," Rose replied without much interest. "Eight o' clock."

Becky met Jack's eyes, "Well, with Mrs de Courtney organising it, it should be a faultless event." She raised her eyebrows, "Seems that everything this woman does is too good to be true."

Jack tried to hear the hidden sarcasm in her voice but there was none. "You could be right," he said not wishing to be drawn any further but knowing he would attend the meeting at the church hall.

Jack showered and changed and then he drove slowly to the church. He would persuade Father Mathews to let him play the guitar at the barbecue; it would impress Mrs de Courtney. Yes, he felt quite pleased with himself as he drove into the car park beside the church hall. Now he glanced round at the parked cars but was unable to locate her BMW. He hesitated and picking up his guitar case slowly wandered into the hall.

The interior of the hall was dark as if wishing to close out the bright evening summer sunlight. Groups of people were standing around with sheets of paper in their hands. There was a drone of voices and the sound of footsteps on wooden floorboards.

"Jack!" Father Mathews, dressed in overalls, came across hand outstretched. "I didn't know you'd volunteered," he looked round, "Brother Martin will introduce you to people."

"Mrs de Courtney, she's not here yet?" Jack asked and he looked round the hall once more.

"No, Mrs de Courtney is late... unusual for her."

Brother Martin took Jack's arm and introduced him to various members of the congregation. Suddenly Jack wished Anna would come and put some organisation into the melee.

Then he heard the hall doors open and as Anna walked in he felt his heart go into its usual excited beat. Dressed in a loose white top and well fitting blue linen skirt and blue open-toed high-heeled shoes and with her hair falling loose round her face.

He stood waiting for her to smile at him. But her eyes merely flickered in his direction with no friendliness in their depths as she swept passed the waiting groups without stopping to talk.

"Sorry I'm late," she said contritely as she apologised to Father Mathews. Then frowning she turned and gave Jack a cursory nod of acknowledgement. He felt shut out and childishly angry that she had ignored him, her eyes refused to meet his. He knew he was sulking like a child left out of a party. He scowled when a woman called Liz came across and asked him what he intended doing. He saw Anna sit behind a makeshift desk and go through the agenda items.

He walked across and stood looking down at her.

"Good evening, Mrs de Courtney."

She did not look up but continued to turn over the documents on the table as she murmured.

"Good evening." Then gathering her papers together she stood up and formally tapped the table and immediately the babble of voices hushed.

"Thank you all for coming," Anna said in a brusque manner. "I'll now go through the detailed arrangements." She did not turn in his direction at any point and Jack knew Anna had deliberately ignored him. He waited until she paused as if she had finished and asked, "So, what do you want me to do?"

"Go home!" she replied.

"Go home?" he repeated, taken aback at her abruptness.

"Yes, you can come on the night and play your guitar, Father tells me you are reasonably talented."

"Would you like me to do some cooking?"

"No thank you." Her answer was flat.

"Just strum the guitar. You can manage that can you?" Her voice was cold and he felt her hostility. The onlookers listened with Father Mathews, taking in the scene.

Jack could only stand and stare, not understanding why she was treating him this way. He knew she was upset - but why humiliate him? He walked out, letting the hall door close itself and slam loudly behind him.

On arriving back at home Jack's mother insisted that he called Mary.

The moment she answered the phone he felt the warmth in Mary's voice, the Irish lilt lulling him and quelling his anger, and he pictured her laughing eyes and smiling mouth.

He listened to her whispered words of love, felt his heart beat and the palms of his hands gripped the receiver and he knew he wished that it was Anna who was saying those words. Mary would be his wife, and he loved her, but Anna was different, he couldn't explain it even to himself.

"I'm going out, Mum," he called as he grabbed his car keys.

Jack had a drink in the local pub, but it had not solved anything nor had it assuaged the anger he felt towards Anna. He had contemplated leaving her and letting her find another gardener, but a niggling voice told him that was stupidity. She was still the woman for his days of grace.

He managed to get up early the next morning, taking a few rounds of bread and a bottle of water in a carrier bag in his determination to arrive at Anna's house on time. He would give her no cause to niggle at his time- keeping.

He drove down the avenue and was about to turn in when

he noticed that the gates were closed. He felt a moment's anger; perhaps she had decided not to continue employing him. He glanced at his watch: a minute to nine o'clock. He was about to alight from the car and go to the intercom when the gates swung open. Trust her to be not a minute too soon or a minute too late, he thought, as he slowly drove the Beetle up the driveway.

Her house was quiet. He parked the car in his usual place and taking his carrier bag he marched past the kitchen, not giving his usual friendly wave. He knew Anna was watching him, but apart from a slight nod of his head acknowledging her presence he did not stop but went on over to the shed.

Anna could tell immediately from his cursory nod that despite the fact he was on time the previous night's events had left him hurt and angry. She knew she had been unkind. She had known when he'd marched so angrily out of the church hall that she had been childish, by her need to show him her displeasure – and her power.

Now she stood and watched as he cranked up the lawnmower before starting the methodical walk up and down to try and produce stripes on the tired lawn. He deliberately ignored her as she opened the kitchen door, about to ask if he wanted some coffee; she waited only a second or two for him to change his mind, but then shrugged her shoulders and returned inside to catch up on some overdue telephone calls.

Jack felt hot and weary; his anger had dissipated with the hard work and now he glanced at his watch; there were ten minutes to go. He'd leave as he had arrived, without contacting her. He took the bottle of water he had brought with him out of the plastic bag, opened it and started to gulp the liquid down, determined to be independent. Then he removed his baseball cap to wipe the sweat off his brow.

"Jack!"

He turned in surprise and some of the water spilt down his chest.

Looking up at Anna standing quietly watching him, he did not reply. He just continued to stare at her, trying to gauge her mood and the reason for her approach. Her eyes were veiled behind the dark glasses, but he caught the faint flush of embarrassment on her cheeks.

"You've finished?"

"Yes." He made a monosyllabic reply as he fiddled with the peak of his cap.

"The grass is still very dry!" she looked down and toed it with her sandal.

"It is. I will put the sprinkler on." He started to walk across to the shed.

"Jack." He turned and waited. "I was very rude to you last night…" he could see she was unused to apologising, and was determined not to help her out. "It was childish of me… I was annoyed."

"There was no need for it," he replied.

"I know…" There was a pause before she said quickly, as if afraid of the words, "I am sorry."

She hesitated and then held out her hand. He raised his eyebrows quizzically as he rubbed his hand on the back of his shorts and grinned before taking her slim hand in his.

"So why?" he asked as his eyes met the blackness of her glasses.

"Why?" She repeated the question.

"Why?" His eyes did not leave her face and she averted her gaze. "Okay so I suppose I was stupid walking out, but I felt…" he shrugged his shoulders and held his hands out, "you were rubbishing me."

She shook her head vehemently, "It's not quite that simple, Jack: I am just not going to fill in a young man's summertime."

"For God's sake, I'm not chatting you up," his voice was rough, " I'm not some toy-boy wanting to bed an older woman. I like you - is there anything wrong in that?"

She stared at him, realising her mind was in a turmoil of indecision.

"Look: yesterday I kissed you... I thought that's what you wanted me to do..." he held his hand up seeing the expression on her face. "No, I misread the signals... I shouldn't have presumed just because you were... well, turning me on..."

She raised her eyes and met his and then turned away, but he felt rather than saw a faint glimmer of understanding in her eyes.

"Anna, you're a beautiful woman and I'm no saint... are you still annoyed?" His voice was appealing and she met his eyes, realising it was the first time he had used her Christian name.

"I suppose I should be flattered... but, as I said, I really do not want a summer dalliance," she replied quietly.

"A dalliance, now there's a nice word," and he laughed and quite unexpectedly Anna laughed too.

"I like you and I just wish...!"

"And what do you wish, Jack?" He heard the light teasing note in her voice. He felt a change in the atmosphere: gone was the frost and in place had come a touch of spring.

"Anna I don't want to quarrel with you," he murmured.

"Would you like some coffee?" she temporised.

He followed her down the pathway and into the kitchen. She could feel his presence behind her, so close, and for a brief moment she wondered what it would be like to lie in his arms. To have his lips caressing her body... a young firm masculine form beside her. His kiss: to have his mouth on hers, exploring. Yes, he attracted her... but those thoughts had to remain in her mind... the temptation had to be controlled.

Jack could tell by her nervous movements that she was still unsure and as he walked across to where she was preparing the cafetiere, she turned suddenly and the boiling coffee spilled across the working surface to drip onto the floor.

"Damn!" He heard the anguish and frustration in her voice and knew she was near to tears.

"Hey, it's no disaster," and instinctively he reached out and took her gently into his arms, comforting her as one would a child; but imperceptibly he held her closer. And his lips touched her dark hair. And he so desperately wanted her.

She did not pull away, although he knew she too must be aware of his need; instead she turned her face so her eyes looked up at him and unable to resist the temptation he lowered his head and kissed her on the mouth. For a brief moment he felt her respond. Then she tore herself out of his arms and stood in the puddle of coffee, her eyes blazing with anger.

"My apology did not give you the right to presume..." She stopped and ran her tongue over her lips; she was emotionally distressed.

He frowned, for he was sure he had not misread the signals or the response, however brief it had been.

"Get out, just go. Now, Jack..."

"Look, Anna," he smiled disarmingly. "I think this is all coming out wrong." He started to protest, but without warning the back of her clenched hand had caught his cheek in a savage blow.

Taken completely by surprise he stared at her, seeing now the undisguised anger in her eyes that blazed at him from a face contorted in rage. A different Anna now stood before him, one he did not know, but there was passion he saw that in her eyes and it appealed to him. He knew her anger was due both to her own need, and to her guilt in succumbing to his kiss.

He wanted to hold her: even to be the target of her anger was better than being the object of her indifference.

He tried to placate her: "Look..." But it took no time to realise that he had spoiled his chance and had no option but to leave.

CHAPTER SIX

*A*s he mowed the lawn at his next client Jack asked why he was bothering with Anna at all; she was upsetting him, and he was getting absolutely nowhere. He had been sure she was throwing out signals… but perhaps he'd been too hopeful, too carried away by his own imagination.

She had been on his mind from the moment he'd met her. Okay so he wanted to feel her body beneath his… to hear her moan and, yes… yell! He didn't think she had yelled in climax for a long time – if ever. He wanted to feel her tongue in his mouth, wanting him. No: demanding him…

He stopped mowing and lit a cigarette; it was all fantasy. But she intrigued him by her moods and most of all her beauty. He had set his sights on making love to Anna, and that was that.

Even if it meant he would lose his job, he had to return to the house and clear the air.

It was late evening when he approached the closed gates. He got out of his car and waited for the intercom to respond.

"Who is it?" came her voice, distorted by the speaker.

"Jack…" he waited. The pause seemed to grow in length and he coughed to remind her he had not received an answer. The gates remain closed.

Anna had stayed by the pool all evening imagining he would return. She had even taken the small phone that was linked to the gates with her. An apology, she tried to lie to herself that that was all she wanted... but it wasn't... Her day had been full of doubts. She had to admit she had waited for a phone call or an appearance. At eight o'clock she had given up. Now he was actually there, at the gate to her house... and to her sexuality?

Here was a chance to experience a sexual fulfilment... a last moment to taste a passion she had been denied. He had awakened a need she had thought had abated - or was it only dormant? Now there was a wanting, soon she would be too old to attract a young virile man... soon her body would age whilst her desires remained.

"Are you still there?" he asked.

"Yes, but it is late, Jack and I am rather tired." The voice was ice cold, but her body was tense.

"Please, can't we talk, we have to clear this up."

There was a pause and he was about to turn away when the gates started to swing open. He dashed to the car and threw himself in and drove up the driveway to park outside the front door.

The house was dark and he walked round to the side. He just knew she would be by the pool, sitting on a cushioned chair beneath the large umbrella. He stood looking over at her; she was dressed as she always seemed to be, in a colourful skirt, sleeveless top, sandals. Her long and luxurious hair hung down her back. Her eyes were trapped behind dark glasses and at the sound of his footsteps she turned quickly and then stood up, straightening her skirt; but she did not remove her glasses.

"Yes, Jack?" her voice was brittle and uninviting.

He stood awkwardly, wondering why he had bothered to

come. There was a pause and he shrugged his shoulders and walked across to the pool and sat down on one of the chairs and without asking took out a packet of cigarettes and lit one.

She saw his youth and vulnerability and felt a wave of embarrassment and accepted she was losing control of the situation.

"I can't fathom out your moods," he said, as he watched her fidget uncomfortably.

"Jack, young men do not kiss married women in the manner you kissed me, it is, well..." She stopped.

"I accept you are married," he interrupted her, "I also accept you are a good Catholic," he stretched his legs out and leaned back in a nonchalant manner. "Look, if you and I have another big row then I'll get up and walk away... you'll be without a gardener and the church barbecue will be without a guitarist. We would both be worse off," his voice was mild. She had to accept the wisdom of his statement and lowered her eyes. To dismiss him would mean she was safe.

"I am not your 'days of grace'!" she said quietly.

"Oh, forget them; I don't think they are for someone like you anyway, Anna!"

"I beg your pardon!" she replied indignantly.

"You have too many principles; I couldn't live up to your high standard of life. I bet you've never used contraceptives, I bet you've never missed confession, I bet you adhere to the rule book by the letter..."

"Please refrain from setting me on some moral high ground. You have no right to talk to me like this," her voice was hard and cold.

"Days of grace are love and laughter... you don't need love and you can't laugh."

She stared at him. "I really do think you should leave, you are rude and presuming. I have given you no reason to think that I was at all interested in you." Her voice was angry and she recognised as the words flowed out she was goading him.

"No," he said bleakly as he stubbed his cigarette out. "Shall I?" he pointed to the anti-mosquito flare and when she nodded he leaned forward and struck a match and waited until the small red glow appeared and the wisp of repellent came. "Do you want one of your own drinks?" he asked as he rocked back on his heels, wanting to prolong his stay.

"I have some minutes to read for a meeting tomorrow." Her manner had relaxed a little and he felt on safer ground.

"Minutes!" he stared at her.

"You have heard of them?"

"I've never known anyone sit reading minutes on a beautiful summer's evening."

"Well now you have, and if I am to read them then I do need to concentrate." She had changed her mood again, and he felt confusion, he was used to sexual innuendoes and banter, but this was a maze of hidden obstacles.

"You really are asking me to go?"

"Yes, I am."

"Okay, Mrs de Courtney, I admit defeat… if you want to read your minutes so be it. The alternative would have been to sit back and have a nice relaxing drink and listen to my dreadful jokes."

She stared at him from behind her *Raybans* and quite suddenly she felt her heart begin to thump and there was a dryness in her throat. She closed her eyes and said a silent prayer a mixture of forgiveness and thankfulness, unsure why.

He was relaxed watching her, his mind in a turmoil of uncertainty as he stretched his face into a grin and said.

"Read the minutes tomorrow."

"Are you implying that I enjoy being boring?"

"Well you sometimes look boring. Your hair, it's always

scraped back, you never have it loose, except for tonight of course, and your glasses... its as if you want to hide your beauty... as if you want to be thought of as old... settled, uninteresting. I've been with girls of my age who are stupid and boring, and I've know old women who are alive and interesting."

"The scraping back of my hair, as you so delicately put it, is for practicality: my glasses are to aid vision. I am therefore not in the first category you indicate," the language was rigid and he saw her hand tightly clasped so her knuckles shone through the translucent skin.

"You put yourself down all the time," he leaned forward, his voice and expression now intent, "I know you are about to sack me, okay. But you're a stunningly beautiful woman. When I saw you at Mass I wanted to get to know you."

"Please..." she held a hand out in protest, "I don't want to hear this."

"Don't you? Don't you really want to hear that a man young enough to be your son finds you so bloody sexual he can't get you out of his mind? There's something I have to do, or my life will go to ruin: I want to make love to you, Anna."

She got up and made to slap him across the face, but he was ready for her and grasped her wrist and, despite her struggling, forced it back to her side. She stood back, breathing hard, her eyes wide and staring.

"Get out. GET OUT! Please just go... and this time don't you DARE come back!"

He heard the wild anger in the voice and knew that he had now really lost her.

Anna sat still until she heard the car moving away. Then she ran a hand through her hair and automatically gathered it together, replaced the clasp and straightened her blouse. As she picked up her glasses she found that her hands were shaking, as the moment overwhelmed her with its tangled web of emotions: shame, disappointment, loss, relief, and even excitement.

The sun woke her; it was a new day. Would he come? Surely Jack wasn't that stupid but suddenly she found that she wanted to see him again, wanted him telling her his silly jokes. Was she being fair to him? She showered and dressed and then sat in front of the mirror, staring at her reflection: she looked the same… She peered closely at her face as she picked up her brush and started to tidy her hair, which fell to just below her shoulders. She picked up the clasp and went to pull her hair back to the nape of her neck. And then she stopped. No: today she would leave it loose. She saw her glasses and picked them up: today she would use them only for reading. She stared at her reflection and then grabbed her hair and scraped it back tightly and severely and replaced her glasses on her nose.

Jack arrived determined that he would tell Anna he was quitting as her gardener. He had spent a restless night going over the events of the previous day. He couldn't cope with her stop and start signals; the end did not justify the means.

The gates were open and he drove in, got out of the Beetle and slammed the door shut and then walked by the side of the house, his head down, not wishing to see if she was at the kitchen window waiting. He wanted to tell her he was leaving before she sacked him.

"So you've returned, after all, even after what I told you last night; you come creeping back…" He heard her voice, with its taunting tone, and saw her standing in the open kitchen doorway. Then, "I have looked round the garden: there seems to be very little improvement in the small vegetable patch!" her voice was now more even, but still in control, the voice of an employer.

He took a deep intake of breath and then raised his eyes to meet hers. "Mrs de Courtney, I would be glad if you would pay

me what is owed. I have decided to quit working for you…"
He'd said it, the words were out. He saw her frown and knew
he had taken her by surprise. She bit her lip and then gave a
faint shrug.

"If that is how you want it, I will make out a cheque." She
did not invite him into the kitchen and he remained standing
at the back door. He lit a cigarette.

"Here!" Anna thrust the cheque into his hands. "I would
have thought you could have completed the work we agreed."

"I can't work here, and well you know it; you told me to go
and not come back," he snapped now as anger took over.
"And I don't like being hit by employers in any shape or
form…"

"And I do not like being kissed, slobbered over, by my
gardener," Anna replied sharply. "You have your cheque, I
have nothing more to add…" She turned and fumbled with the
door and he wondered if she was crying and then dismissed
the thought as part of his fantasy about her.

He stuffed the cheque into the top pocket of his shirt and
turned and started to walk back to his car, kicking the gravel
pathway.

"Jack," he heard her voice and stopped and then slowly
turned round.

She was standing her hair loosened her glasses removed
and he could see the tears on her cheeks. "You were right, I
have been unfair to you, I am unused to so many
compliments…" She wanted to add, "… I am unused to love
and sexual encounters."

He went back towards her, fearing she might retreat, but
she stood firm, and let him stand up close to her. Instinctively
he took her in his arms knowing, or at least hoping, she would
respond. He wanted to kiss her, but was afraid to make the
move. He felt her body relax against his and knew that there
had been a sudden change of direction in their relationship.

"Mrs de Courtney," he said as they drew apart. "Do you still want a gardener?"

"You know I do, Jack," she murmured and he saw the faint embarrassment on her face at her admittance.

"Coffee?" Anna turned and walked into the kitchen; Jack followed. There was a decidedly restrained atmosphere, each waiting now for the other to make a move.

Eventually, after exhausting the small talk he said, "Look, I mean say No, if you want…" He ran a hand through his hair. "There is so much I want to tell you, so much I want to ask," he paused trying to gauge her mood. "Would you have a day out with me?"

Her eyes met his. "You are asking me for a date?" there was amusement in her voice.

"Well, yes." He was conscious it all sounded very amateurish and he gave a self-deprecatory shrug.

"That would be…"

He held his breath.

"Very nice," she replied quietly.

Jack congratulated himself as he drove home. Finally he was going to take Mrs Anna de Courtney out. But where? Although he had thought of nothing else but having a day out with her, the actual location remained obscure. It needed to be planned; Anna would expect and deserve that consideration. It could be costly too.

He'd been impulsive with the invitation, as usual. He parked his car in the narrow street and then strode up the path and into the house. Rose was out and for once he was glad that only Becky was around.

She was sitting on a deckchair in their pocket-sized garden, clad in a brief bikini and smothering herself with barrier cream. Her face was burnt red and he swiftly contrasted her with Anna, who always seemed so cool and at ease with any situation.

"Hi!" Becky said: she yawned loudly, without looking up.

Jack smiled. "God, it's a real scorcher, too hot for gardening."

Becky turned. "Jack, get me a can of something from the fridge."

He was about to tell her to get off her backside and then remembered he wanted a favour. He returned with two cans and a tattered road map. He handed her the unopened can and ripped the ring pull off his own. Then he took his tee shirt off and threw it onto Becky's rug and sprawled out next to her.

"I've got a problem!" he said. "I need your help."

"I was hoping for a quiet afternoon," Becky said pointedly.

"Sorry, but I have a crisis!"

Becky frowned as she removed her sunglasses and peered down, seeing him flicking through the map. "What's that for?" she asked as she slurped from the can.

"This is the problem," Jack said and hesitantly told her of his invitation to Anna.

There was a deadly silence.

Becky stared at him incredulously and finally unable to contain her anger snapped. "Are you stupid?"

Jack shrugged. "No, of course not," he blustered. "I just asked her out... she's lonely... family away..."

Becky's expression indicated both her scepticism and her dislike of the situation. She issued a warning as to the consequences of any friendship with an older woman, and a married one, too.

Jack dismissed it all with a wave of the hand.

"And what the hell happens if Mary finds out?" Becky went on.

"She won't," Jack replied simply.

Becky could not understand Jack and the obsession he had with this woman called Anna. She and Rose had laughed about it but now it was getting into the realms of seriously affecting his life.

"Look, you're engaged to Mary... I like Mary, we get on, what the hell are you messing about for? This woman, she's old... probably looking for a bit on the side... think what you're doing!"

Jack glared at her, knowing that what she said was not exactly true and he attempted to placate her. "Look it's to satisfy my vanity, I just want to take her out for the day. She's not what you and Mum think she is. She's a lonely married woman... I just feel sorry for her!"

"Pure rubbish and you know it. She's twice your age at least," Becky went on.

"Okay, okay... I 'm sorry I mentioned it," he said sulkily and lay on his back and stared up at the sky. "Just give me a clue as to where to take her," he murmured after a moment's pause. "Please!"

Becky gave a faint inward smile as she quickly thought of a place that would really be the biggest yawn she could think of. Somewhere that Mrs de Courtney would not enjoy. Yes, if Jack was intent on this ludicrous outing then she was determined that he would see this wonderful Anna in a different light. Well, kids, crowds and romance just don't go together. It had to be a tourist-infested place... Then she had it: Stratford! Oh how the elegant Mrs de Courtney would hate those crowds! Giving a silent smirk she said seriously.

"Why not a little culture? I'm sure she'd appreciate an afternoon in Stratford, a walk along the banks of the Avon... dead romantic!" and she smirked inwardly.

"You think so?"

"I can give you the name of a pub, *The Dirty Duck*, doesn't sound very Mrs de Courtney... but it's okay!" She yawned again and closed her eyes, remembering the vibrant, crowded hostelry. Anyone but Mrs Anna de Courtney! She was sure there would be no further outings between them after this fiasco. Becky sighed satisfied she had done all she could for Mary.

Jack thought it out and then nodded enthusiastically. "Fine, we'll drive to Stratford, I'm sure she'll like walking along the river. Don't mention this to Mum!" He slapped his hand against the map and smiled gratefully at the silent Becky.

"I suppose you also intend taking her in that old tatty car! I mean, she's used to five-star treatment." Becky could not resist the final dig.

He stared at her, his exuberance for the day gone. He felt deflated. She was right.

"Any suggestions?"

"No, sorry," Becky said, pleased she had put a final dampener on his day out.

Anna had watched as Jack chugged down the drive in his Beetle. A date! A day out with her gardener, whatever had possessed her? The brief moment when he had taken her into his arms, well, she had known then that the physical attraction was mutual.

She should have declined his invitation. He was really too young. Well, perhaps not that young. Suddenly she thought of Charles and felt a moment's sadness. She couldn't talk to anyone about Charles. Once, she had phoned *The Samaritans*. It had been in the early hours of the morning. She had heard the sleepy voice on the other end of the phone. "Samaritans, can I help you?" She had felt the sweat on her hands as she'd sat on the edge of Charles's chair in the study.

She had gripped the receiver.

"Hello, are you there?" someone had said.

She had managed to whisper, "Yes." But that had been all; slowly she'd replaced the receiver. There was no solution, but to talk about it would have helped. It was Charles' secret and her unwitting one. Was her life built on secrets? It seemed extraordinary that she and Charles had been married for over twenty years and they both shared a secret each. Would Jack be a second secret for her?

She walked into the conservatory and listened to Hector as he sat on the window ledge spitting at the birds, who teased him because they were out of his reach.

Hector knew all their secrets.

She was becoming morbid; she sat down and thought about Jack. Where would he take her? She should phone him and cancel it. But no. Curiosity got the better of her; here was a young brash man who thought he was God's gift to women and now he was being put to the test. She laughed inwardly to herself. His car; she couldn't be seen in that dreadful old banger. No, she would use her own car. He could drive. She yawned as she rested her head against the chair back and closed her eyes.

Although Anna had previously rejected a summer dalliance with Jack, she did not look upon an afternoon out as anything other than what it was. At least it would be safe: in the public eye, away from the house and entirely under her control. Perfect.

CHAPTER SEVEN

*J*ack arrived at Anna's just after lunch; he had dressed in a clean casual denim shirt, black jeans and casual tan leather shoes. Anna sensed immediately that he had taken time and trouble in choosing what to wear and she knew that he wanted the afternoon to be a success. Anna too had given it some thought, and ended up in a sleeveless white cotton blouse, a swirling summery skirt and white high heeled summer shoes. She deliberately wore her hair loose and held the fringe back with a red band.

"Hi!" He gave her an approving stare as she came out with Seth on the lead.

"I'd like to take him, can we?"

Jack hesitated for a moment then nodded; he breathed a sigh of relief as Anna, without comment, handed him the keys of her BMW.

"So?" Anna asked as she watched Jack's firm hands on the steering wheel as he guided her car out of the drive. "Where are we going?"

"Stratford. We can walk on the towpath and give Seth a run. Is that all right?"

She nodded her approval and asked. "Have you been to the theatre there?" Suddenly she realised how little she knew about his likes or dislikes. Conversation was proving difficult as there seemed to be an unbridgeable constraint between them.

Although he appeared to be a good driver, she sensed Jack was ill at ease driving her car; but his choice of venue, Stratford, had pleased her. His suggestion to make it an afternoon outing, and being agreeable for Seth to accompany them, meant no hotels and no formality. Anna approved of well executed plans.

"I would like to go, but it's really a little beyond my budget, at the moment. And you?" He too was conscious of the restraining atmosphere that existed between them and wondered if he had made a mistake in listening to Becky's advice.

"We used to go, occasionally, but I don't think Charles really enjoyed it," she sighed.

Jack wanted to ask, why? He wanted to ask what sort of a man is this Charles who allows his beautiful wife to feel neglected, and who leaves her alone whilst he goes away on long business trips. He wanted to ask her if she loved Charles, but he decided it wasn't quite the right moment.

As they finally reached Stratford Anna instructed him, "Down here, there's a car park," and watched as he competently reversed the car into the marked out parking space.

He laughed as he finished the manoeuvre. "I once went out with a girl who couldn't reverse her car; everywhere she went she had to be sure she could drive straight out!"

Anna involuntarily laughed, "Yes, very awkward!"

He made no further comment and got out and walked round to open her door, and then let Seth out from the rear. As he fumbled for the parking fee she almost offered to pay, but then thought it might embarrass him and let him get on with it. He returned to stick the ticket on the windscreen, and watched as she put her sunglasses on her head and called Seth to heel.

"Why do women always wear their sunglasses in their hair?" Jack asked lightly.

"Force of habit," she replied and as Jack held out his hand

to her she chose to ignore it, putting Seth on the lead and placing the dog between them. They walked through the Memorial Park, over the small wooden bridge and across the green square.

The sun was shining down and he could see she was hot.

"How about an ice cream?" he suggested desperately trying to relax the tension, as they stopped for Seth's needs.

She frowned and briefly shook her head. He sensed she did not approve of eating food in public, but he ignored her and went across to the ice-cream van parked at the side of the road and returned with two huge vanilla cones, which were already dripping. Anna had always stipulated to her children that one should ever buy food from vendors, especially those with dirty vans, but she knew she had no choice and reluctantly took the cone; she wondered if the vendor had used a clean scoop. She saw Jack start to devour the ice cream and nibble at the cornet. Not wishing to hurt his feelings she sat with him on the small wall, took a paper tissue from her handbag, placed it round the cone and delicately started to lick the ice cream.

"Well?" he asked as he threw the remains of the cone down for Seth to lick up.

"Very good!" she admitted before placing a generous portion down for Seth. "Although I still don't approve of eating in the street." He heard the puritanical tone in her voice and laughed as she wiped her hands with the paper tissue and then replaced it in her bag.

"What are you laughing at?" She stared at him.

He shrugged, "I am laughing at your middle class attitude; we live in a street eating society, you should be glad you can always get something when you want it..." He stopped as he saw the closed expression creep over her face. Anna wondered whether to accept his criticism or react to it; she quickly chose to ignore it.

"Come on." He got up and held his hand out to her. She

hesitated and then allowed him to pull her up from the wall. They walked slowly past the *Royal Shakespeare Theatre,* glancing at the forthcoming productions.

"Oh, the *Taming of the Shrew,*" she exclaimed.

"I like Shakespeare," he offered, not too truthfully.

Anna frowned, "I wouldn't have thought Shakespeare would have been your forte."

"Well you're wrong." Suddenly it came to him, a long forgotten memory, and he couldn't help but feel extremely pleased with himself as he said, "*You lie, in faith; for you are call'd plain Kate, and bonny Kate and sometimes Kate the curst.*" He stopped and started to laugh as he saw the amazement in her eyes. "I played Petruchio in a school play," he confessed.

"You surprise me sometimes," she replied, a thoughtful expression now on her face.

They continued to stroll along.

"Come on, I could do with a beer." He pointed across the road to the pub.

"*The Dirty Duck.*" He heard the faint intonation in her tone as she looked up and read the pub's name. He gave her a sideways glance, but her face was expressionless.

Taking her hand in his he guided her across the road and then up the few steps to the pub. It was crowded but as they stood glancing round the patio a couple got up from their table and Jack moved swiftly across and gestured for Anna to follow.

She paused before saying, "Could you take the glasses away please, Jack?" She brushed a hand over the seat and sat down, pushing the ashtrays and crisps packet to one side with disdain.

"Okay here?" He waited until she had settled down and Seth had flopped beside her. "What'll it be… beer…white wine… G and T?"

She held her hands out, "Oh, not in the afternoon…"

He raised his eyebrows, "Never?" he asked and the suggestion was not lost on her.

"Depends who's asking…" she laughed as she joined in his game of innuendo.

"I'm asking…"

"What?" she smiled and he frowned.

"What would you like to drink?"

"Oh, that!"

He grinned realising she was playing him at his own game.

"A shandy; a small shandy, please," she amended and watched him go to the bar with a perplexed expression on his face.

He returned, placed the drinks on the table and produced two packets of crisps from his pocket. Then she watched as he went back to the bar, to return with a large ashtray full of water which he placed down on the floor for Seth, who lapped it up gratefully. She smiled, acknowledging his thoughtful gesture.

"Thank you." She tried to make her voice sound grateful as he opened the packet of crisps for her, but half a pint of shandy and a packet of salt and vinegar in a crowded pub just wasn't her idea of afternoon refreshments. Jack watched as she delicately picked up the half pint and took a hesitant sip as he leaned back and lit a cigarette. They talked in staccato fashion to start with and then slowly she relaxed again in his company.

She saw the eyes of the two teenage girls at the next table sweep over her and then stare at Jack curiously. Anna could see they were trying to assess the situation, and suddenly it amused her. She knew they wondered whether she was mother or lover. Now one of the girls flicked her hair back from her face, her eyes bold and knowledgeable as she ran a tongue lightly over her scarlet lips in a tantalising gesture. They nudged one another and giggled audibly.

"I think they want your attention," Anna whispered as she took another sip of her drink.

Jack too had been aware of them; he had seen the provocative movements of their body, known what they wanted. It amused him, and he had wondered at Anna's reaction.

"I think they are trying to discover if I am your mother!" she said in an amused voice; she turned and gave him a quizzical glance.

"Shall we show them you're not?" he asked joining in the game as he leaned forward and placed his arm round her shoulder.

"Jack," she murmured surprised at herself for she was not embarrassed. Instead she could only feel an odd pleasure in the sense of victory. Anna's eyes met those of the girls and she found herself raising her eyebrows in an acknowledgement of possession. Then on impulse she turned and laughed into Jack's face. It was an intimate gesture that left the onlooker in no doubt as to their relationship. It also indicated to Jack that they had gone out with the boundaries of friendship and tentatively entered a flirtatious mood.

"Oh I am wicked," Anna murmured.

"I could never see you being wicked," Jack replied seriously.

The smile was momentarily wiped off Anna's face as she remembered her secret and felt the pangs of guilt as they conflicted with the carefree attitude she was displaying. Perhaps she was trying to recapture some of the lost years and make up for the disappointment and trauma that marrying Charles had caused her. Perhaps not.

"You look very pensive." Jack saw the shadow cross her face and realised her mood had imperceptibly changed from joy to almost sadness.

"I was just thinking," she replied; but she did not elaborate.

They got up and he picked up Seth's leash; then Jack held his hand out to her and now she grasped it as they walked out of the pub. Across the road was the *Collegiate Church of Holy Trinity*.

They walked into the sombre graveyard with overhanging trees that obstructed the sunlight and stood for a moment just looking at the moss-covered tombstones.

"It's depressing," Jack observed as he saw Anna reading one of the inscriptions.

Graves always reminded Anna of her mother; she did not want any more of those unpleasant thoughts to invade her mind and spoil what was turning out to be an enjoyable afternoon. She walked slowly with Seth on the lead round the tombstones, peering at the names and dates. Then she glanced across to see Jack looking at a grave and watched as he bent down to study one of the gravestones; she saw a sadness on his face so she knew he was thinking of his father. After a few minutes she went across and placed a hand on his shoulder and whispered.

"*Do not stand at my grave and weep, I am not there, I do not sleep.*"

He stood up, took her hand in his and kissed it. Anna still found outward affection in public embarrassing, but she continued to allow him to hold her hand as they walked to the large porch.

"Shall we go into the church?" he asked. She hesitated and he saw her uncertainty but then she nodded.

"Will Seth be okay tied here?" he enquired.

"As long as he can lie down in the shade he'll be fine." She watched as Jack tied the lead round a metal post.

"You know, I've never been inside an Anglican church, except once for a wedding," she admitted as they stood in the porch. He moved forward to click open the ancient latch on the inner door.

"Mind your head!" he read the notice and obeyed it as he passed through.

In contrast to the warm day, the church was cool; it was well lit and they stood amongst the other visitors, looking around at the old pews and the magnificence of the stained glass windows. It gave Anna the feeling that this was a well-used and well-loved church. They stood for a moment as they let their gaze take in the surroundings. Jack watched as Anna walked to the centre aisle of the church and, with habit born of old, and disregarding some curious stares, genuflected to the altar. Jack hesitated and then allowed his knee to bend in acknowledgement that he was in the house of the Lord.

"There isn't much reverence in here, is there?" Anna commented, as they followed a group of chattering women.

"Look at these!" Anna now stopped as she pointed to the beautifully embroidered kneelers that hung in lines on hooks on the back of the pews in front. They turned to the rear of the church, fingered the baptismal font and saw the reserved pews.

"*Church Warden!*" she read from the sign.

"Perhaps they have reserved places in heaven as well!" Jack said humorously as he glanced through a prayer sheet. They walked down the aisle to the pulpit.

"It is a beautiful church," Anna murmured.

"Look at this carving," Jack pointed to a screen between the choir stalls and the altar. "They used to serve the Eucharist behind this screen and they rang the bell to tell the congregation that the sacrament was being blessed. This is a very old church," he acknowledged.

They walked to the steps leading to the choir stalls and stopped; there was a man sitting at a small table with a large notice affixed on a stand. "Fifty pence to see the grave of Shakespeare," Jack read, and then turned to her with a querying expression, but she had walked away.

"I don't think it is right to ask for money to see a grave," she whispered. "This is not a museum, it is God's house, a place for peace and prayer."

He was surprised to hear the self-righteous tone in her voice but was getting used to it.

"I suppose it is like paying to see the resting place of Princess Diana," he replied.

"Doesn't make it right," Anna said coldly, and then she added, "It is not peaceful. You really couldn't sit here and pray. It is too noisy. There is no solemnity." She stopped and he watched as she placed an offering in the collection box and then he followed her out. "It's all different routes to God, I suppose," she said bending to release an anxious Seth from the metal post. "I did once think of becoming a nun, but then I realised I did not have any saintly qualities."

He laughed, "I'd would have thought you had all the saintly qualities one would ever need."

She gave him a sharp under-the-lid glance: was he being sarcastic? "Now why do you say that?"

"Because you're a good person, Anna."

They stopped walking and turned to face each other. There was a lingering empathetic moment as Jack gazed into the depths of her blue eyes. She saw quite clearly what the look portended and she decided it was time to go. They started to walk down the cobbled pathway of the church.

"Do you go to Mass every Sunday?" Jack asked as he held the gate open for her.

She nodded. "Yes, I try to. My family do not attend Mass now. Steven has lost interest and Kate, well, she comes occasionally with me."

"Your husband?" he asked guiding her round the parked cars.

"Charles?" she gave a bitter laugh. "He is too interested in his business at the moment. But I believe that everyone returns, or wishes to return, to a belief as mortality draws nearer. I think in adversity you do find the need for faith."

"I suppose so, I can't say I've given it much thought. I bet you're a good Catholic..."

"No!" her voice rose sharply. "Please don't call me a good Catholic, there is no such thing as being a good Catholic: I am merely a practising Catholic and try to be a good Christian."

He stared at her, surprised at the faint tinge of venom in her reply.

"Okay, but you're helping with the church barbecue, so you must be committed."

"I help with arranging the barbecue because Father Mathews asked me to but that does not make me a good Catholic..."

He frowned, her reply seemed unusually sharp and he placed an arm round her shoulders and gave her an impulsive hug, but she pulled away and they walked in silence until he said.

"Come on, let's walk back along the river." He took her hand again and swung it in time to the pace. They stopped to watch the swans gliding past, and then at the narrowboats moored to the banks of the Avon.

"I always thought I'd like a boat and just meander along through the canals," he said, as he released her hand and reached into the top pocket of his shirt to take out a cigarette. "I often thought it would be satisfying to be on a boat writing a book or painting a masterpiece. But I've done neither; my days will be accounting... just figures."

"Accountants make a good living," Anna murmured reassuringly, countering his note of dissent.

"I guess so." He gave a rueful grin and seeing Seth bounding towards him, reached down to pick up a stick and threw it into the distance. Seth eagerly ran after it and Jack played with the dog for a while as Anna stood watching them.

"Let's sit down." He finally walked across to a wooden seat and flopped down and then lit his cigarette.

She bent down and told Seth to go into the shade.

"It's a peaceful spot, nice watching the river and the boats," she murmured. She was conscious that he had placed his arm along the back of the seat, but seemed to have accepted his gesture: not welcoming it, but not tensing in rejection either. She turned toward him. "I want to ask you a question," she said simply.

Jack shrugged. "Ask away!"

"Why me?"

He stared at her, unable to answer immediately. Then he gave a wide grin, "Because you are so beautiful. I don't mean beauty as in looks; I mean you look stunning but you're also beautiful in manner and character. I just fell for you the minute I saw you…it was a challenge."

She frowned.

"Oh, come on," he went on, "you know how good you look."

"And the challenge?" She gave a disarming smile.

"To be your friend," he said lightly. He could tell his reply did not satisfy her but she would not let her curiosity take the line of conversation further.

Two elderly ladies tottered past, obviously sharing a joke, and hearing their laughter. Anna suddenly remembered the many times she had walked along this very path with her mother and how they had laughed together. It seemed a lifetime ago. She shuddered violently, and acquired a solemn aspect.

Jack noticed her change of mood as a reflective expression came into her eyes. "Are you all right?" He moved his arm round her shoulders and he wondered what memory had been evoked.

"Just a ghost walking over my grave," and suddenly she

was glad to feel the heat of his hand through the thin texture of her clothes.

"You've no ghosts, surely?"

"We all have ghosts lurking in the shadows. The devil is never far away."

Jack looked at her surprised by the seriousness in her voice. "How can you look like an angel and have the soul of the devil?" he asked.

Anna didn't reply. She couldn't let this flashback break into the sunny, warm day, her first chance to relax: she hadn't been able to sort out her own mind yet, let alone reveal its secrets to a stranger on a park bench. He repeated his question, pulling her slightly toward him so she had to look up and meet his eyes.

"Small sins," she countered.

"Oh come on, going through a red traffic light is hardly the same as killing someone is it?"

She turned away and bent down to stroke Seth. It was time to leave.

They arrived back at Kinellan House at six-thirty.

"I can't ask you in," Anna said, and saw the disappointment in his face. "I have a meeting with LATE tonight. But thank you, Jack," she reached forward and kissed him on the cheek, "it was a lovely afternoon."

CHAPTER EIGHT

*J*ack arrived home feeling elated. It had been his first day of grace with Anna. As a memory he knew it would be hard to better. His exuberance was not lost on Rose or Becky.

"You've caught the sun?" Rose said as he walked into the living room.

"All that gardening for Mrs de Courtney." Becky gave him a sly wink as he sat down and stretched his legs out and threw her a cigarette before lighting his own.

"Was it successful; did it all go well?" Becky whispered as Rose left the room.

"Absolutely," he beamed at her and mistook her flash of irritation as one of conspiracy. They made idle conversation before Rose came back into the room.

"Time for my bus! To take me to Allan House." She gave Jack a meaningful glance but he did not reciprocate by offering her a lift. He didn't want Anna to see him dropping his mother off.

"My, Mrs de Courtney works her volunteers hard!" and Becky winked at Jack.

"So tell me?" Becky asked when they heard the front door slam behind Rose, "how did it go?"

Jack gave her a swift account of the day and Becky heard the faint admiration in his tone at the mention of Anna's name.

"You like her don't you," Becky cut in, "I mean *really* like her?"

He hesitated and then nodded. "Yes, I do."

"You're not surely going to sleep with her, because if you do I'll have no choice but to tell Mary."

Jack shook his head. "Don't be bloody stupid. No, of course I'm not going to sleep with her. I love Mary, you know that..." He smiled reassuringly at Becky but she could see the smile did not reach his eyes. "Anna is just a friend..."

"Oh so it's Anna is it?" Becky remarked sarcastically.

"I can hardly take her out and keep on calling her Mrs de Courtney; anyhow everyone is on a first-name basis these days," he snapped.

"What on earth do you see in her?" Becky asked curiously. "Mary's so vibrant, I mean..." she shrugged her shoulders. "Don't bugger up your life because of, well, an infatuation for this woman."

He drew deeply on his cigarette and stared down at the carpet. He wanted to tell her to mind her own business, but he knew he would have to be careful. Better placate her than row with her. Becky walked towards the door, but before she got there Jack called her back.

"You ask me what I see in Anna, well let me tell you. She takes pride in her appearance. She is interesting, well-educated, not afraid to speak her mind on topics she disapproves of. She's good company has a sense of humour and..."

Becky interrupted him, "Oh please, why not just say she's a paragon of virtue?" she said as a parting shot and left the room.

The bus had been crowded and if truth be known Rose wished the evening meeting had been cancelled. It was a quarter to eight when Rose finally reached Allan House. She glanced at her watch as she hurried across the car park and saw with annoyance Anna's white BMW. Why was that woman always punctual, she wondered annoyed that she had not left home earlier.

Once inside the offices of LATE she saw the meeting had only just started. Making a hasty apology to the other volunteers she squashed into one of the two remaining seats. Rose glanced through the proposed volunteers' schedules. She was feeling hot, tired, and irritable.

Plastic cups of water from the provided chilled water container were passed along the table and she gulped hers down, knowing as she did that it had suddenly made her face flush beacon red. Her entire body now seemed to be on fire and she wished she had chosen a more suitable attire; man-made fibres always clung to her with body heat and she was conscious she looked overweight, hot and exhausted.

"Good evening, ladies." Rose heard the light bright voice and knew it belonged to Anna de Courtney. She glanced round at the familiar faces of the other volunteers before her eyes finally rested on the slim cool figure of Anna, dressed in a lightweight beige flecked linen suit. Her hair loose round her face, her make-up impeccable. Rose always felt ill at ease with Anna, who to her epitomised so much she would have liked to have been herself. Smart, rich slim and competent.

The meeting rumbled on with items under discussion, such as transport, driver rotas, volunteers, day group activities, in fact all the subjects Rose felt the least likely to consider on a hot summer's evening. It was when the reports for the day club catering were read out that Rose pointed out two discrepancies she had found on the schedules; also her concern regarding the lack of drivers available during the summer for the ambulances.

"Well spotted." Anna nodded her approval, and Rose felt her face burn even brighter. Anna swiftly called on June the elderly secretary and gave concise instructions to her as to the action required. Rose listened to an efficient and polite Anna; it was not long before the situation was in hand with the appropriate amendments. Even when Anna faintly rebuked June for her typing errors, the criticism came out as complimentary and Rose had to admire the way Anna handled all her staff.

With the meeting drawing to a close Rose was the last to leave the building. She heard the sound of an engine and then the familiar voice of Anna calling from her car.

"Let me give you a lift home!"

Rose hesitated and then not wishing to appear churlish nodded her acceptance. The drive home was without incident and Rose had temporised with letting Anna know that she was Jack's mother, but for his sake and the embarrassment she knew it would cause she decided to say nothing. They engaged in banalities and it was not long before Anna drew up outside the small terraced house.

"Thank you for the lift," Rose said as she struggled from the car.

"It's the least I could do," Anna murmured and as the passenger door closed, she checked her mirrors before moving off. But she failed to see Jack's battered orange Beetle parked at the side of the road.

When Anna arrived back home, on the doorstep she found a single red rose with a card saying: *Thanks for a lovely day, Jack.*

Obviously Jack had used his ingenuity as to how to get into the garden; the gates had been closed all evening. She smiled inwardly as she carried the rose indoors, but the elation was dissipated when the quietness of the house and the ever-present memories of her past flooded back to invade her mind.

Jack had spent the following morning at an old lady's house monotonously mowing the lawn. His thoughts were not on his work but with Anna. He had heard his mother's detailed account of the previous night's meeting and was glad that Rose had given Anna praise, as it confirmed his original assessment that she was a good person.

In the early afternoon Jack found himself back at Kinellan House. He had planned a surprise afternoon with Anna and he hoped she would be agreeable.

Anna came out of the back door and again her attractiveness caught him off-guard. She was a woman who did not try to be beautiful, and yet she unwittingly was. He contrasted her unfairly with Becky, who would plaster make-up on in the belief it made her appealing, and Mary, who had a vibrant beauty but not a natural one.

"Anna!" His voice was full of enthusiasm. "It's a beautiful day, we'll drive to Malvern and climb the Hills... we'll have a dinner in some pub... you'll love it!"

Anna frowned, "I thought you were coming here to do the garden?" she said jokingly.

"Come on," he cajoled, and it was not long before she found herself in Kate's bedroom staring at herself in the mirror as she fastened the clasp of the leather belt with its ornate buckle on the waistband of her daughter's jeans.

She looked again at herself. The image was not of Anna who would proclaim in a superior tone, "Oh I never wear jeans, not even slacks... they are just not me!" No, this reflection in hip-hugging jeans was not the Anna everyone knew and she blinked in disbelief.

She searched the wardrobe for a suitable shirt and finding nothing went into Steven's room, but ended up going through Charles's wardrobe to find a cotton shirt which he had never worn.

Jack had been pacing up and down the hallway with growing impatience. Finally he had mounted the stairs. He stood on the galleried landing and walked slowly down the small door-lined passage, seeing the array of pictures on one of the walls. He stopped; they were all family photographs. A young Anna, with two children and a man. It had to be Charles. More school photographs. Anna and a white haired old woman... her mother? He would have liked to spend more time, but he heard Anna's voice.

"Is that you Jack?"

"Yes," he replied, but curiosity got the better of him and he walked into what looked like a guest bedroom.

"What do you think of this?" he heard Anna ask and walking out of the room he turned and they met in the doorway.

"What are you doing in here?" Anna asked sharply and the initial friendliness had gone for the moment.

"Just admiring your house."

"Come and look at this shirt..." She took his hand and guided him from the room. He felt that he had trespassed as she closed the door behind him – and locked it.

She tucked the shirt into the jeans and Jack saw a different Anna looking back at him: the sophisticated clothes had been replaced by mundane clobber.

"If Charles could see me now!" she smiled

"If Mary could see me now," he temporised.

"Will you ever tell Mary?" Anna asked as she rolled back the shirtsleeves.

"I've already done so," he grinned.

"You've what!"

"I told her I met a beautiful, rich, older woman."

"And what did she say?"

"It's an odd quirk of human nature, for when you tell the truth, people don't believe you. Mary just laughed and wished me well..." He walked towards her and placed his hands round her waist, drawing her close.

"I'll never tell her," he whispered. "Some things are best not revealed, and our days together belong to us. Soon we'll have to say goodbye and that will be the end of our days of grace. You will live your life with Charles and your family and I will marry my Mary." She heard the note of sadness in his voice, and knew what he said would have to be.

"Quite a climb!" Anna gasped as they stopped and stood together, windswept at the top of the hill, and looked down at the open English countryside spread out below them. Jack took in Anna's long dark hair ruffled by the breeze, the faint sweat on the brow and the cheeks with the blush of a sun-kiss. Shirt sleeves rolled up, shirt collar unbuttoned to reveal the outline of breasts, the jeans, well-fitting, scuffed and worn and the shoes, expensive brogues for gentlewomen on country walks. Sometimes he felt his time with Anna was unreal, and he had to shake his head to ensure it was no dream.

"My feet!" She untied one of the laces. "It's the first time these walking shoes have really been walked in!"

Reality returned. He sat down on the ground and lay back. "It's dry," he said, seeing her hesitate; he held his hand out and she sat down awkwardly beside him. She watched as he took the inevitable cigarette from the pocket of his shirt and placed it between his lips - his eyes not leaving her face. She wondered why she found the act so sexual; reaching across and removing the unlit cigarette from his lips she ran a hand through his hair and smoothed it back.

Jack stared up at Anna as she turned to rest on her elbow; suddenly he decided he wanted her to take the initiative. She had removed her sunglasses and her eyes were scanning his face. He ran his tongue lightly over his lips and he heard the sudden intake of her breath and he knew she wanted him. Then as she lowered her head he closed his eyes; then he felt her lips on his forehead, his cheek and finally on his mouth.

"I think we should continue our walk," she said firmly, staggering to her feet, flustered and unsure.

"Ouch!" she yelled, screwing her face up in pain as her foot touched the ground.

"I think you've got yourself a blister." He knelt down and eased her shoe off and then the sock. The blister was large and water-filled and the surrounding skin red and sore.

"Why the hell didn't you say something?" he looked up at her, "there's no point in being a martyr."

"I wasn't," she snapped.

He reached across to the small haversack he'd brought and took out a first-aid kit, gently punctured the blister, squeezed out the water and pressed the skin back onto the heel. Then he took and placed a plaster over the deflated blister. He'd learned his first aid skills in Romania, he said.

"I think you'll have to take it slowly, you don't want the sock to rub it too much... see how you go. Next time, get some proper walking boots!" he exclaimed in exasperation.

"Next time?" she asked as she watched him pull her sock into position and then ease her foot back into the uncomfortable shoes.

"Sure, next time we'll do a mountain!" and he grinned as he stood up and gave her a brief kiss on the lips. "Give me your hand, lean on me. Let's go down into the village and have a cup of tea."

He kept her amused with information and small talk, so she forgot the agony of her foot. His views were sometimes immature but never boring and she found herself looking at things through his eyes. He made her laugh at stupid things she would have disapproved of. They entered the beer garden of the pub holding hands.

"Get a table I'll order a pot of tea and some cakes," he instructed, and she knew he had been there before, with Mary perhaps, and for a moment she felt a trespasser on forbidden territory.

"I've ordered," he said, coming to sit beside her on the wooden bench. When he reached across the table to take her hand in his she tried to pull it loose, conscious of the eyes of others at nearby tables. But he held it firmly and brought it to his lips.

"Jack, please!" she murmured as his eyes held hers. "I get embarrassed."

"Don't be," he whispered. "No one is interested in you, except me!"

"I will have so much to confess," she closed her eyes and he stared at her, waiting for her to continue, but she merely shrugged her shoulders. A young girl came with a large tray which she placed down and smiled at them.

"Right, ma'am," Jack removed his hand, "that looks really good." He eyed the large pot of tea, the jug of hot water and the plate of warm scones, butter, strawberry jam and a dish of cream.

"Go on," Anna laughed, "have a scone!"

He grinned and put a plate and paper serviette on the table, took a scone, split it and inserted the cream and jam, then he watched as she poured out his cup of tea.

"A nice strong cup," she declared, handing it to him and pointing to the milk and sugar.

"There's a change!"

She raised her eyebrows.

"Well, it's a better cuppa than you make!" he said; there was amusement in his eyes as he picked up the cup and took a sip of the hot liquid.

"I'm sorry?" she said frowning.

"Well to put it bluntly you make a lousy cuppa, Anna!" he laughed.

She stared at him and he could see the flicker of annoyance in her eyes.

"You've never complained," she snapped.

"I've never had the courage."

He saw the two red spot of anger appear on her cheeks and knew she did not like his criticism. "What do you mean? You've never had the courage."

"It would have seemed rude!"

"Oh, and you're never rude!" she remarked sarcastically; there was a tinge of frost in her tone as she added, "Well, you don't have to drink it."

"I'm winding you up," he laughed and then she grimaced and slapped his hand and joined him as he laughed at her.

"I want you like I have wanted no other woman," he whispered as he moved his legs against hers.

"Not even Mary?"

He shook his head. "Not even Mary!"

"Well," Jack said almost an hour later, "I have to go and get the car." He bent and kissed her, and strode off without a backward glance. Anna agreed she would sit in the beer garden resting her foot until Jack returned, and she cursed herself for her stupidity in not wearing trainers or Kate's walking boots.

Jack glanced at his watch: it was five o'clock. He felt the sweat pouring down his face; this was not the leisurely afternoon he had planned. Whoever walked in heavy brogues? He remembered the last time he had done the Malvern Hills with Mary. She was always well equipped for walking, striding ahead of him, her red hair like burnished copper. But he couldn't think of Mary, not today.

Anna soon became bored with sitting in the pub garden. She took the stout stick Jack had found for her and slowly managed to amble round the small village, sitting eventually on a white painted bench overlooking the green. She wished she had given him her mobile phone, some means of communicating with him. He was unused to her car, an accident - he could have crashed. Even lost his way. She could be sitting for hours waiting and wondering. Her mind now started to conjure up all sorts of situations, for he seemed to have been gone an eternity. Had he stolen her car? She dismissed the thought even as it manifested itself in her mind.

Then, just as she was thinking of hobbling back to the Inn and telephoning someone, she hadn't decided who, she heard three hoots of a car horn and saw her BMW pass, and then stop a few yards down the road as her waving stick caught Jack's attention. She clambered into the car and sank back gratefully into the leather passenger seat. Jack looked tired.

"Six o'clock," she murmured looking at the dashboard clock. "Drive into Malvern," she instructed. "It's a nice little place. We'll stop at the *Abbey Hotel* and have dinner there… you've earned it."

He turned the car into the reserved car parking area of the attractive ivy clad hotel. "I could do with a shower," he said looking down at his jeans and sleeveless tee shirt.

They sat in the corner of the dining room, conscious only of each other, their eyes and hands constantly straying to make contact as the meal progressed.

It was only when a family of two young children with their parents and grandmother sat at the next table that Jack noticed a curious change in Anna's manner. He thought at first it was embarrassment at his attire, but then realised it was something deeper. She suddenly seemed remote, inaccessible. Her laughter was forced and her attention distracted. Jack couldn't put his finger on it but noticed Anna's eyes constantly looking over to the family, who seemed to be celebrating the grandmother's birthday.

"Anything wrong?" he asked; it had been quite clear she had not been listening to anything he'd said.

"I beg your pardon?" She jerked back to reality.

"Anything wrong?" he repeated.

"No, why should there be?" and she placed her hand over

his. "I think I'm tired, it has been quite a day." But he wasn't convinced.

When the bill folder arrived Anna said quietly, "This is on me," and covered the bill with her hand. "No protest, please." The receptionist's eyes flickered from Jack and back to Anna with a knowing look as Anna dug into her bag and produced a small wallet from which she extracted a gold credit card. The receptionist looked on with interest as Jack watched Anna sign and return the slip and card to its folder. If Anna expected Jack to be embarrassed she was disappointed; she tucked her arm through his and allowed him to pull her close.

"Won't your husband check on his statement?" Jack asked.

"Really, Jack, this is my own account... every woman should have one, remember, it goes with our independence."

"And indiscretion, perhaps!" he ventured, but she appeared not to have heard.

He helped her walk slowly out of the front entrance and then stood looking back at the hotel. Suddenly Anna reached up and kissed him briefly on the mouth. Jack was comforted by this return to her former happy self, but found himself wondering if he had only imagined her change of mood at dinner.

Once in the car she settled herself back in the seat; as he pulled out of Malvern he saw her chin drop to her chest, and her eyes close. Jack felt a sense of contentment; despite the blister, it had been a good day and he hoped the night ahead would be one to remember. He relaxed and listened to the faint drone of the tyres as they sped over the tarmac. It was quiet with a faint crescent moon appearing and the stars watchful eyes in the heavens.

He remembered another night under the stars, when there had been nothing but hopelessness. Then there had been just a priest and the children accompanied by gunfire. The country road was winding and apart from spasmodic light from other passing vehicles it seemed endless and as Jack felt his eyelids start to close he leaned forward and switched on the radio.

Suddenly there was a hard thud from underneath the car. Instinctively he jammed his foot on the brake and the car slid to a swift halt. The impact jolted Anna forward in her seat and she awoke abruptly.

"What's happened?" she said blinking her eyes sleepily.

"Dunno, but it was a hell of a thud. I'll get out and see." Jack pushed open the door and he got out and walked up to the front of the car.

"Can't see anything!" he muttered as he stared to walk round, inspecting the bodywork.

"Take this," Anna said. She was standing beside him with a torch in her hand. Jack bent down and she shone the beam; neither of them could see any sign of an impact, or damage.

"It must have been a bird!" he said dismissively and stood up, brushed the knees of his jeans and was about to walk back to the car when Anna called from the rear of the vehicle. Her voice was shrill with acute distress.

"Oh my God! You poor poor thing," she cried. He walked across to where she was bending down by the grass verge, shining her torch at the bundle of black and white fur. The cat lay crying in distress. "It's terribly injured, oh Jack what can we do?"

He sighed and knelt beside the limp animal, its opaque eyes staring up at him in helpless terror; momentarily those nights in Romania returned. He swallowed and blinked his eyes and peered at the animal.

"It's taken a hell of a knock. It's probably a farm cat... there's not much we can do, no collar." He grimaced as he noticed now the blood seeping onto the grass. Involuntarily, he shivered.

"Well," Anna said decisively as she too stood up, "we can't leave the poor thing in agony to die. Get me the car rug from the boot."

"You're not taking it with you, are you?"

"And what do you suggest I do, just leave it to die?"

"No, of course not, but it'll mess your car up!" he muttered.

"Jack!" he heard the condemnation and shrugged his shoulders and walked back to the car, returning with a tartan rug.

He stood and watched as Anna, disregarding the blood and dirt, bent down and gently eased the frightened cat onto the rug. He noticed the blood smeared on her hands and the red stain on her jeans and sweater as she rolled the cat up into the rug and carefully carried the bundle back to the car. She placed the rug and cat on the back seat, and then got in beside it. Stroking its head she whispered soothing words.

"So what do we do now?" Jack asked. He had got back into the driving seat and was tapping his fingers on the steering wheel.

"We take it to my vet. Please, pass me my phone."

Jack gave Anna her mobile telephone and as he started the engine he heard her talking to the vet. It was immediately apparent that she knew him of old; they were on first name terms. He overheard her say that she would be there within forty minutes.

As Jack headed for the motorway he was conscious of a stream of distressing cries from the back seat. He saw through the driver's mirror Anna comfort the cat by gently stroking it repeatedly, disregarding the blood-soaked rug , and he listened to her soothing tones. Bizarrely, he thought he could now hear the cat actually purring. His own disgruntled feeling at the abrupt end of what should have been a perfect day dissipated; in the shadow of her care and compassion he suddenly felt ashamed.

The journey seemed interminable. Once off the motorway every traffic light was red and the roads seemed full of Sunday drivers. Following Anna's instructions Jack slowed up outside the large Victorian house before turning into the tarmacadamed front garden, now a car park.

Without hesitation Anna leapt out and scooped the bundle into her arms. "Ouch!" she murmured as a claw caught her arm.

Jack went ahead of her to the door marked *Surgery* and rang the bell. The door was opened almost at once by a middle-aged man of slim build. Dressed in a short sleeve shirt and denim jeans he was staring at Jack; but as soon as he saw Anna coming up the path clutching the blood stained rug, Jack heard the affection in the vet's voice as he greeted her and took the bundle from her arms.

"Hello Miles, sorry to call so late..." Anna said as she followed him up the path.

You are a wonderwoman, Anna!" said Miles, and there was no denying the admiration and affection in the tone. Jack watched as she gently shook her head.

"Hardly, we ran it over!" she replied and then turned to him and smiled.

"Miles, this is Jack," the vet gave him a casual nod as he followed them into the surgery. Miles placed the now blood-soaked car rug down on the examination table; Jack saw that Anna's arms were scratched and she had blood on her shirt.

"Wash your hands," Jack advised. Miles pointed to the washbasin and paper towels, but Anna merely nodded as she watched the vet pull back the rug and peer at the cat's gaping, bleeding wounds. Jack could see the tears in Anna's eyes as she gently stroked one of the paws.

"Well, that's another of your nine lives gone," Miles said gently as he started to examine the limp body. "Nothing looks broken, but she'll need an X-ray, and stitching up. I'll give her an injection now and we'll do whatever is necessary. Keep her in overnight and we'll know more tomorrow."

Anna walked across to the wash hand basin and sluiced

water over her bloody hands and dabbed at the scratch marks on her arm. "I'll pay whatever it costs." She suddenly yawned and murmured, "Sorry! It's been a traumatic day."

"Go home, Anna," Miles said solicitously, "nothing more you can do. Phone me in the morning." He turned towards Jack. "You drive her home carefully now."

Jack waited as Anna kissed Miles lightly on the cheek and then he took her arm and guided her towards the door.

"Well," Jack said, as he helped Anna back into the passenger seat, "that's a night to remember!" He got into the driving seat and turned with an affectionate smile on his face. "You know you really are a terrific person, Anna. You'll take the cat if it gets better, won't you?"

She nodded.

CHAPTER NINE

*A*nna awoke early as sunlight and bird song entered her bedroom. She stretched her naked body. Feeling the ache in her thighs she instantly recalled the night before and Jack's passionate love-making.

When they had arrived back at the house she had discarded the bloodstained clothes into the laundry basket and then stood in the shower with the warm water washing away the dried blood... but all the water in the world could not now wash away her sins. She thought of Jack, his youthful idolisation and the night that followed: he had been there in the bedroom waiting for her as she emerged clad only in her towel.

His love-making had surprised her. There had been no short kisses, no swift covering of her body and quick jab into her, no short sharp huffs and puffs, no heaving before the swift withdrawal of release without concern for her satisfaction. No turning over and goodnight.

For the first time she had experienced the intimacy of foreplay, relished her own lack of inhibition as he had swept her up in his arms and held her close, the towel relinquished to the floor. She had not protested when he had laid her down carefully on the large double bed.

She bit her lip as she thought of her passion, Jack's body over hers, his gentle insistence, his arousing caresses. Then, her reticence completely banished, her expression of total submission as she cried out her frank desire for him. She waited to feel shame, remorse, even guilt. But she could only remember the pleasure, the final explosion as her body met his in a passion she hadn't known she possessed.

She had lain beside him, her mind in turmoil, her body spent of passion; he lay on his side, looking down at her.

"I love you, Anna!" his eyes had swept over her nakedness. "I've wanted to fuck the hell out of you ever since I saw you in church..." She flinched at his choice of words but he bent his head and placed his lips on her mouth to silence any protest she might make.

She felt a flood of embarrassment and guilt sweep over her now as she remembered it all. Her heights of pleasure, her explosive passion needing a demanding man to trigger the soaring climax. He had wanted to stay the rest of night with her, but she had managed to say 'no'. The temptation had been great, but how could she have faced him this morning?

He had left in the early hours. She had a vague recollection of watching the tail-lights of his car disappearing down the drive. She had sat at the breakfast bar sipping a mug of coffee, seeing Hector's sleepy eyes watching her. She had tried to dredge up a morsel of regret, a flicker of guilt, but there was none. She already had enough guilt – for a greater crime than adultery. Poor Charles, he flitted so briefly through her thoughts. But he was another problem, and one yet to be overcome.

She got out of bed and stood by the window. She realised she had slept without the aid of any sleeping pill, but contemplation of the reason for this merely compounded her guilt.

After showering and dressing she looked at herself in the mirror. Was she different? Her eyes seemed a deeper violet and she had let her hair flow loosely round her shoulders... she really did look and feel younger.

She gave a half hearted good morning to Hector and this reminded her of the poor cat at the vet's. She then retrieved the morning's mail and saw the two postcards.

Hi Mum, extending our trip for another four weeks so we can take in more. Have met up with some Aussies - a real laugh! Love Kate and Steven and scrawled in minute writing at the bottom: *Hope you are okay*. She smiled, shook her head, and pinned it on the corkboard in the kitchen.

The second card was from a friend: *Really recommend Saga holidays... when you are getting older, they look after you*. This one went straight into the bin.

On her way past the kitchen mirror she peered at her face; not many laugh lines – more lines of an inner despair. Jack made her laugh, made her suddenly feel young. It was an interlude romance, she knew that: no pressure, no commitment. What could go wrong?

She wondered again how she would greet him? How would he face her? Would they feel embarrassed with each other, or at ease, sexually and companionably. Lovers! She flinched at the word... and yet he was now her lover. Not wishing to think of the consequences of her action she walked into the study, picked up the telephone and pressing the stored vet's number and went on to enquire as to the cat's condition. Her face creased to a smile when she heard the cat's wounds had been stitched up and it would be ready for collection in a few days.

Jack had let himself into his house late the previous night, knowing Rose would be fast asleep. But not Becky; she had crept downstairs and joined him in the kitchen.

"How could you?" she said, her eyes full of condemnation, her voice full of anger. "I can see it all over your face, just what's happened. You really do disgust me." She turned to walk out of the kitchen but Jack grabbed her.

"It wasn't like that," he started to explain, but she viciously pushed his hands away.

"It never is with men, you always come up with some lousy excuse. I'm telling Mary!"

Jack shook her by the shoulders.

"No!"

"Give me one good reason why I shouldn't!"

"Because I'm not married to Mary, so I can't have been unfaithful to her. How do I know she's not sleeping with someone?" The moment he said it he wished he hadn't.

"How can you even think that. Mary loves you, and how do you repay her – by sleeping with a middle-aged slag." And with that Becky turned and marched out of the room.

But Jack was not interested in his sister's moralistic views. He had lain awake and remembered how beautiful Anna was, and how passionate. He knew he truly loved her. Not in the same way he loved Mary. No, Anna was different. He knew it had been an awakening for her, that she had been surprised by her own passion. He had expected her to pull away from him, but he realised almost at once how great was her need. He could still feel her legs wrapped eagerly round his body and her wanton kisses on his lips.

They'd lain together and he had gently turned her face to look at him.

"No regrets?" he'd asked gently.

"It is too late for regrets," she had murmured, "and no, I have no regrets. The sin is mine."

"There is no sin in love, Anna."

"No, but I will have to live with deception."

He had smothered her then with kisses, tried to distract and comfort her.

Now as he lay back looking at the ceiling of his own bedroom he wondered if she would still be overcome with guilt, would Catholic conscience overtake passion? Had he been the sinful one pursuing her... for that is what he'd done. Should he too feel a guilt, a guilt at betraying Mary... lusting and loving another woman? He thought momentarily of Anna's constant references to 'sin' – a word, a concept, that seemed somewhat outdated in the modern world – when everything seemed to be accepted. Even by Catholics.

But Becky was right, he didn't deserve Mary.

Two days had passed since their night together, two days of Jack wondering whether their relationship would ever be the same. Had he taken advantage of Anna? Anna in turn had spent the Tuesday wondering when she would see Jack again. Although he was not scheduled to do her garden until the Thursday she had thought he would return to her and became disappointed when he didn't. Now that he had slept with her, would he still come round? Had he just used her? Thoughts cascaded through her mind, but were soon discarded. Jack wasn't like that.

With a committee meeting lasting all day Wednesday and the evening organising the church barbecue Anna had found little time to wonder what Jack's next move would be. She had collected the cat on the Wednesday afternoon and named it Malvern – it would not be an indoor cat but would merely live in the grounds of the house and come in for food whilst she tried to find it a caring home.

Then late on the Wednesday night a telephone call had come from Jack: would she have a day out with him in Oxford? She had been happy to hear from him and readily agreed, but made it plain that it would be her treat this time.

Early on the Thursday morning Anna watched as a polished black shoe emerged from the Beetle, followed by Jack. She blinked on seeing his blue linen trousers, his open necked white shirt and the creamy linen jacket. He walked rather self-consciously towards the door and he had smiled at the approval in her eyes.

"You look smart!" She reached up and kissed him on the mouth. "Where have you been for the last two days?"

"Working!" he said as he returned her kiss.

"I want our day in Oxford to be special," he confessed as he bent and kissed her again before stepping back to admire her sleeveless body-tight dress. She did not tell him she had again robbed Kate's wardrobe for something suitable: most of her own things now looked a trifle old and staid for her new self. Her hair was loose about her shoulders and he felt a surge of love for her as she handed him the keys to her car.

He settled himself into the driving seat; he admitted knowing that he had a definite smirk of satisfaction on his face as he felt the steering wheel within his hands and brought the car to life.

"I thought of you this morning," he said after they had driven for a short while in silence. "I wanted to wake up and see you beside me. Did you think of me?" He gave her a swift querying glance.

"Oh yes, and immediately felt guilty again. I've never cheated or lied to Charles. I don't want to hurt him. Or Mary."

Jack did not reply and as he approached the motorway she knew he was thinking about his betrayal of Mary and her faith.

"You are, aren't you?" she asked. "Thinking of Mary?"

He smiled involuntarily, "Yes, I suppose I am!"

"Feel guilty?"

"No, no. I know it sounds hard and cruel but I don't. When I saw you in church, I didn't just want to sleep with you, I wanted to know you."

Anna blushed and said in a matter of fact tone. "Well now you've done both."

"Don't be offended," he said turning to look at her, "I've known many girls, and slept with a quite few of them, but I have never held anyone in the same esteem as I hold you."

Anna bit her lip and turned away, feeling a touch embarrassed.

To her surprise Jack left the motorway at the first exit to take a quieter secondary road. Anna had settled back in the passenger seat with what Jack assumed was a look of contentment.

"Where will I park?" he asked as they approached Oxford and joined the inevitable line of cars and buses and coaches.

"Turn right at the *Randolph Hotel*" she directed, "and a first left…"

He signalled and followed her directions to find himself in the car park. "I'll go in and book lunch, meet me round the front," she instructed.

He wasn't sure he was going to enjoy this outing, he wasn't sure he really liked Oxford and he certainly didn't like her taking so much control. He wondered why he minded; money and women paying for him hadn't mattered in the past. He would have liked to have been in charge of the day out, but accepted that with his limited resources and a woman like Anna that wasn't going to be possible.

He made his way to the front of the hotel and watched her come down the red carpeted steps, her hair blowing in the faint breeze. She did not notice him immediately and he saw the flash of uncertainty in her eyes and then she was aware of him standing looking somewhat lost at the front of the hotel.

"Are you cross?" she asked as she put her hand through his arm. "You suddenly don't like taking instructions… is that it?"

He faced her and saw the understanding in her eyes and knew his stupidity could blow the relationship apart. He bent and kissed her, oblivious of the people passing.

"What do you suggest we do?" he asked.

"I think we should get an open top bus tour!"

They walked down towards the centre of the town and

along by one of the colleges. In the distance they saw the green and yellow, tourist open topped bus slowly approaching.

"Come on!" She grabbed his hand and he allowed her to pull him to the bus stop. He clambered up the stairs, leaving her to pay the driver. The female guide welcomed them as Anna settled on the inside seat and he placed his arm round her so he could lean forward and look down on the throng below. The bus jerked slowly forward and the guide pointed out the numerous colleges.

"This is the Carfax, the centre of the old city where four important streets meet, High Street, St Aldate's, Queen Street and Cornmarket."

Jack felt the glow of the sun on his face as he turned and smiled at Anna. "It's interesting," he commented.

"I thought it would be," She glanced at her watch, "We'll go the full route. Can you sustain your hunger?" He grimaced and shrugged his shoulders.

"After lunch I'd like to look round a bit," he said.

The bus stopped and people got on and off and the guide welcomed new faces. The commentary continued.

"The University was founded about eleven hundred. Of course today many of you will associate Oxford with the television series of *Inspector Morse*," the guide went on, "but did you know that many of the scenes for the series were actually shot in Cambridge?" There was a murmur of surprise from the passengers as the guide babbled on.

Jack had been listening; some of the information was interesting and other parts were just plain boring and he had not realised how hot the opened decked bus would be with the sun blazing down. It had completed its circular tour and Jack noted they were coming back to where they had hopped on.

"I could really do with a beer," Jack said. He glanced down at his watch and frowned, "Bloody thing's always stopping." He leaned across and picked up her left wrist and peered down at her watch to check the time: she was wearing a gold ladies *Cartier Santos*.

"God, I'd give anything for one of those," he smiled, saying, "Come on, the tour's finished."

They thanked the guide and left the bus. He took her hand and they went into a small bar, which was crowded with tourists, visitors and summer students. He saw her frown and realised that this probably wasn't for her. She slowly moved in past a group of pint-drinking men who gave her an appreciative smile as Jack managed to find her a stool at the bar.

"Not your scene, I know!" he said as he ordered a pint and a glass of chilled white wine. He moved in close and placed a hand on her knee as a mark of ownership. He felt the warmth of her body through the thinness of her dress and his own sweat running down his cheek. She opened her shoulder bag and took out a packet of tissues and gently wiped his face, and he laughed at her.

They engaged in more small talk before she said, "Come on: lunch, I think!" and waited for him to help her down from the stool.

She had booked a table in the corner of the dining room at the Randolph. Jack entered feeling this wasn't such a good idea. He felt that the stuffiness of the atmosphere was oppressive, and wished he could suggest they go down the road for a *McDonald's*. But he knew Anna was at home in these surroundings and he had no wish to upset her. They settled themselves down at the table.

The waiter handed them the menus and hovered. Jack glanced down; having seen the prices he gave a small prayer of thanks that he wasn't paying.

"I think I need another beer whilst I decide!" He looked across at Anna.

"A dry white wine," she replied, "French."

"I'll inform the sommelier," the waiter replied, with the natural pomposity of someone who had always wanted to work in a top class hotel.

"So what will madam have... I can recommend..." and made several suggestions, all of them inappropriate.

Anna shook her head, "Prawn cocktail."

The waiter looked disappointed as Jack dismissed some exotic sounding dishes and ask for Duck Pate followed by Sirloin steak, whilst Anna ordered the salmon.

As the waiter left Jack leaned across the table and took her hands: if there were any glances from the surrounding tables he remained entirely oblivious of them. He sat just staring at her. Once she would have been embarrassed by such an outward display of love and naked wanting, but now she was slowly feeling at peace with the situation: she was a woman desired by a young good-looking man and enjoying the envious glances of other women.

The wine waiter hovered with practised discretion as they drew apart, then announced, "Your beer sir," and placed two stemmed glasses down in front of Jack. "I'm afraid we don't serve tankards at the table," he murmured.

"No, of course," Jack replied with mock seriousness, and winked at Anna.

The starters arrived and Jack spread the pate thickly on the slices of toast and then took a bread roll and cut it in half. Anna was about to say, 'you break the roll, you don't cut it' and stopped. Did it matter? Did it matter that he now held his knife like a pen? No, it didn't. He met her gaze with a querying expression, as if knowing what she was thinking.

"Sorry, I forgot," he said.

She frowned, "Forgot what?"

"To hold my knife and fork properly. I remembered before, but not here!"

She laughed inwardly, "Jack, just be yourself." She was

surprised at the frankness of her statement. Not long ago she would have looked in horror at someone with bad table manners, let alone share a table with them.

Suddenly she thought of her son, Steven, and she took a sip of wine, conscious she hadn't thought about her family for the past two days; all her thoughts had been on Jack.

"So…?" he asked as the faint shadow crossed her eyes. She smiled at his perception; Charles never noticed a mood change or a problem.

"I was just thinking about my family."

"But are they thinking about you?" Jack replied.

"If they could see me now!" and she laughed. "Kate my daughter, she always accuses me of being so upright – she would say uptight – so conscious of what people will think and is convinced I am quite out of touch." She gave a faint gentle shake of her head.

Their lunch proved to be much better than Jack had anticipated. He had mellowed into the atmosphere and talked to Anna as if he had known her for years. They had discussed numerous topics, from Jack's friends to religious prejudices, and touched momentarily on his future with Mary. It was only at the end of the meal that Jack realised that although Anna talked and laughed with him she had given very little personal information away.

To avoid embarrassing Jack Anna gestured to the waiter to present her with the bill. Without opening the bill folder she placed her gold credit card on top; Jack appreciated that she had been entirely discreet.

The heat caught them as they left the hotel and walked arm in arm slowly down to the Carfax.

They stood on the bridge, looking at the River Cherwell below and the masses of punts and boats. Then he took her hand once more and they had a leisurely stroll past the Botanical

Gardens and she listened as he talked now about his father.

Then down the pathway to stop and sit on a hard green bench and laugh at the people who passed by, acting like lovers as they kissed and sat arms entwined gazing into each other's eyes, oblivious of those who turned to look at them.

Then on to Merton and Corpus Christi, to stop at Christ Church and to enter the coolness of the Cloisters and catch up with a guided tour.

"The College occupies the site of the Priory of Saint Fridewide, the patron saint of Oxford. Saint Fridewide was probably the founder of the priory in her name, and the story goes that she was an eighth century princess who was trying to escape the advances of an importunate suitor from the Midlands..."

The guide paused and Jack looked up as Anna murmured, "I know the feeling..." and she blushed at the accompanying laughter from the group.

They continued to follow the group as it entered the Cathedral.

"The college was founded by Cardinal Wolsey in 1525." The guide had stopped. "On his fall from grace in 1529 the half completed building was taken over and refounded as King Henry VIII's College. In 1546 the King created Christ Church, combining the college with the Cathedral of the Diocese of Oxford."

Anna had moved to one side and was standing quietly contemplating. "Are you all right?" Jack asked.

"The building has seen so much hasn't it? It breathes so many happenings..."

He didn't reply but merely took her arm and followed the crowds into the quad to stand and admire tradition and continuity.

They had left Oxford at four thirty; this time Jack used the motorway and had them back at Anna's house within one and a half hours. As they drove down the Avenue Jack asked if he could have a swim, at this she nodded. He drew the car up to the front door, pulled her into his arms and kissed her briefly on the cheek. The remainder of the evening was spent by the pool flirting with each other.

"I want to wake up and find you beside me in the morning," he whispered; he had no intention of leaving her on her own that night.

CHAPTER TEN

*A*nna opened her eyes and yawned; the sunlight was flooding into the bedroom window, and she frowned on seeing the unfamiliar furniture and patterned wallpaper. She was in the guest room again; she smiled as she slowly turned on her side, remembering their second night of passion. It had been a long time since she had woken to find an indentation on the pillow, telling her that a man had slept beside her. She blinked and glanced round the room, expecting to hear the shower; instead she heard the clatter of a plate being dropped in the kitchen. She wanted to luxuriate in the memory of the night and wait in the hope he would bring her breakfast in bed.

She had forgotten the heights of passion that Jack seemed to be able to so easily awake in her. So she had not thought of Charles; they had grown so far apart, had she become too impatient, dismissive of his needs? Resentful? She examined her conscience and closed her eyes, remembering the little incidents she had chosen to forget.

Poor Charles. She suddenly felt a compassion she had not felt before and tears welled up in her eyes. She had betrayed him, put her need before their vows. But hadn't he betrayed her in a different way?

Jack had risen early, determined to bring Anna breakfast in bed. He had looked down at the peaceful, well satisfied form of

141

Anna as she slept naked beside him. Her fervent responses the night before had almost outstripped his own.

He'd draped a towelling robe round his own naked form and padded across the landing. Her house intrigued him, it seemed so cold and remote for a family home and yet it was very luxurious. He had a peer into the bedrooms now, seeing Steven's room with the posters, computer and an array of cassettes and books, in untidy heaps. Kate's bedroom neat and tidy for a girl, giving little away.

He remembered being momentarily in the fifth bedroom before, when Anna was changing for their walk on Malvern Hills. She had whisked him out and locked the door behind them. The door was still shut and locked to his touch, but the key remained in the lock so he turned it and wandered in. A small box room, the size of his own bedroom at home. A full length mirror on a stand, and two mirrors at odd angles on the wall. A small television set with a built in video recorder. No bed, just a dressing table with an array of make-up. He picked up a small bottle of green nail polish and shuddered, surely not Anna... maybe the daughter, but why in this room?

He pulled open the drawers of the dressing table and stared down in surprise to see some scanty black lace underwear. Not Anna, sadly she was not a black lace person. He fingered a padded bra and then pushed it back in the drawer. He glanced round the room; it gave nothing away. Whose room was it? His curiosity aroused he walked to the wall of wardrobes and opened them. He stared in disbelief at the array of clothes. Dresses, skirts, blouses: all of garish style and colour. A long raincoat. He took one of the dresses down from the rail, and stared at the size. It was marked eighteen. Certainly not Anna! The shoes too seemed overly large. He glanced up in amazement as he saw the shelf with an array of wigs on stands. Long blonde haired wigs, short dark haired wigs and one outrageous ginger wig. He opened one of the drawers and saw the video boxes, neatly stacked but unlabelled. Another drawer revealed three catalogues of women's clothing; glancing through one he saw some items had been ringed round with a red felt-tip pen.

He frowned; although it was none of his business, his curiosity had certainly been aroused. He closed the door behind him and returned to the kitchen where Hector watched him with suspicion.

"Good morning," Jack said as he came into the guest room bearing a tray.

"I've seen this done on old movies. It always looked so romantic, but in actual fact, it's bloody hard work. I couldn't find a vase to put that single red rose in... where the hell is the bread, and the butter seemed to be invisible." He lowered the tray onto the bed. "The teapot has a leaky spout, the toaster burnt the bread; apart from that, you are out of marmalade and I made a mess of boiling the eggs!"

She stared up at him and then shook with laughter as she gazed down at the tray. "Jack, it looks very nice." She reached for the teapot and poured herself a cup of tea, ignoring the dripping liquid splashing over her bed sheet and the fact she always had coffee for breakfast.

Jack sat on the edge of the bed and seemed to be watching every mouthful she took until in desperation she handed him a piece of toast. "Here," she said, thankful to pass the burnt offering to him.

He watched until she had finished and then removed the tray and slipped back into bed beside her. The morning stretched into midday.

"We should get up," Anna murmured as she gazed down into his eyes. She laughed and got out of bed and pulled him to stand beside her. "Shower. Come into our room, we have a large shower!" she raised her eyebrows and the invitation was clear.

In the late afternoon they lay on the loungers by the pool.

Anna had discarded her bikini top. He had moved across to lie beside her, his hand on her breast. He heard the deepening of her breath but it was overshadowed by the faint noise on the driveway and they both sat up.

"Did you shut the gates after last night?"

"I think so." Anna frowned before saying, "No!" She scrambled to her feet. "Where's the top of my bikini?" She was now flustered and Jack had moved cautiously to the side of the house.

"It's a blue car," he said, "Looks like a small Rover…"

"Oh my God, it's Mavis… she's only the vice-chairman of LATE," Anna muttered.

"Pretend you're out," he said.

"With the gates open, and my car at the front, don't sound stupid," her voice was tetchy. "What is she doing coming unexpectedly? She must be suspicious, Mavis never comes out of the blue. I should have known, you shouldn't have stayed… I must have been mad. Your car… she'll see it."

Anna rushed into the outside shower room and grabbed a white towelling robe from the back of the door and struggled into it. "I'll take her into the kitchen. You slip round the front of the house…"

"I've no gardening clothes!"

"Pretend, use some intelligence. You are here to estimate for something…"

"I've used it all up on you!" he grinned.

"Jack stop acting like a bloody fool: if Mavis finds out then our days of grace are finished." Anna ran a hand through her untidy hair.

"You'd better cover that up," Jack grinned as he pointed to the visible love-bite on her neck. They heard Seth barking and a car door slam.

He reached forward and kissed her. "Good luck!"

"Get dressed, for goodness sake…"

"I can't!"

"Why not?"

"I left my clothes in the bedroom…"

She closed her eyes, remembering.

"I'll sneak out… don't worry."

"Oh I'll not worry," her voice was laden with sarcasm. Anna entered the house via the back door and into the kitchen seeing the glasses, the obvious signs of two people who had eaten. She picked up the dishes, "go away Hector!" she said as she threw what she could into the dishwasher. The kitchen looked an absolute mess. No time for a plaster on her neck now, so she drew the collar closer and took three deep breaths and tightened the cord of the bath robe tighter round her waist as she walked to the front door. The bell rang again. She padded swiftly across to the hall, conscious of her bare feet. She remembered the barbecue, they had barely cleared it away. Glasses, had she left them out? The champagne! Her bikini thrown aside in a moment of abandonment.

"Mavis," she tried to inflect surprise into her voice as she pretended to yawn and rub her eyes. "I overslept." She saw Mavis's eyes flicker over the robe, the bare feet and then back to Anna's face.

"Four o'clock in the afternoon, that's not like you, Anna!" her voice and eyes were critical. Anna gulped as she took in Mavis's disapproval, the pale blue slightly bulbous eyes, the finely wrinkled forehead and thin bitter mouth beneath tightly pinched nostrils. Her hair splattered grey and black, cut in what Steven called Mavis's *pudding-bowl haircut,* dressed in an old-fashioned knee length flowery dress and carrying as she always did a large brown leather handbag. "I came the other day but you were out!" Suspicious eyes met Anna's who merely smiled as she walked into the kitchen.

"I know…"

"You know?"

"Yes, I know I was out."

"That young man told you?"

"Yes of course, the gardener."

"Mmm!" Mavis pulled out one of the chairs and sat down at the breakfast table, picking up crumbs between her fingers, a look of surprise on her face as she saw the disorder.

"Have I come at an inconvenient moment?" Mavis tried to smile to take the criticism from her voice. This was not the Chairman of LATE the woman she admired for her neatness and razor sharp mind. "You look as if you've had a party?" there was disbelief in her voice.

"Just a meeting about the church barbecue... it lasted late!" Anna started to move some of the dishes and felt her robe slip away.

"What's that nasty mark on your neck?" Mavis asked her nose wrinkling up as she peered for a second before Anna managed to pull the collar up again.

"A bite!" she replied, "from some insect... last night."

"Peculiar insect!"

"I know." Anna turned and filled the coffee cafeteria with ground coffee, not freshly made as she usually did, but some she had bought a month previous.

"Wasn't that the gardener's car I saw at the front?" Mavis got straight to the point.

"Er... oh yes, it must be... I asked him to estimate."

"Mmmm..." Mavis allowed Anna to place a mug of coffee before her and slowly poured in the milk.

"I didn't see him?" she said after taking a sip and grimacing.

"Oh he's around somewhere..." Anna went to the window and peered out; Jack was furtively tidying up the pool area.

"Is he out there?" Mavis made to get up, curiosity and suspicion written all over her face.

"No, no it's the dog... he's waiting for his walk," Anna felt herself flushing from the heat of the robe and the unwanted coffee.

There was a loud meow as Hector with his tail up high walked into the kitchen and jumped on the table.

"Shoo!" Mavis flicked a hand in his direction but he merely yawned and lay down. "He shouldn't be on the table," Mavis said frowning.

"Come on, Hector," Anna scooped him up and placed him on the kitchen floor. Then glancing down she saw Hector tapping at something with his paw. It was the champagne cork. She bent down but it was too late the cork had been taken up in Hector's mouth and he jumped back onto the table and deposited it in front of Mavis.

"What is it?" she drew her mouth into a thin line of disgust as she picked it up. "A champagne cork!" There was no disputing the suspicion in her eyes now.

"From the meeting last night," Anna said hastily.

"Must have been some meeting!"

"It was," and Anna knew she was smiling, or was it a smirk of self-satisfaction - she hoped not.

"Mmmm..."

"More coffee?"

"No thank you."

"Biscuits?"

"If it's no trouble..." She watched as Anna padded still barefooted to take out her wooden biscuit barrel. "I have some business to relate," Mavis said as she opened her bag and took out a folder. "You should read that before the next meeting..." Mavis babbled on and Anna found her mind wandering away from the problems of LATE and the elderly.

"Are you listening, Anna?" Mavis asked sharply

"Of course, just leave the papers and I'll sort it out," Anna said reassuringly as she took the folder and moved it onto a small table.

"Your heels look red and sore?" Mavis observed.

"Yes, a tight pair of shoes…"

"Mmm."

There was a knock on the outer back door and Anna smiled at Mavis. "Ah, he must have done the estimate," she said as she went through the utility room.

"Good afternoon," she raised her voice as she opened the door and winked at Jack. "You were rather late…"

"Yes I was," he shouted back and they both started to giggle.

"Would you like a coffee?"

"No, I'll go now…"

"You will put the estimate in writing?" she asked and tried to contain her laughter as he reached forward and pulled the cord of her gown so it opened to reveal her naked form. His hand momentarily touched her breast and she gasped. He leaned forward and kissed her.

"Anna!" they pulled apart as Mavis came noisily into the room.

"Oh you're the young man I met the other night?" Anna pulled her robe together, pretending to adjust the cord.

"Yes…" Jack smiled and turned to leave

Mavis sniffed and Anna gazed in horror at the back of Jack's once white shirt, which now displayed a large brown patch of barbecue sauce.

"What's that on your shirt?" Mavis asked with disgust on her face.

"Oil!" Anna said as she moved to finger the stain.

"Er, the car… yes I had an oil leak…"

"On your back?" Mavis glanced from one to the other and then peered at the barbecue.

"Gets everywhere, that oil…" Jack shrugged his shoulders. "Goodbye Mrs de Courtney… I'll send in the estimate."

Anna sighed and turned and walked back to the kitchen.

"Forward young man…!" Mavis muttered, "but do you always meet tradesman in your dressing gown?"

Anna could not think of a suitable reply and merely mumbled, "I think he knows Steven," Anna tried to make it sound vague, and then glanced at the clock.

"Mavis I am sorry, but I really must get changed... I've a... a... meeting at church." She held her hands out.

"I just wondered if you were lonely with Charles and the family away?" Mavis said diffidently. "We could have a day out together..."

Anna stared at her and ran a tongue over her lips as her mind raced into overdrive to think up a suitable reason for not accepting Mavis's offer.

"Oh how kind," she gushed as she put her hands out towards Mavis, "but only yesterday, Joan... you remember Joan...?"

"No!"

"Well, I think you met her, she's a friend... she said she would come and stay and I said, well I said... do come!"

There was disappointment on Mavis's face. "Is she staying long?"

"I don't know, I think so... but I have also planned a weekend away."

"On your own, perhaps I will..."

"No, no, not on my own... with another friend... Another friend... yes, yes, Jane, she wanted to go to... to Canterbury... I said I'd go with her."

"You seem very busy, you don't usually have people to stay or go away for weekends. Who's looking after Hector and Seth?"

"Oh he's looking after them!"

"Who?"

"Jack...yes, he'll pop in and see to Seth."

Mavis raised her eyebrows. "I thought it would be nice for you and I to sit and talk over plans for LATE."

Gently Anna started to usher Mavis towards the front

door. "I am sorry, Mavis, I must change." The door was finally reached and opened.

"How is Charles?"

"Well and working."

"And the children ?"

"Well and not working!"

There was a pause and Mavis hovered on the front step. "You are very fortunate, Anna, in having such a lovely home, such a good husband and family... I hope you realise how lonely it is to be on your own, to have no one..." the eyes peered into Anna who managed a weak smile. "Count your blessings..." she leaned forward and kissed Anna on the cheek.

"That's a nasty mark on your neck... it almost looks like a love bite!"

Anna drew the collar of the robe up closer as Mavis's chilling words hit home.

As she closed the door the phone rang. She walked swiftly into the study. It was Charles. She heard the weariness in his voice, knowing it was late and he would be lying on the bed with papers and reports scattered round. There was despondency in his tone and she listened perhaps for the first time to the unsaid words, the worry and, yes, his loneliness... why had she not heard that before... for she always imagined he was enjoying his visits to the east. There was no tetchiness now... just tiredness and wish to come home and that surprised her.

"Are you really all right?" she asked and listened to his reply, feeling also guilt at having to reassure him. "Of course I care..." she heard his hesitation and tried for the first time in years to sympathise. She replaced the receiver wondering why the call had suddenly unnerved her. She picked up the silver framed family photograph from his desk. Kate, Steven, Charles and herself and as she gazed at them she knew she didn't want to lose them... love was an easy word, but caring, companionship and family were far more important. She padded back into the kitchen.

Jack knew he should have phoned, taken Anna's advice and told his mother he would be late home… late home, that was a joke, he was almost twenty-four hours overdue. The reception he received as he turned his key into the front door lock and entered the small hallway was just as he'd anticipated.

Rose stood arms akimbo her face set in anger as she greeted him.

"For God's sake Jack, where on earth have you been?" the words were hurtled out with vitriolic anger.

"Look, I can explain…" he tried to say but Rose cut him short.

"Mary phoned you three times last night she was upset because you had not kept a promise to contact her. She wondered, and so did I, were you were?" He met the suspicion in her eyes as he tried to brush past her wanting only to get to his bedroom and have a change of clothes. "Well?" his mother was nothing if not persistent.

"I meant to phone but you know, I'd been drinking with Gordon and well… we played cards and I got drunk and ended up crashing on his sofa." He realised he wasn't succeeding in convincing her. For even to his ears it didn't sound like the truth.

"I don't believe you, Jack… God help you if you cheat on Mary!"

"Trust me, Mum," he kissed her cheek.

"I wish I could," she pulled away from him and sniffed. "And what is that smell?"

"A joke, someone poured sauce over me…." he turned round and she gasped.

"Oh Jack that was a new shirt. You'll have nothing left to wear on your honeymoon if you keep on like this." His mother flipped a hand at him. "I'll be glad when you are safely married, my lad, and so no doubt will Mary. She talked of coming over next weekend!"

"Did she?" he tried to inject enthusiasm into his voice. "I'll phone her."

"You'd better, I think she's suspicious that you are sowing wild oats before the wedding…"

"Oh Mum!" Jack laughed as he walked into the kitchen.

"Don't oh Mum me!" Rose replied and he saw she was serious. "I want no problems from you, Jack."

"Trust me… now I've a phone call to make. Can I have a bit of privacy?" He gave Rose a meaningful look as he brushed past her and into the hallway where he picked up the phone and dialled the number he had jotted down.

"Who are you phoning now?" Rose asked.

"The most important woman in my life, who else?" he replied and with that he picked up the receiver as Rose shrugged and walked into the kitchen. She was at least thankful Jack was going to telephone Mary.

But Jack did not dial Mary's number. It was Anna he phoned, to invite her out for the evening.

CHAPTER ELEVEN

That evening Jack arrived at the Kinellan House on time, and was pleased to see Anna had reversed her car out of the garage and he knew he would be driving it again.

He waited in the hall for Anna to get ready and she emerged at the top of the stairs with her hair loose, her smile welcoming, wearing a long white summer skirt with a matching blouse with a scooped out neck that showed off her excellent figure. He was relieved that he too had decided to dress casually for the heat in light slacks and an open-necked shirt.

"You look cool and beautiful," he bent and kissed her and then escorted her to her car.

He had booked a table in an Italian restaurant that someone had recommended to him months ago. Anna had been a little wary of being seen together in public, but Jack had assured her the restaurant was small, tucked away, and not the place her friends would visit. As they drove she told him about the rest of Mavis's visit, making it into an amusing anecdote.

He pulled the car into the small car park adjacent to the restaurant and as he unclipped his seat belt he leaned across and kissed her and they smiled into each other's eyes.

The restaurant was two small adjoining rooms, oak beamed with a stone floor. The tables were brightly covered in red chequered tablecloths and the lighting was from candles in wine bottles. The walls had faded framed photographs, some brassware, and it gave of an air of intimacy. It was crowded, and Jack knew if he had not booked they would not have been able to eat there. They were shown to a small corner table. Anna admired his choice and commented on the relaxed ambience. He leaned across the small table and took her hand into his.

"Have you been here before?" she asked.

"No, this is my first time."

"I am glad," she murmured. "I hope the food is as good as the atmosphere."

Jack ordered a lager whilst Anna studied the menu with care and finally ordered Parma Ham followed by a chicken dish, whilst Jack went for more substantial Cannelloni followed by Ham Tagliatelle.

The meal was excellent and they were both in a happy mood. Jack had taken her hand again, holding it in both of his. His eyes visibly making love to her, his legs entwined round hers beneath the table.

"Please," she whispered as she ran her tongue lightly over her lips, and he could tell from the flush on her cheeks that she was imagining the night ahead.

"Shall I order coffee or get the cheque?" he asked.

"I think we'll have coffee back home." She was conscious of her heart beating, and the wanting within her as she slowly dabbed her mouth with her napkin.

Anna noted the lines of worry appear on Jack's face. She had come to know when he was in deep thought and asked him if there was something on his mind. He hesitated before saying.

"It's just curiosity and none of my business," he started off and she felt a sense of unease but knew she had to let him have his say.

"So, what is it?"

"Well, this morning, when you were asleep, I was looking

round your house," he saw a wary flash come into her eyes. "The bedrooms, and…"

"And?" she prompted him.

"Okay I opened the locked bedroom door. The key was in, I know it was sheer nosiness."

"Yes it was, a locked door implies keep out. "

He heard the tone of her voice and it was like when he had first met her, cold, distant and remote.

"I'm sorry," he said lowering his eyes.

"So you obviously went into the room and I am assuming you looked round?"

He looked sheepishly at her. "Yes, I did."

Anna realised that to sustain their relationship she had no option but to tell him the truth. It was their first test; embarrassment played no part in this, not after what they had done together in bed. He could see her indecision and felt obliged to say.

"Leave it, forget whatever it is you don't want me to know."

She tapped her fingers on the table and looked into his eyes. "So, Jack, what did you surmise from the contents of the room?"

"Someone's dressing room?" he guessed.

"Exactly, and do you wish to know who uses that room?" She was tantalising him now, and he shrugged his shoulders. "Well, you obviously saw the clothes, the wigs and of course the shoes… ah yes, the shoes, now they were too large for my feet, so what conclusion did you arrive at?"

He stared at her. "I just don't know!"

"I think we should have coffee here, rather than return home," Anna said, decisively raising her hand to catch the attention of the waiter. Jack could see she was totally unsure of herself now. He wished he had not mentioned the room and its odd contents if it meant spoiling their evening.

She waited until the coffee had arrived in two huge cups with a separate jug of cream and a bowl of sugar. She allowed a generous splash of cream to form a milky surface over the coffee before she took her teaspoon and slowly stirred the contents round and round.

"Anna, if it's something you don't wish to talk about…"

She shook her head and her eyes remained downcast. She hesitated for a brief second, momentarily uncertain whether to take him into her confidence, but their relationship was such that they were more than just friends, they had become passionate, trusting lovers. Her voice was a low monotone and Jack knew instinctively she was re-living a painful moment in her life.

"It all started for me five years after we had married," she said in a low voice, "Steven was a baby and I had just given birth to Kate. We were happy, not ecstatic; our marriage wasn't based on outright passion, more on mutual interest and respect." She saw his sceptical expression. "I should explain, Charles is twenty years older than me. There was always a small part of Charles that had been cut off from me; I used to put it down to the age difference. He was an avid amateur radio enthusiast. He had a room upstairs laid out with his equipment. He would go up there and supposedly communicate with people all over the world. He was, or so he told me, a member of the local amateur radio association. He would spend many evenings up in the room and it didn't worry me."

Anna took another sip of her coffee and went on.

"In the early days I used to read a great deal, and, of course, I had two babies. There was a nanny, but she didn't sleep in and my mother lived with us. It was her house then," she sighed and paused before continuing. "Mother had a self-contained room and we had our own routines.

"It was a Saturday evening, the end of a family day. Mother

had retired to her room to watch television. Charles had gone up to his room to fiddle with his radio, or so I thought.

"I don't know why, but I suddenly felt that I wanted to see what Charles was doing. I cannot recall the exact reason but I remember getting up and walking into the hall. The house was quiet – I couldn't even hear him speaking and I felt it strange. I went up the stairs and stood outside the door of Charles's room. There was silence from behind it. Sometimes in the past the door had been locked. Charles said it was to keep dust and the children off the equipment. He is very fussy about all his possessions."

Jack listened hearing Anna talking in a staccato fashion, the words almost being dragged from her lips.

"I remember going to the door, I raised my hand and was about to knock on it and then on impulse I tried the handle. It was not locked and it slid open. The room was brightly lit."

Jack now saw the flash of agitation in her eyes as she clenched her hands so the knuckles shone white against her skin.

"Anna," Jack reached across the table and took the clenched hand into his. He could not imagine what could be so distressing.

"Charles was not there... there was..." she paused and lowered her eyes.

Jack frowned and waited for her to continue.

"There was this apparition... I can't describe it as anything else, for that was how I saw it then and how I see it now." She lowered her head onto her hands. "It will be etched on my mind forever, Charles standing in front of the mirror, except it wasn't Charles. It was a grotesque caricature of a woman... a large woman in a badly fitting dress of horrendous design, with a large padded bosom, a red wig that didn't fit and raddled make-up. I stared and Charles turned and I remember waiting for him to laugh and say, 'It's a joke,' or something

157

similar. He didn't, he just started to cry. The mascara tracked black rivers down his rouged cheeks, the lipstick smeared like a clown, and then he removed the wig and I remember I felt physically sick.

'What are you doing?' I asked and this sad figure knelt down before me. Apparently he had to do it, so he said, a compulsion to dress up. The radio was all a front. The wardrobe was full of clothes. Jewellery, make-up. He grovelled at my feet, and I don't know what disgusted me the more." She paused and Jack saw the distress in her eyes.

He had listened intently, feeling a sudden need to burst into laughter for what she was saying seemed too bizarre to comprehend. But he saw the anguish on her face and knew this was no joke and a wrong move would mean Anna would clam up and never trust him again. He arranged his face into a sympathetic composure.

"You're saying Charles is a cross-dresser?" he started tentatively.

"A transvestite!" She ran her tongue across her lips and he could see she could barely say the word as she closed her eyes. "You and Father Mathews are the only two people I have said that word to." She saw the querying expression in his eyes. "Oh yes, Steven and Kate know, they were told when it became necessary. They accepted much more easily than I could."

Jack nodded but knew in his case he couldn't have accepted or understood his Dad dressing up as a woman and his mother would have laughed - sympathetically of course, but she had no time for sexual malfunctions.

Anna was continuing. "Over the years I've read so much about this terrible problem. Some women are very brave. I have tried to lock it away. I still can't accept that when Charles leaves the house in the morning dressed in his suit, underneath he is wearing women's silk underwear. I just pray he will never have an accident and have to go to hospital."

Jack's mind boggled as he tried to imagine the situation but deep down he realised it was a very sad affair.

Anna went on. "Charles doesn't wish to be cured, even supposing there is a cure. It's a psychological problem. So I've been told. " She wiped away a tear.

"Oh Anna!" Jack's voice was full of sympathy. He knew the strain it had been to tell him, but wondered too why she had felt the need to share her burden with him. Secrets he did not really wish to know; it seemed to make him a integral part of her family. Almost a bonding between them.

"You are not disgusted?" she asked after a pause.

He shook his head. "Not disgusted, no; confused, I don't honestly know why men find the need. But obviously Charles does. But you, I mean how do you cope?"

"With great difficulty. My 'good works' sublimate." She painted the quotation marks in the air with her forefingers. "It was, of course, a complete sexual turn-off," she ran a tongue over her lips. "I tried to help, we talked, but over the years it has become his life, now he goes out in the Morris Traveller you noticed in the garage. He looks quite ghastly, and almost laughable… but I can't laugh." He heard the sob in her voice. "Thank you for not laughing," she whispered.

They had not talked very much on the journey home. Anna had sat wondering if she had been wise to confide so much that was so wretchedly private. He had driven up to the house and helped her from the car and gone to the front door, waited until she had switched off the burglar alarm and then, seeing the waiting in her eyes, he'd said, "Goodnight, Anna. I wish I could stay, but mother is getting rattled and I can't use Gordon as an excuse again." He kissed her and knew she had expected him to stay, to comfort her.

Back in his own car, Jack drove home knowing the confession had shaken him and he wanted time to assess what had been said. He was unsure what difference the information made, except he knew it was faintly disturbing and also embarrassing. How could Anna live with him? How could Charles dress like that, make his face up and stand admiring himself in front of the mirror? Was it an offence? Could a man go out dressed as a woman? What happened if he went into the ladies' toilets? His mind was full of thoughts about this bizarre situation. Anna so perfect, the last person to have a transvestite for a husband. Suddenly he found himself laughing at the totally absurdity of the situation. Then he also knew Anna would be the last person who would tell anyone and he realised now the trust and esteem she had placed on his shoulders. He felt sorry for her in divulging the family secret. Her marriage seemed a total sham. It was a shame because Anna deserved so much better.

He should have stayed the night, held her in his arms and whispered he loved her. Obviously Charles had rejected her to dress up. Poor Anna, and he felt an overwhelming pity for her. He parked the car alongside his house, got out and opened the front door.

He knew he had to telephone her.

He was glad Rose was glued to the television and Becky was out. Before announcing his return he picked up the receiver and dialled her number.

Anna replaced the receiver, she had wondered how he would react to her disclosure. She knew it had been the right decision to tell him. She could still see the wave of disbelief flicker across his face when she had said the words 'Charles is a transvestite'. He hadn't laughed, he didn't mock Charles and he showed no false pity for her. He had listened and analysed what had been said. She couldn't really blame him for not wishing to stay the night and was quite thankful that he had chosen to leave her the way he did. They both needed time to think. She knew now she could trust Jack.

His telephone call had been welcome, a day out with a secret destination for the day after tomorrow. He would pick her up early on Thursday morning.

Where would he take her, she wondered but knew only that she wanted to see him. The destination was unimportant.

At eight o'clock on the Thursday morning, Jack, as promised arrived. Anna had opened the door and he had seen the gladness in her eyes as without hesitation she opened her arms to him and he held her close, feeling her body against his, knowing she had missed him. He pulled away and stared down into her face, meeting the smile on her lips, seeing her hair loose and held back by a band, the way he liked it to be. Her summer skirt and usual sleeveless blouse avoided any attempt at sophistication, and matched his casual jeans and shirt.

Anna had spent the previous evening going over the incident in the restaurant. She felt it had been a betrayal of Charles but knew also that Jack was not a person to laugh or gossip. Now, she could see he was eagerly awaiting the day ahead, her confession about Charles forgotten.

"Come on, it's a long way!"

She handed him the keys of the BMW.

They had driven northwards up the M6, stopping off at a service station for a late breakfast. Anna had had coffee and toast and watched as they sat opposite to one another staring down at the passing traffic and then into each other's eyes as Jack ate his plateful of eggs, bacon and sausage.

"This is madness, you do know that!" she had laughed and reached across to take his hand as he pushed the plate away. "Where are we going?"

He wiped his hand across his moustache. "Wait and see!"

She watched the signposts of the motorway, seeing Liverpool and then Manchester. It had to be the Lake District, there was no where else. Then suddenly he was turning off the M6 and she looked up at the sign.

"Blackpool!" he grinned. "I bet you've never been and walked along the golden mile. Eaten fish and chips and had your fortune told?"

She did not tell him she felt she could live without such an experience but merely nodded.

"There's the tower," he pointed across the flat terrain. "The Paris of the north," he commented dryly.

"But without the sophistication!" she added quietly.

Blackpool was hot and crowded as they had driven along the front looking for a parking space. Finally she had seen the hotel, a bastion of respectability amongst the plebeian terraces.

"Park there!" she had instructed and he had turned in, ignoring the *Residents only* sign.

"Phew!" he got out feeling the heat on his body.

"I'm sure you could do with a cool beer?" She held her hand out to him and they walked into the foyer, she excused herself. He hesitated and then sat down in the large airy lounge with two beers and a plate of sandwiches. Last time he had been in Blackpool he'd been with his Mum and Dad, and that was a long time ago. He stood up and smiled as she approached freshly made up, her hair brushed and cascading round her face. He stood up and held his hands out to her. "You look wonderful."

They drank and ate the sandwiches before wandering out to join the throngs walking down the promenade to stop and stare at the murky grey waters. He had kissed her and they'd walked arm in arm. As the day went on, they'd eaten ice creams, got caught up in candy floss and laughed.

"You know what Blackpool is famous for, apart from the tower, sticks of rock and the fun fair?" he grinned at her.

"No, but you'll tell me," she replied.

"Fortune telling. There's cards, crystals and palms to be read. They all claim to know your future…"

"But can they tell my past?"

"Angels don't have pasts, do they? Come on," Jack pointed to the large yellow billboards displayed outside the tented premises. "They all claim to have Romany blood, whatever that supposed to mean." He stopped and pointed. "A palmist… go on it's only fun!"

Anna saw the old woman sitting on a stool knitting outside her tent. Without warning she looked up and Anna was taken aback as the black eyes seemed to bore into her.

"You go in," Jack said and Anna found herself being manipulated into the tent to be followed by the old woman.

"Sit there," a bejewelled hand pointed to an uncomfortable wooden chair the other side of a small rickety table covered with a white cloth on which stood a rather grubby looking crystal ball. The old woman pulled a bead- encrusted curtain across the opening. The dim light and the scent of a joss stick burning in a holder gave off an aroma and Anna felt a smile creep onto her lips; this was quite ludicrous, no one would believe that she could sit in such surroundings looking into the future.

"Ten pounds or five pounds?" the old woman had sat down and was peering intently into Anna's face.

Anna was about to ask what the difference would be and then found herself shrugging and digging into the pocket of her jacket and handing over a ten pound note. She watched as the note immediately disappeared somewhere in the folds of the long voluminous skirt.

The old woman nodded and then taking a piece of black velvet wiped over the surface of the crystal ball and peered intently into what to Anna appeared to be a piece of glass reflecting the light.

"Mmmm!" she sniffed and then looked up at Anna. "You

have secrets my dear, black secrets. I see an old woman..." She looked up but Anna remained impassive, she wasn't going to feed this woman information. Everyone knew an old woman... it meant nothing. It was just rubbish.

"There is a young man..." She stopped and shook her head slowly from side to side. "I see trouble." She pushed the crystal away and covered it with the black velvet.

"Give me your hands" She took hold of both of Anna's hands and with a dirt ingrained forefinger nail she slowly traced the lines and Anna sat back and listened to what seemed to be the usual patter of health and wealth.

"You are married and I see a boy and a girl... a decision and secrets always secrets around you. The young man will bring you trouble... beware... he is not all he seems to be." She stopped abruptly. "It is a troubled hand my dear. You are at a cross-roads in your life." Old, knowledgeable eyes met hers. "Be wary of the decisions you make, the people you trust."

Anna got up and gave her thanks to the old woman, unsure as to what she had heard. Although she realised the dangerous territory she was on, it also seemed incongruous that Jack could bring her any form of trouble. She had the whole relationship under firm control and dismissed the predictions as rubbish. She greeted the sunlight outside the tent with relief and saw Jack standing grinning at her from the railings of the promenade.

"So, what did she say?" he asked and listened as she told him.

"Doesn't sound much to me, a troubled hand; well, my old dear told me I would marry and have four children, be happy, healthy and rich!"

"An easy way to earn ten pounds," Anna said sceptically.

Jack had persuaded her into the fairground and they had walked round holding hands. It had been a world Anna knew little about, hords of people, angry parents and screaming kids. He'd persuaded her to go on the roller-coaster called *The Big One* and she had clung to him as the car climbed to the top of the steep incline. She yelled at the top of her voice, her hair blowing behind her as the car plunged at a frightening speed to an alarming depth.

"That was the most frightening experience of my life," she had laughed, knowing that wasn't entirely true. He had kissed her as they walked on through the funfair. On impulse he went across to one of the stalls.

"A memento!" He placed the small bear dressed in goggles and wearing a flying jacket with a red scarf round his throat and a white tee-shirt with an imprint, *The Big One*, written across it, into her hands.

She stared at it and then laughed. "A boastful message," and she had reached up and kissed him. "He's lovely, what shall I call him?"

"Gregory... after my first teddy bear," Jack said.

"Gregory he is!" and she had hugged the small brown bear.

They took a tram ride and walked along the pier and then he'd said. "You can't come to Blackpool and not have fish and chips." She had grimaced but gave way and they'd sat on a seat on the promenade.

"If my daughter could see me now, eating with my fingers!" Anna laughed as she wiped her hands on a paper tissue.

"Well, I see you've not left any!" Jack noted as he peered into her empty chip paper.

He sat back reflectively and lit a cigarette. He saw the children on the beach, the donkeys, men selling gas balloons and suddenly he remembered a scene of children, broken children, who had trampled from one village to another. Thin, emaciated bodies, eyes wide and staring, arms thin and bellies huge. He remembered how he and his companions had made a fire and cooked bowls of rice.

"You look thoughtful?" Anna said seeing the sadness on his face. "Share them?"

He had never discussed this with her, but now he told her of those six dreadful months. "Man destroying man, for land that they will die and leave, blood-soaked land, rotting bodies and why? Killing a brother because he looks different, because he believes differently. Those awful children. It seems so terribly wrong and yet, it is the unfairness of life. Perhaps we also live in a cohabited existence with those in hell." He paused and stared ahead at the incoming tide. "I couldn't hack it, you know. It got to me, the terrible suffering. I pretended I could do it. I saw the priest, who was so caring. It made me sick, the sores on their bodies... I left a month early. I went off to America to live it up. I've told no one what a bloody coward I was. I couldn't take the poverty. Unlike your confrontation with Charles, you had the courage to remain. I've only ever had the courage to run away." He stopped and bowed his head and then lit another cigarette and she reached across and placed her arm round his shoulder knowing she had shared his nightmare, as he had shared *one* of hers.

Eventually he turned and smiled at her and then kissed her gently on the lips. She saw his light-hearted manner return and knew he had filed the memory away.

He took her hand and they walked slowly back towards the hotel. "I've really enjoyed today," she said, "I wish these days of grace could continue forever..."

As they walked along the sea front towards *The Imperial Hotel*, Jack noticed a second-hand record shop. On impulse he instructed Anna to wait outside whilst he went and rummaged through the boxes of old 45rpm records. It was a long shot, he realised, but nevertheless worth a try. Finally he located what he had been searching for and paid the assistant the princely sum of fifty pence.

"What's that?" Anna asked as she looked at the thin paper bag.

"I'll give it to you tonight... it's almost our story."

She gave him a querulous glance. "I'll look forward to hearing it," she said.

They walked up the steps to the hotel foyer.

Anna sat in front of the large mirror in the ladies' powder room and stared at her reflection; the sun had caught her face and she could see the smear of salt from the chips round her mouth. She thought of his small confession; it had surprised her for behind his carefree exterior it seemed there was sensitivity and understanding of his own short-comings. Pain too: he had not been able to see and bear the suffering. Small secrets... unwittingly shared. She stared at Gregory sitting at the corner of the make-up table. She had forgotten her family, their problems, forgotten Charles, she had felt young for the first time in years. Secrets... and she saw the flash of pain in her eyes as she slowly repaired her make-up.

CHAPTER TWELVE

*S*he joined Jack in the bar and accepted gratefully the gin and tonic he had ordered for her.

"Future Prime Ministers might have sat where you're sitting," she had told him as he gazed round the beautiful wood panelled *Number Ten Bar*.

He'd raised his eyebrows.

"This is a political party conference hotel..." she had replied.

They had managed to get a corner table in the restaurant. "I look a sight!" she had murmured, but he'd kissed her all the same.

The dinner was served in a typical four-star tradition. Jack knew that Anna preferred this type of restaurant to the fast-food outlets he and Mary frequented. Although he had pointed out that they would be very late returning, Anna merely shrugged and said, "So phone your mother!"

Jack could not make head nor tail of the menu and listened as Anna competently ordered Potage aux Topinambours followed by Sole Bonne Femme. Finally after much deliberation Jack ordered a Tomato Juice followed by Sirloin Steak – well cooked – and French fries. He felt safer with what he knew.

Over coffee Anna invited Jack to go with her to the church barbecue.

"If I remember correctly, last time I went to the rehearsals, you ignored me..." he said with a smirk on his face.

"Oh now come on!" Anna cajoled, "I think we've moved on from that incident, don't you?"

He smiled, "Sorry! But won't you mind being seen with me?"

She shook her head, "Why should I, you're a member of the church and so am I, what else will people read in to it?"

He frowned at her naivety but nodded, "I'd be happy to escort you," he said and drained the remaining coffee from his cup.

They enjoyed a final walk down the pier, listening to the waves meandering into the shore, seeing the lovers and melting into their background.

The long drive home, her legs curled up on the passenger seat, her fingers caressing the nape of his neck, her words of endearment into his ear. Their love-making when he had pulled off the motorway into a side road to find a lay-by.

She had laughed in the back seat.

"I said it would be a day to remember," he had whispered.

He had kissed her beneath the porch of her house waiting for her to invite him into her bed again but she merely said.

"Go home, your mother will worry!"

He nodded and handed her the record he had bought. "It's almost our story – but not quite."

Tears formed in Anna's eyes when, after fiddling with the hi-fi system in Steven's bedroom she heard the words to the song; *the uptown uptempo woman and the downtown downbeat guy* sung by Randy Eddelman. She wondered – would Jack desert her like the song said?

On the Friday morning Jack arrived at the house on time. He had half hoped that Anna would tell him not to bother with the garden, but would suggest they spent another day out. It would take his mind off home – it was getting difficult and the atmosphere was tense.

Rose had been waiting for him the previous night. It had not been until two in the morning before Jack came in. Standing in the kitchen in her dressing gown, Rose's face was full of anger. She had not minced her words, they were harsh and unyielding.

"Mary phoned again, I told her I didn't know where you were... but I did. I phoned Mrs de Courtney's house, there was no answer. You told me you were gardening. You lied didn't you? Leaving here in the early hours of the morning, creeping in now, just look at the time. You've been with that woman, you're having an affair..."

"Mind your own business," Jack had yelled at her. "There is nothing going on... I was with Gordon," he lied.

"I don't believe you. Mary was upset, you haven't phoned her. She is a good girl, you're jeopardising your life, for what, a quick fling with another woman..."

"Mum," he had gone to put his arms round her, but she had pulled away angrily. "Why can't you just be content with what you have?"

He had lain in his bed watching the dawn break. Perhaps his mother had been right. His thoughts returned to Anna and then to Mary knowing he wanted both of them for different reasons. After only a few hours sleep he wakened. He would take his mother a cup of tea in bed; a peace offering. He would phone Mary and lie again about his whereabouts the previous night.

As Jack stopped the Beetle outside Anna's front door he noticed her car was out in readiness. He grinned, glad he had thought to bring a change of clothes.

The front door opened and he got out to greet her.

"Hi!" He saw she was formally dressed with her hair tied back.

"Oh Jack," she gave him a swift kiss, "I have a meeting, the preparations for the church barbecue on Saturday, I'll be out all day."

She saw the disappointment on his face and reached forward and kissed him again. "Believe me, if I could have avoided it I would." Anna sighed as he walked with her to open the car door. "Get the garden sorted out, I'll phone you later."

"I'll miss you!" he said as he raised his hand, watching as the car drove out down the drive and through the open gates.

He strolled round to the rear of the house and knocked on the kitchen door. Did she have faith in him? Would she have left it open or not? Slowly he turned the handle and watched as the door opened. He went into the kitchen at lunch time and made himself something to eat. He looked round and was tempted now to explore the house more closely but he didn't. Anna did not deserve that.

Anna arrived at the church at precisely half past nine. She walked across to press the intercom button to announce her arrival, and waited until the door swung slowly open.

She had arranged to meet Father Mathews in the church hall along with the chairman of the fund-raising committee and the chairman of the Parish Council to discuss the final preparations for the annual barbecue. She walked down the stone floored corridor of the Friary building, admiring, as she always did, the beautiful wooden panelling. Imagining what it must have been like all those years ago when the monks had been in residence; now only two priests and a handful of brothers occupied the building. She paused at the door of the

Day Chapel and then slowly pushed it open and entered to stand quietly in the silence for a moment, contemplating the suffering figure on the cross.

Memories of her mother flooded unexpectedly into her mind and she felt the tears prick behind her eyes. She sighed, would these thoughts every leave her?

"Forgive me," she murmured and as she turned to leave she saw the watchful figure of Father Mathews standing in the doorway.

"Anna!" he gave her a worried smile, for he had observed the droop of her shoulders.

"Good morning, Father." Her voice was bright now and he walked with her down the corridor to enter the rear of the hall.

"Peter is going to be late," Father Mathews said as they stood glancing round. "But Vincent should be here any minute." He pursed his lips and then added. "So how are you, Anna?"

She saw his penetrating blue eyes surveying her and smiled as she replied. "Busy as usual!"

"The family still away?"

She nodded and the Father continued. "You must be lonely?" and before she could reply he said, "I suppose Jack is still gardening for you? I saw you both passing in the car the other day." Now his eyes seemed to bore into her. "He's a good man, and I like Mary."

Anna was not sure if she imagined the faint note of censure in the priest's voice as she turned and met his eyes.

"I'm sure they will make a wonderful couple," she equivocated.

"Sorry, I'm late Father." The door burst open and they both turned.

"Vincent!" There was warmth in Father Matthew's voice as he turned and welcomed the middle-aged man who bore down on them, clip-board in hand. He was dressed in an inappropriate heavy tweed jacket and formal shirt and sporting a bow tie. He pushed his overly long grey hair back from his red face then adjusted his glasses.

"Hello Anna, how's Charles?" Vincent asked shaking Anna's hand.

"He'll be home soon," Anna murmured as she brought out her notebook from her capacious shoulder bag. "I think we should be getting down to arrangements, stalls and helpers..."

The meeting took longer than she had anticipated. She had forgotten how indecisive Vincent could be. Finally a small sketch had been drawn and a list of volunteers and their duties made up.

"Oh," she said in what she hoped sounded a casual manner. "Jack Fearnley has offered to come along and help."

She saw Father Mathews give her a sharp glance but before he could say anything Vincent had cut in saying with undisguised enthusiasm.

"Great, that's really great. He plays the guitar doesn't he?"

"So he tells me," Anna smiled gratefully at Vincent and then started to gather her papers together.

"Time I must be going," she said nodding to Vincent and the Father. "I'll be in touch, let's hope the weather stays fine."

Anna nodded her goodbyes and walked to the door of the library. Had she imagined the faint look of disapproval in the Father's eyes? It was ironic that he had introduced them; did he know more than he let on? Suddenly Anna wished she had not asked Jack to accompany her to the barbecue but it would be too hurtful at this stage to suggest he arrived separately.

Jack worked hard, feeling the heat draining his energy, but was determined Anna would return and be pleased with the work he had put in. At four o'clock she drove up the drive. He smiled as he walked towards her.

"I was expecting you back earlier!"

Anna frowned; she did not approve of having to explain

her whereabouts. "I went to LATE and found a home for the cat you ran over!"

Jack picked up the faint acquisitive tone but said nothing. Due to the cat's injuries the vet had kept it longer than anticipated. As Anna walked to the front door she said, "that little lot cost me four hundred pounds…"

Jack was surprised. When Anna had taken the cat into the vet in her blood-stained clothes, he had admired her act of compassion and now he had felt it had somehow been soured as it now had a price. "Where is the cat, I thought you were bringing it back here?"

"Oh, don't be stupid," she said tetchily, opening the front door. "I can't have a stray in with Hector."

Once in the hall Anna turned in an attempt to justify her actions. "I have found a good caring home for the cat."

He was disappointed, he didn't know why but felt compelled to ask. "Who?"

"Oh some volunteer in LATE." She entered the kitchen and went over to the coffee machine and poured herself a cup.

Jack felt cut off as she had obviously closed the topic and the cat was obviously of no more importance. For a brief moment he wondered if his relationship would end as abruptly. "So?" he went on, determined to extract more information. "Is this person a cat lover?"

She walked across and placed a mug of coffee in front of him and gently ruffled his hair. "Oh, she's a simple person who needs to be liked. She and the cat will get on well." After his coffee Jack had cleared up his tools and left Anna talking on the phone.

Jack drove home wondering why he felt a sense of being let down. He dismissed this thought after considering what Anna had done for the cat. Even to her, four hundred pounds was a lot of money and his initial assessment of her was correct. She was still an angel in his eyes.

He parked his Beetle and walked up the path, pushed open the front door and as he walked into the kitchen he could hear Rose in the lounge.

"Jack!" she said, "Come here…"

He walked into the room and was astonished to see his mother holding the cat that he had run over.

"Isn't she adorable?" Rose said, "Mrs de Courtney gave her to me."

"Gave?" Jack queried.

"Well," Rose went on, "she said it would go to the cat's home if no one would take it. Look it has all these stitches; who would want it in this condition, it would end up being put to sleep." Rose glanced down at the cat and muttered, "Poor little Puss, nobody wanted you – except me."

Jack felt a sense of betrayal and irritation and remembered how Anna had described the person who had taken the cat. It had been an unfair description.

"You look a bit miffed – what's the matter?" Rose asked.

"Nothing," he muttered, but surely Anna would not have had the cat taken to the cats' home? It seemed so out of character with her caring attitude.

"It's the church barbecue, remember, I did tell you?" Jack saw the suspicion in his mother's eyes as he walked into the living room dressed up for another night out.

He picked up his guitar and checked his appearance once more in the hall mirror. Jeans with the thick tooled belt, denim shirt, sleeves rolled to the elbow, open to reveal his sun tanned chest and the leather toggle, his boots would be hot for a summers evening but part of the gear and the old Stetson with the leather band… a memory of a girl who had worn it and memory of a night given over to rather more than a snog. He picked up his canvas guitar case and strolled to his car.

The car gave a near death groan as it laboriously lurched and slowly moved forward. Her automatic BMW had spoiled him and he wondered how Mary would react if he suggested a new car.

He wished now that he had not agreed to be the entertainment; he would have preferred to sit back as a guest just watching Anna. He reached into his top pocket of his shirt and put a cigarette between his lips; he had almost stopped smoking, as Anna didn't like the smell on his clothes or the taste of tobacco when they kissed. But now he lit it and inhaled deeply watching as the smoke curled out of the window.

He had offered to go and accompany Anna but she had decided she would go early and meet him there. The church car park was full. He could hear the sound of music and saw the balloons and banners. He managed to manoeuvre his car into a small space and glanced round for her BMW. She had obviously been one of the first to arrive and that meant the last to leave. He gave a silent curse and then remembered where he was going and amended it to a prayer that she wouldn't be too conscientious at the end and feel a need to clear away and then wash *every* dish.

He opened the car door and stretched his long legs out, he hadn't realised how cramped the Beetle had become now. He dragged the guitar out, stood up and yawned and then reached into the back seat for his hat.

"Hi Jack!"

He turned and frowned, not immediately recognising the face belonging to the voice.

"You've forgotten me!" She was young, about seventeen he judged, with long brownish hair and a wide open face. Brown eyes laughed at him from beneath dark brows. He let his eyes roam her slim body encased in very tight jeans and an unbuttoned open-necked shirt that outlined bra-less breasts, with the tails tied together over her torso to reveal a gap of flesh. He searched his memory and shrugged his shoulders not terribly interested in who she was.

"Karen... you've not forgotten?"

He had but he managed to smile nevertheless.

"Hi! Karen." He locked the car door and walked towards the large grassy garden at the side of the church near to the cemetery.

"You alone?" She had sidled up to him and he found they were walking together.

"Well..." he hesitated and then admitted a "yes!"

"So am I, lucky we met!"

No, he thought.

He wanted to tell her to go, but she clung to him, smirking at the other girls as they passed. "You haven't got a regular girlfriend then?" she asked and there was a provocative note in her voice.

"No girlfriend – just a fiancée!"

He could see the cloud of disappointment in her eyes. "She's not here? You said you were alone!"

"She's away!"

"So the cat can play," she turned to leer up at him.

"Don't mention cats!" his voice was sharp.

She frowned.

"Private joke!" he smiled before adding, "I'm here to sing a few songs," he gesticulated to his guitar. "The entertainment!"

He wished she would leave him but she stuck to his side chattering about inconsequentiality's.

"Look, you must have friends here?" he asked in desperation. "I've got to go soon."

"Don't you like me?" her voice was petulant.

"I don't know you," he replied without interest. He stopped and stared down into her face, there was an open invitation in her eyes as she placed her teeth over her lower lip. They walked round the various stalls and he could smell the aroma of meat sizzling; fairy lights had been strung over where they were selling beer and soft drinks. He carefully allowed his eyes to wander round the crowds of people who were either standing around or who had taken their places at the wooden tables that had been covered with bright paper tablecloths.

Then he saw Anna talking to Father Mathews, and he felt a surge of disappointment for she was as she had been; the austere Mrs de Courtney, hair tied back, printed skirt and sleeveless top. Their eyes met and he knew his mirrored his disappointment as he gave her a wry smile and tipped his hat.

"You know her?" Karen asked sharply not missing the gesture.

He shrugged, "No." He felt the lie and wished it didn't have to be so. He quickened his pace, turning now in Anna's direction, but Karen was not to be dissuaded – she clung like a limpet.

It was later, when Jack found himself on his own that he approached Anna.

"Good evening, Jack," her voice was formal but her eyes gave him the message he wanted to see.

"Hi!" he gave a faint smile. "I have managed to extricate myself from that Karen… she says she knows you, or rather Steven!"

Her eyes did not leave his and he read the wanting he too felt. "Yes, we all had a brief encounter with Karen, what can one say about her that is charitable?"

He laughed.

"You look…" as he pointed to her hair.

"Efficient, I hope!"

"Well, I was going to say remote and unobtainable." They remained in a brief encapsulated moment, until Jack reached across and used a finger to brush a strand of hair from her eyes and she gave him an intimate smile. Father Mathews had noticed the gesture and coughed as he approached. They both turned and met the disapproval in his eyes.

"How is Mary?" It was a pointed remark and Jack saw

Anna move away as he stood answering the Father's questions. "Are you still gardening for Mrs de Courtney?"

Jack gave a faint nod. "She is a hard task-master," he tried to make it sound a joke and then saw Anna standing by the barbecue. Even as she tried now to look her staid best, he still saw her beauty, he could still feel his heart beating and he knew now that he truly loved her, deeply and passionately and that he always would. He took out a cigarette and lit it, he thought of Mary, picturing her here with him. He thought of marriage and commitment, and then of the time he had spent with Anna and he knew then it was Anna he wanted to spend the rest of his life with.

The barbecue had proved successful. Over two hundred people had attended and when dusk came, a circle had been formed and Jack, in the middle had started to ask for requests. It had proved a little restrained at the beginning, but the atmosphere relaxed and it was not long before everyone joined in.

In the flickering flames, Jack remembered the victims in Romania, where he too had sung to them. In particular he remembered a seventeen year old girl who came and sung *I'd like to teach the world to sing* with him. The church barbecue did not evoke the same feeling of togetherness but it was a happy occasion.

He frequently glanced across and saw Anna sitting with a reflective expression on her face and he wondered what her thoughts were.

"What a day!" Jack said with an air of exhaustion as he followed Anna out of the church hall and into the car park. "Well, the barbecue seemed to be pretty successful, but what on earth made you buy all this junk?" He glanced down at the carton she had asked him to carry across to her car.

Anna shook her head, pushing her hair back as she

179

struggled with his cumbersome guitar case, "I honestly don't know, I think I felt so sorry for the craft stalls, the women had spent so much time making things and very few people were offering to buy them."

"What did they make?"

"Oh, you know those knee rugs and knitted dolls and things," she replied with a laugh.

"Really Anna, what do you want with knee rugs and dolls?" He shook his head in despair and sighed. He remembered how she had gone round all the stalls giving encouragement to the stallholders and all the participants. Why she felt the need to purchase items as well, God only knew!

"You've put so much effort into this event, it's really been you who instigated it all… they should have given you something as a thank you."

Anna smiled inwardly. It was a constant topic of conversation in her house as to how much she did and how little thanks she received, but she had long since realised that voluntary work was often a thankless task.

"People who give their time voluntarily do it not only to help others but also in a way to help themselves," she replied seriously.

He stopped and stared at her. "Is that why you do so much?" he asked curiously.

"Perhaps!" she gave an oblique smile.

"You mean you have a need to help?"

She started to walk on saying. "I have so much, Jack, I am well-blessed. I want to give something back into the community, if that is a need then yes. It has also been a very difficult time with Charles. I realised then how it helps people to talk over problems… I had no one to talk to. My mother wouldn't have understood, and friends, well… I've never really wished to discuss my problems outside the family. I coped, but it sure wasn't easy… I suppose the end result gave me a perception on life I did not possess before. Then my need was to take my mind off my own problems and that is why I got involved with LATE."

"Does this work help you?"

Anna nodded.

"So it fills two roles?" He frowned, remembering his mother and her restlessness after the death of his father. Her need to have more than a part-time job. Her depression until someone had suggested she volunteered for LATE. It had saved her, shown others had a need as great as hers. He wondered briefly what Anna's need really was; it had to be more than Charles.

She smiled at him. "Oh yes, it does. It helps those who give and those who receive."

"Well, I suppose you're right. You're certainly always busy, like today; what have you got out of this evening?"

"Oh Jack, being with you, of course!" She threw her head back and laughed a light carefree sound. He wanted to put the carton down and take her in his arms, kiss her. She encompassed all his thoughts, he could not imagine a time in his life now without her. He had fleeting moment of wanting to break off his engagement, take Anna and run away with her. But it was all fantasy, he knew that.

"You volunteered for Romania?" She went on, not seeing the flash of pain that swept over his face as she continued. "You felt a need after your father died... you don't do this sort of work for thanks, you do it because you want to." He nodded. "Look," she explained in a matter of fact tone. "The money we've raised and the pleasure people got from the day is really all the thanks I could have wished for." Jack felt a mixture of tiredness after helping to clear up and elation because they would soon be alone.

He stood by the car and waited until she opened the boot and then stowed the carton inside. Then she handed him his guitar case. He waited until she had got in and fastened her seat belt before closing the driver's door of her car.

She laughed softly as she gazed into his eyes, and he wanted to kiss her.

"Good night Anna!" he heard the voices of people passing and pulled back and joined Anna as she waved and called the various good nights. He walked back to his car and waited until she drove slowly past him and out of the church car park. He drove impatiently behind her. Eventually he parked his Beetle alongside the BMW in the driveway of her house and stood waiting for her to walk towards him.

"Hello, stranger!" He took her into his arms and kissed her and she pressed her body against his.

"What was it you wanted, a cool beer, a swim and...?"

"You!" he finished with a grin as he followed her into the house and watched as she scooped Hector into her arms and kissed him. He'd not told her that the stray cat she'd paid for had ended up in his home and was now renamed Custard.

"You know where the beer and the pool are," she said, "help yourself. I'm going up to change, I feel hot and in need of a quick shower." She placed Hector down on the hall floor and walked across to Jack. "Are you hungry?" she asked as an after-thought.

He grinned and swept her into his arms bending her over the kitchen table. "I'm always hungry," he whispered as he bent to kiss her. She disentangled herself and ran her hand through her hair and pulled her blouse together.

"Really, Jack," she chided him but here was a sensuality in the words and he knew she had wanted him as he needed her. "Do you want any food?"

"Only you!" He lunged forward.

"Oh be serious," she laughed placing a hand on his chest and gently pushing him away.

"We'll have a midnight snack," he replied.

"If I can keep awake that long!" she laughed.

"Oh, you will, I guarantee you that."

"You do, do you?" she raised her eyes provocatively.

"Yes. Come into the pool, let's have a swim!"

He saw the flicker of desire in her eyes as she bit her lower lip in a hesitant manner. "You mean in the nude?"

"Exactly!"

Anna hesitated, "I don't know."

"Don't be so puritanical. Come on… it's just the night for a swim." There was a goading note in his voice.

"Suppose someone saw us?" she prevaricated.

"Who, there's only Seth and Hector. And we've shut the gates this time!"

She stared at him for a moment and then replied. "I'll change, you turn the pool side lights on and get some drinks."

He blew her a kiss and went outside, feeling the heat of the dying day. He lit the flares and then sat down on a pool-side chair and yawned before lighting a cigarette. The lights round the pool broke up the dusk. He would miss the luxury of her lifestyle. He wanted it to last forever.

Jack finished his cigarette and then discarded his clothes and plunged into the pool. He felt the cool water around his naked body as he did a couple of lengths; then he relaxed and floated on his back, gazing up at the perfect star-lit sky. He heard the splash and felt Anna beside him they swam together before he turned to take her in his arms, feeling her naked body next to his.

They laughed, swam, made love and drank beer and at midnight they lay stretched out in light towelling robes together on one of the pool side loungers.

Anna raised herself on an elbow and the folds of her robe opened to expose her naked breast. Not so long ago she would have hastily pulled the robe together in embarrassment, but not now. She enjoyed the admiration and wanting in his eyes as they hungrily met hers. Now looking down at the face below hers and gently tracing the lines across his forehead Anna knew that at this moment she could so easily fall headlong into love with Jack. 'Could'. She analysed the word – perhaps she was already in love.

He saw the varying emotions in eyes that glowed in the dusk and reflected the poolside lights. He reached up and drew her close so her head rested on his chest, her fingers entwining the thick hair. She remembered Charles's hairless body and suddenly the years of celibacy stretched interminably and she felt a sadness overwhelm her and she bent and kissed Jack's warm, open lips.

He felt her passion and sadness in the desperation of her kiss. This extraordinary relationship would end soon, he knew that, and he wished there was more time. They drew apart and she moved to lie back so they looked to the darkness of the sky.

"It's late," she murmured, "we should go indoors."

She got up and folded the cushions on the loungers whilst he picked up the beer cans and his clothes and followed her into the kitchen.

"We never did have any supper," she said as she walked towards the fridge to take out a bottle of champagne. "If you open the champagne I've some smoked salmon sandwiches I made earlier."

"Sounds good." He bent and kissed her and stood watching as she took the foil-wrapped platter from the fridge. He took the champagne and cooler and glasses and she took the platter of sandwiches up the stairs and into the guest bedroom.

"I'll always associate smoked salmon sandwiches and champagne with a night of love," she said with a contented laugh and watched as he poured the champagne into two flutes and handed one to her.

She could see the serious expression on his face as he raised his glass. "Oh Anna… I think I am in love with you," the words took her by surprise and she stared at him.

"It's the heat of the night," she whispered.

"No, it's you!"

She placed a forefinger on his lips. "Please, we can't think such thoughts. We both knew from the beginning that this was a casual dalliance… Days of Grace, remember?"

"It's no dalliance for me, " he said quietly. "You are the most beautiful woman I have ever known, look, I mean beautiful inside as well as outside. That sounds a bit, you know, well I'm not good with sentimental words, they come out all wrong. Poets have the edge on scenes like this…" He stopped and shook his head, "but I do know you are the most amazing person I've ever met. I'll never forget you." And she could see he was faintly embarrassed.

"Oh Jack, I can't tell you how much our time together has meant to me. Bring the champagne over and the sandwiches, let's be totally decadent and have a picnic in bed," she laughed.

They propped the pillows up and she turned the overhead lights off and switched on the gentle glow of the bedside light. He poured her another glass of champagne and she watched as he munched through the sandwiches. I love him, she thought, and a warm glow spread through her body.

"These few weeks will be our secret," she sighed. "No one will ever be able to share these moments. I'll lock the memory away forever."

"You won't tell Charles?"

"No, I certainly won't tell Charles," she whispered.

"Or your children?"

"Maybe one day there may be a need to tell Kate. I don't know," she said thoughtfully. "I'll have to be old, really old."

"I wonder how they'd react to a mother having an affair with her young gardener?" He grinned at her.

"Oh a very special gardener, one who will never be forgotten. One who wakened me with a kiss. But nobody will ever know. Every woman is entitled to have a life outside her family. I'd never have said that a few months ago… you really have changed me." She reached up and kissed him. "And you, will you tell your Mary?"

He shook his head. "No, like you say, this is our secret."

"And your mother?"

"Certainly not my mother, although I sometimes think she suspects something. But not this, sitting in bed with the chairman of LATE naked, drinking champagne and about to make love…"

He took the glass from her hand and placed it on the bedside table and then he slowly opened her robe.

"Our secret," he murmured as he bent his head down so his mouth cupped her breast. "Don't you feel a pang of guilt?"

"Guilt?" He heard her repeat the word as her body moved sharply away and he turned to rest on his elbow. The word penetrated through her subconscious and suddenly, like a fast forward moving video, the scene of her mother's death replayed itself.

"Guilt, of course I feel guilt," she heard her voice say as if from a long tunnel, as she pulled away from his embrace. He felt her withdrawal and cursed himself for mentioning the word.

They lay in polarised silence and then he turned and kissed her gently on the forehead. "Anna, we haven't hurt anyone, it'll always be our secret," he whispered comfortingly. Then when she didn't respond he continued, "Hey, come on, it's too late for hang-ups. Everyone feels guilty at some stage or another, it's a symptom of being human. Only animals don't feel guilty."

"Animals don't sin," she replied abruptly.

He stared down at her face and remembering how often the words sin and guilt had been mentioned during their brief time together.

"You're always on about 'sin', it bothers you. What is sin?

And what could you ever have done that is sinful?" He turned and ran his fingers through her hair. "You are too beautiful in mind and spirit, Anna, to be sinful." He remembered how she had picked up the injured cat, her compassion and care. All right she'd found a good home for it but it would have been dead without Anna. So many small acts of kindness, and yes, he admitted, some inhibitions, but who wouldn't have with a cross-dresser for a husband?

Anna flinched inwardly at his patronising attitude.

"Oh Anna," he whispered into her hair. "We are friends as well as lovers… place whatever burden you have on my shoulders. I promise I won't walk away." He knew he sounded overly sentimental; slushy, Mary would call it. But the wine had loosened his tongue and he wanted to embrace Anna in his compassion. It was a retribution for the lack of compassion and commitment he'd made to all those he'd run away from in Romania. He too had guilt on his soul and he doubted her sin could match his.

There was a long silence as they lay together, each locked in their own prison of guilt. Anna realised their relationship had entered a crucial stage. He loved her, she did not doubt that, and suddenly she wanted to unburden all the guilt that lay hidden in her mind. The mythical *Scales of Maas* when, in her case, the guilt of taking her mother's life would be weighed against a feather. It was a need to expunge herself. Suddenly there seemed a glimmer of hope that she could unburden herself to sympathetic ears.

"Sin and guilt and secrets," she said, breaking through the silence in an attempt to steer the conversation in another direction. "We all have acts and deed and memories stored away under lock and key. We are afraid to open a door to confess so the burden grows. My God, how it grows…"

He felt her shudder and whispered, "Not another ghost walking over your grave?" and expected her to laugh but instead he heard her give a faint sob.

"What do you mean by that?"

"A ghost walked over your grave in Stratford, as I remember? Anna, I know there is something on your mind. Tell me. There is nothing that would shock me."

She remembered her confession about Charles, his sympathy and understanding. Apparently nothing would shock him... he would understand, perhaps at last she could unburden her guilt. Share it with another. He would listen and then kiss her and hold her in his arms, it would be her guilt shared, her secret placed on his shoulders. A bonding, something that only the two of them would know.

"I told you what happened when I was in Romania – we are not all perfect," he paused. "Are you trying to tell me you've had another affair before me, because if you have I can understand. You've had problems with Charles, it would well..." he stopped, unsure how to continue. Anna wished it was that simple. An affair she could deal with. An affair people could understand.

"Darling Jack," she murmured and he heard the endearment and was comforted. When he felt her lips on his cheek the kiss was not one of passion but of compassion. "Not every man is a warrior. You have admitted your weakness, what more does Jesus ask of any of us?" she replied.

"So," Jack said breaking the silence that ensued, "tell me your secret, admit your own weakness, Anna."

He had turned on his side and was smiling down into her face. She ran her tongue over her dry lips, and the wish to unburden her nightmares and guilt overwhelmed her. To feel his arms round her holding her close and listen to his words of comfort. He'd told her he would not walk away, the time had come to put him to the test.

He saw the conflict flicker in her eyes.

"Anna, you told me about Charles...this cannot be worse!"

"I have tried so often to Confess. Will you hate me, I wonder?" she asked.

"I could never hate you; my God, Anna, you make it sound as if you've committed some horrible crime. I know you, I love you… tell me!"

Why, she asked herself after such a perfect day had they suddenly chosen this time to display their secrets. She closed her eyes and then as if in a dream she slowly told him about her mother. Their love and friendship, and how supportive her mother had been to her. The death of her father and the ridiculous conditions of his will. Jack did not interrupt and she felt the tears coursing down her cheeks.

"My mother was such a proud, independent person, such good company; she loved her Gin and Tonic and family dinners. She was a good Catholic, an excellent bridge player and had a very sharp brain and was well read," Anna paused. "You can never pinpoint the time when disorientation starts, when the mind suddenly goes into reverse. Dementia creeps on its victims, be they the sufferer or the carer." She paused and he could feel her distress.

"She got lost," Anna continued. "We had gone on a shopping expedition and always had an hour to do our own thing and then we'd meet up for lunch. One day she didn't arrive, and I found her just wandering round the shops, oblivious of the time and without any recollection of where she was supposed to meet me. I thought it would be easy to cope with. But of course the disease progresses. My mother started to wander, she would get up in the middle of the night, then she started going to bed in the afternoon." She stopped and heard his murmur of sympathy and was encouraged to continue.

"Charles was really very understanding; he had taken over the running of the house when we married and now arranged for the alterations so mother did not have the stairs to contend with." Anna described the room, the nurses and the constant smell of urine. The times she was alone trying to cope when Charles was away. The burden of voluntary work and her mother. She left nothing out of the hardship that dementia entailed for the carer. The horror of her mother unable to talk or remember, her own growing impatience, the need to restrain her mother for fear she would have an accident and harm herself. But most of all her own lack of compassion.

"You are too hard on yourself," Jack said when she paused. "You did all you could. Impatience, you make it sound like cruelty. It's obvious you loved her Anna... what more could you have done?"

She gave a faint sob. "I could have let her live until God decided it was her time to die." Her voice was barely audible. There was a heavy silence as she waited for his response.

"I'm sorry?" he replied and she knew by the tone of his voice he had not really understood.

"Leave it, forget what I said," she said hastily wishing to recover the situation.

"No, you said you could have let her live. What do you mean?"

Anna knew she had to continue, make him understand. "Oh Jack!" and she turned and clung to him. "My Mother was so feeble, she was doubly incontinent. She didn't know me, she was not the mother I loved, that person had died years ago. I tried to break the clause in my father's will on grounds of compassion: he wanted her to spend her remaining days at home whilst I wanted her to spend the last days in proper care and not with agency nurses. In the beginning I seldom saw the same nurse twice, some were caring and helpful, others just wanted the money. It was only when I asked for continuity did a nurse called Helen become at all regular.

"But despite that I just I couldn't go on... I was alone one night, she had messed in the bed. I stood in her room, the nightlight was casting shadows on the walls. I saw the crucifix above her bed and I prayed, prayed so hard for help, help for me, not for her, she was far past any help…. Tried not to think I would ever do anything to harm my mother…. I remember Hector came into the room, and knocked her rosary onto the floor. Then, O God!" she shook her head, "She messed up the clean bed again… she had no quality of life left, no dignity or self-respect. I wanted to scream. I took one of the pillows; the blank eyes stared into mine before I placed it over her face. Her thin, bony hands fluttered and then lay quiet. I ended my mother's life, that is my sin."

She realised she had not told it at all in the way she intended; she had wanted to make more of the problems. The anxieties, the sheer hard work, night as well as day, the terrible tiredness. The weakening of her resolve, her decreasing lack of control over her temper. How could she have told him how it had happened, or had time dimmed the act; perhaps she was afraid to confess that this outwardly calm, collected person did after all have a darker side. She sobbed and felt the tears running down her cheeks as she waited to feel his arms round her, to hear the words of comfort, to feel his tender kiss on her cheek.

"Oh Jack, you don't know the relief it is to tell someone…" she turned towards him, but he did not reach out to comfort her; instead she heard his voice, accusing:

"I have got this right, Anna: you killed your mother?"

"No!" she stared at him in horror, "you make it sound like murder. It was an act of mercy. Surely you of all people can understand." Now she felt a need to justify her action. She heard him sigh and watched as he turned away from her. "You are condemning me?" there was fear in her voice.

"No," he said, but even to his ears it didn't sound convincing. "It's just, well, your own mother…"

Anna sighed. "She was ill, Jack, the mother I knew had long

since died, it was just her shell!"

"But she was alive, Anna, the faith tells us we have a soul... you are Catholic, surely you can see it's wrong... it's..."

"Murder, go on say it," she snapped as she pulled her robe across her nakedness. "Don't you think I haven't said that a thousand times to myself over the years. But I thought you would understand..."

"I do, I do, believe me. Caring is difficult. But no one lives forever, there is an end and that isn't ours to decide." He sighed as Anna cried silently, waiting for the comfort that he seemed incapable of giving.

"I don't know what to say....you're a Magistrate, you know the law as well as I do."

"The law, what has the law to do with it?"

"Well, you've committed a crime!" he mumbled.

"Is that all you can say by way of consolation. Of course it's a crime, I know that. I've never agreed with Euthanasia but suddenly I couldn't take any more. My mother had lost all her dignity. She had become the sort of person she was afraid of becoming. She would have understood."

"But you'll never know, will you?"

"You don't understand," she struggled to sit up in bed. "I used to be so convinced in all my beliefs. Sadly I learned life isn't black and white; the grey in the middle is how we have to live. I always thought I was strong, law-abiding and faithful to all the laws, of God as well as of Man .... my sin is, that I am none of these things, Jack."

"You're right, Anna, I don't understand. Your family? Didn't anyone suspect?"

"Suspect I had killed my mother? Of course not. The sudden death of an demented old woman. I was the devoted daughter, remember?"

"You never confessed to Father Mathews?"

He saw Anna lower her eyes.

"Bloody hell, Anna…" He tailed off, unsure what to say. Anna felt a perceptible change in his attitude and knew she had made the wrong decision. Telling him was a moment of inner weakness and belief he loved her sufficiently to understand.

"No. I've wanted to confess, believe me." She paused. "Jack, can you at least forgive me?"

There was a silence before he said. "I am not the one you have to ask for forgiveness." He stopped realising how sanctimonious he sounded. "Look, I can't get my head round it, Anna. I mean, well, you're so caring…"

"And helping my mother to die wasn't caring?"

"Of course it was to you, but it's not right… it was to help yourself more than it was to help her."

As they both subsided into an anxious silence, she stared at him in stunned disbelief.

He was unsure what to do: to turn over and make love meant he acquiesced and he wasn't sure if he could accept her confession. Slowly he got out of bed and she watched as he fumbled with his jeans and shirt.

"You're not leaving?" She struggled into her housecoat. "Please don't go, I thought you, of all people, would understand. I beg you, Jack, don't leave me." Her voice had risen. "You are condemning me. You've never nursed someone with dementia… you would have had to walk a mile in my shoes, Jack, to understand."

He lit his cigarette; his hands were shaking as he stared at her. He was surprised how her action had affected him. He felt repugnance that she could have deliberately taken a pillow and placed it over an old woman's face.

"Look, I don't understand how you could do it. I have been with an old person, and one who's sick, and needs constant attention. I watched my father die. The disease made him confused and virtually paralysed. We had to do everything for

193

him, we'd no money for nurses, we relied on what could be provided. My Dad had no quality of life. He suffered, Anna, I mean really suffered. So did my Mum, God, looking back at it, she was a Saint. Mum brought him out of the hospital so he could die at home with his family, in dignity. He was doubly incontinent in the end, always in pain... and yet, I couldn't have done what you did. My Mum would say *The Lord giveth and the Lord taketh away* – when he is ready. I know that sounds hard and I'm sorry. Really sorry." He held his hand out and shrugged his shoulders as he saw the tears in her eyes. "You saved the cat's life, Anna, and yet you put your own mother down. It doesn't make sense!"

She stared up at him, annoyed that she had told him, dismayed by his lack of understanding, mortified by his condemnation. "I told you, Jack, the grey areas of life seldom make sense, but that is where most people live, trying to do the right thing. Trying, that is the best we can do. The best that is asked of us. Sometimes we fail, I have failed myself: my mother, my family, my faith. But if we always succeeded then there would be no need for recompense. Christ came to save sinners." She paused and turned to take a tissue from the box on the bedside table. She sniffed and dabbed her eyes. "You have a lot of learning to do. Your own cowardice, Jack. Your own grey area. You ran away from those who needed you... you hadn't the guts to help and save others... you just wanted life to be neat and tidy, well it isn't, neat and tidy. It's bloody hard."

He stared at her, not wishing to comprehend what she had said, wanting only to leave.

"I think it's time I left."

"We've ended it, you and I, is that what you're saying... it's over?" As she stared at him he was shocked to see her face quite disfigured by lines of worry – he could not even imagine her former beauty. "Oh you coward... I thought you would comfort me. You said you'd not walk away from me. I wish to God I'd not told you."

"I wish to God you hadn't...!" he shouted at her as he opened the door.

"You selfish bastard" she cried out. But he had left.

CHAPTER THIRTEEN

*I*t was just after one o'clock in the morning when Jack spun his orange Beetle down the drive and out through the gates of Kinellan House. It was over, and he couldn't really believe it – but he couldn't understand how anyone could kill the person they loved. A pillow over the face, a horrible, selfish act. He shuddered as he drove round and round trying to clear his thoughts before pulling up outside his house. Anna's disclosure had knocked him for six, suddenly her burden was now his. What should he do? Thoughts of going to the police station crept into his mind, but that would mean revealing their affair, and this would hurt his mother, and Mary, and ruin Anna's life. It would also mean doing the ethical thing of reporting a murder. He sighed, 'murder'! Yes, that was the name for the deed. Anna was a murderess.

He tiptoed quietly into the house, patted Custard and then went into the kitchen and opened the fridge to take out a beer. He ripped the can open and took two swift gulps and then sat down on the kitchen stool and lit a cigarette. He realised he was hungry and opened the fridge again to take out a jar of peanut butter and a packet of water biscuits. Not much after a midnight feast of smoked salmon sandwiches and champagne.

He found it hard to come to terms with his moralistic outlook. He should have taken Anna in his arms, comforted her and then made love. But no, he felt that that would have cheapened him – he would have colluded with her. Suddenly he felt frightened by her disclosure. It was not a nice thought to live with and for the first time since meeting Anna he felt that their affair had been a mistake. If only she had kept her own counsel; he knew it was an inevitable irony about their relationship – Anna was no Saint.

Her confession had been like the shattering of a mirror, the image that you had seen and believed to be perfection had been disfigured by cracks and flaking paint. Nothing could ever be the same between them. He found himself imagining her mother, dispossessed of dignity. Anna had suffered, he accepted that. But his own mother had cared for his Dad, in a small house with little money; they were confined and lived with the knowledge that death was near, but they prayed together by his bedside. When he died they cried. He wondered who had cried for Anna's mother. Had Anna?

The taking of a life and those poor emaciated people in Romania, starving, dying, hoping that despite all their suffering and hardship they would live to see another day. Whilst some in the West now viewed the taking of a life of suffering with such little thought.

"Life isn't meant to be easy, son," his Mum had said when he'd ranted at God for letting his Dad suffer. "It's a testing ground to see how we cope. If there was no suffering then we'd all be in heaven!" She had a simplistic faith and suddenly he realised she might not be slim, beautiful or clever, but she had an inner goodness. Anna, he felt, had let him down – she was a goddess with feet of clay.

Anna awoke the following morning with a headache and puffy eyes from crying, to be confronted with the platter of stale sandwiches, the half-empty bottle of champagne and the two glasses.

She had placed compassion on Jack's shoulders and in

return she had received rejection. She dragged herself into the shower room and was baptised with the warmth of the water turned up to its hottest.

He would return; she was confident that his need for her would drive him back. But their time together, their Days of Grace, was running out: Kate and Steven would be back in the UK in ten days.

She and Jack needed time; it had been an emotional night, he would reflect on it and see she had no other choice. Murder! Had he really accused her of that? Not euthanasia, but murder. How could he think she would have murdered her mother? It was ludicrous, she had done a terrible deed, she knew that, but she had put her mother out of her misery. Anna towelled herself down and walked back into the bedroom to dress and clear away the debris of the night.

She had toyed with the idea of going to early Mass, but the time had dripped away and she had been forced to attend the eleven o'clock service. She had dressed with care, but she saw, as she looked into the mirror, a tired woman approaching middle age. There would only be Charles, watching him growing older and older, seeing his face raddled and lined with its red smeary lipstick, the panda eye-shadow a throwback from the sixties era. Incongruous wigs and dresses. No, she couldn't stand that any more... but what else was there?

She drove to the church and as she entered the car park she glanced round, wondering if the orange Beetle would be parked somewhere.

"Excellent do last night, Anna!" She heard the words of praise as she got out of the car. She tried to smile, tried to be Mrs Anna de Courtney, always in charge of herself and any given situation. But today, it was extremely hard.

She felt a vulnerability she had not felt before knowing there was another person who knew her secret; could she trust him? As she walked to the Narthex she chided herself for ever taking Jack into her confidence.

On entering the Narthex she noticed the stand for LATE was again in disarray but ignored it and strode purposefully to her pew and after genuflecting she knelt down, her head resting in her hands.

The days passed and she felt more let down and angry at Jack's withdrawal but then she reminded herself he'd scurried out of Romania at the first sign of hardship. She tried to self-justify her actions: Jack had been young, not fully understanding the trauma of her situation. She sighed, she was patronising him, he knew only too well the consequences of what she had told him.

She toyed with the idea of phoning him, but dismissed it; she would not crawl. She had sat at the pool-side remembering that it had only been the previous Saturday when they had laughed and there had been empathy.

Anna waited for Jack to make his usual gardening visit to her on the Wednesday morning, but he did not arrive, neither did he phone. Instead she received confirmation from Charles that he would be returning the day after the children arrived. It was all tumbling too quickly and she wished Jack would come, say he forgave her, so they could at least have one last day together.

The following day Anna left the house to drive to Allan House for a meeting. As she turned the car out of the village she saw the battered orange Beetle parked at the side of the road and slowed down, imagining that Jack had broken down. Then she saw him, naked to the waist, the sweat gleaming off his body as he pushed a lawn mower back and forth in someone's garden. She drew into the side of the road, opened the driver's window and called him over.

He turned and she saw the flash of indecision on his face.

Then he shrugged and switched the machine off and walked without enthusiasm across to the car.

"What happened to you yesterday?" She tried to keep her voice light, not wishing to sound possessive or demanding. "The garden's getting an awful mess again…"

He looked shame-faced, his eyes flickering away from her stare. Eventually he mumbled, "Something else came up, another job."

"Oh for goodness sake, Jack, don't lie to me – you're avoiding me!"

He gave a deprecatory shrug. "No, I was occupied, I'm sorry."

"Jack," she said in a more modified tone, "it was my confession… you felt, and probably still feel, that I took the easy road. Please, let's talk."

He shrugged his shoulders. "Look Anna, it's all getting too involved. I'm having to make judgements, I just wanted to be with you, days of love you know. I didn't want to be the keeper of your past."

"You're frightened, like you were in Romania?" there was faint contempt in her voice.

"No, I'm not frightened, I just can't get my head round it. Now seems a good time to admit it has to end. Okay, I should have phoned. He dropped his eyes and she sighed.

"Will you come for dinner tomorrow night. No," she held her hand up, "just a farewell dinner. My family will be back soon; it would, as you say, have had to end… one final dinner, Jack?"

He saw the appeal in her eyes and nodded reluctantly.

Anna had prepared the dinner with care. She had hovered between having it in the dining room,, the kitchen or on the patio. In the end, as it was a fine warm evening, she settled for the patio. She covered the wooden table with a bright red check cloth and placed the mosquito flares round the pool. She had prepared a simple meal: Vichyssoise soup for a starter with warm garlic bread, followed by a fillet steak, chips and tossed salad. She had beer and wine in readiness and an iced pudding. She had stood in front of her bedroom mirror contemplating what to wear; in the end she'd put on a simple sleeveless dress, she brushed her hair so it fell loosely round her face and she had made up with care.

As Jack drove to Kinellan House he wished he were just meeting Gordon for a drink. Suddenly Anna, the house and her secrets seemed less appealing than a pint of lager in a local pub. He was annoyed that the relationship had ended thus, but knew there was no turning back and this time he would definitely not be spending the night. He drove up the drive and parked in his usual space. Feeling a sense of uneasiness he rang the front door bell.

He stood in the front porch, in well pressed lightweight navy trousers, and a navy cotton long-sleeved shirt rolled back at the cuffs. He blinked nervously as she opened the door. He handed her the modest bunch of flowers he'd picked up from the local florist.

Anna accepted the flowers and waited for his usual kiss. She really wanted him to take her in his arms, to hold her close and whisper he loved her, but he merely took her hand in his and made no offer of a kiss. She instantly felt that there was now such a distance between them, it could never be narrowed again.

Jack followed her into the kitchen and she knew from his attitude he felt apprehensive. He stood awkwardly watching her place the flowers in a vase, then walk across to the fridge to hand him his usual can of beer.

"We'll eat on the patio, all right?" She smiled at him and he nodded.

"That's fine." But his voice lacked enthusiasm.

They ate and drank and talk and even laughed occasionally,

but they both knew the old intimacy had gone. She could see that his eyes no longer hungrily watched her every move. He was casual, but polite. Always polite.

"Was it only last week you told me you loved me?" she challenged him as they sat drinking coffee.

He looked across the table at her. He saw the pain in her eyes and knew he had hurt her even more deeply than he had realised. He'd walked away from the woman of his dreams, rejected her. He felt a pang of guilt and sadness, he should have been more understanding.

"I handled it badly, but I still can't accept it," he admitted. "It sounded so brutal. Our time together had to break up. I'm sorry it happened the way it did."

"Well, you missed out on the champagne and smoked salmon sandwiches," she joked lightly, hoping to inject at least a little air of their previous intimacy.

He gave her a faint smile. "Anna, I want us to be friends. Our days out…" he stopped and held his hands out. "Oh God, Anna, of course I love you, I always will. You were the most unobtainable woman, the most beautiful person, of course I want you back in my arms." He stopped.

"But?" her eyes met his.

"I can't explain. In today's world it sounds so insignificant, the taking of life. I suppose, as you say, I am a coward. I'm walking away. I didn't wish to be involved. But I can hold my head up high. I can admit I was a coward. Can you honestly do the same? I just wish you hadn't put the burden of your guilt on my shoulders."

"It is not your guilt, Jack. It's mine, and I have to live with it." She watched as he took out a cigarette and lit it.

"Anna, have you ever thought you might be found out?"

She picked up her coffee cup and took a sip before eyeing him over the rim. "Found out? My mother is dead – and buried – there is nothing to find out."

"Well, what you did is illegal."

"You mean you are going to report me?"

"Good God, no."

She pursed her lips together. "I would soon deny it, of course."

"Anna, I know I've sounded sanctimonious, but it's just the way I see it. Life is life. Sounds trite. We're friends, we both share two secrets, one of love and one of sin."

"So this is really the end?"

He nodded. "Mary comes back next week; but I'll never forget you, Anna."

"Oh, I think you will." She stood up and fiddled with her dress, finding something to do with her hands, straightening it out; obviously, the controlled Mrs Anna de Courtney was finding it hard to cope with the fact that it had all ended so abruptly.

"Jack, will you kiss me – one last time?"

She saw him hesitate, but then he rose from his chair and held his hands out; she grasped them and let him pull her to her feet.

"Oh Anna," he whispered, taking her into his arms. She placed her arms round his neck and drew his face towards hers. Pressing her body to his she remembered their first kiss and the nights of frantic love. She knew he wanted her and she kissed him with passion. "Oh Anna!" His breath was hot on her cheek as they drew apart and she knew he was tempted; all it needed was the slightest hint from her. But pride made her determine she would be the one to walk away now.

"Jack, I've a small present for you. A keepsake of that day in Oxford together." She turned to fumble in her handbag.

Jack frowned as he stared down at the gift-wrapped, oblong package wishing he had thought to buy her something.

He fumbled with the paper and finally extracted the red and gold box embossed, not too discreetly, with the name

Cartier. He hesitated before opening it, knowing what it contained and wishing he had the willpower to refuse the gift. A silver and gold, men's *Cartier Santos* watch. He gasped, incredulity written on his face.

"I can't accept this, Anna, it's far too valuable..." he said making a gesture of rejection.

"Oh, I think you can, Jack!" He heard the faint edge of sarcasm in her voice as she handed him an envelope. He placed the box down on the patio table, opened the envelope and extracted a card. In her own handwriting it read: *If you ever value this token of our friendship more than the friendship itself, you may sell the watch.*

A flicker of indecision hovered on his face.

"It's up to you, Jack," she said, narrowing her eyes. "A choice, a decision!"

They walked slowly down the hall and she saw his eyes glance across to the closed door and she imagined his thoughts.

"That was my mother's room," she acknowledged.

He reached out and gave her arm an awkward caress, but she noticed his step quickened until he reached the front door.

"Goodbye, Anna," he said as they stood in the porch.

"Goodbye, Jack!" She followed him out to the orange Beetle and watched as he got into the driving seat and slammed the door shut. Then she stood in the drive, tears flowing freely down her cheeks as the noisy, rusty, old Volkswagen spluttered its way out through the open gates for the last time. There was no familiar toot of the horn as it turned into the main road. She waited with fading hope, but the familiar rattle of its engine soon faded into silence.

Anna stood for a long time staring down the empty drive with a feeling of desolation. He had come into her life. He had awakened her sexuality. And now he had left. She remembered his tentative kiss and her anger, and then the passion she never thought she would experience. It had ended so bleakly; deeply within herself she knew he could never have come to terms with what she had done – and neither now could she.

Oh, she admitted the deed had been smoothed out in the telling; she could tell no one of the hurt she had inflicted on her mother, mentally and physically. But she had, over the years, managed to hide it all away: the memory, the guilt, the nightmares. She wasn't a wicked woman, just one who hadn't been able to cope at the one time in her life she had found herself at the lowest ebb. The efficient Anna de Courtney could not live with her demented, totally helpless mother… she had failed not only her mother, but herself. But she was the one who deserved all the blame.

She went slowly back into the house; how quiet it seemed. The dishes from their meal still remained in the kitchen. With tears in her eyes she walked outside to the pool where they had swum and made love. It had been so good –how could he have turned his back on her? How could he have left her? Hector arrived on the patio and she bent down and picked him up. She hugged him close to her and let her tears drip onto his coat.

It was very late before Anna finally went to bed. She had sat reflecting on her life, her attitude to Charles, her lack of help and understanding, the derision that she knew was often visible in her eyes. Her hypocritical attitude to her children. Perhaps out of her affair with Jack some good had to emerge. One day perhaps she would confess to Charles, reveal her secrets, before they were locked away forever.

"Well, you're grumpy this morning?" Becky said as she glanced across the table to where Jack sat scowling at his untouched breakfast. "What's up?"

"Nothing's 'up', as you put it!" he snapped back at her.

"You gardening today?"

"No!"

"Oh, not up at the manor house then?"

"Look, give it a rest, will you!" he glared at her.

He pushed his chair back from the table and heard a squawk as the cat dodged his foot. He stared down and the cat stared back at him and he remembered the day on the Malvern Hills. Anna's lack of concern as she placed the blood-stained rug in her car. The gentle soothing words as she'd sat stroking the cat in the back seat. Had she murmured words of love to her mother as she picked up the pillow? What had she thought as she gazed down at the frail figure on the bed, how had she reacted as she lowered the pillow and saw the hand helpless trying to push it away. The scene horrified him. That poor old woman, helplessly trying to stop her daughter suffocating her.

He walked out of the room and up the stairs to his bedroom; he sat on the bed and felt beneath his pillow to take out the shiny red box and stare down at the watch Anna had given him. He didn't have to read the inscription on the card, it was imprinted on his memory.

"I love her," he said to himself, "and yet I've just walked away." He had thought of little else but her confession. He had tried to rationalise it, make sense of why anyone could put a pillow over a fragile old lady's face and keep it there until the last breath of life had been expelled. He had tried to find some excuse, not wanting to moralise, but it had all seemed so hypocritical. Anna out doing good works, helping the elderly and yet unable to help her own mother. He thought of Rose, the tireless work she put into LATE, her admiration for Anna, and yet basically Rose was honest, whereas now, in his eyes, Anna was not.

He thought of his Dad, who had spent months lying on the bed in the back bedroom, his Mum working in a part time job to get money to help out. The stained, putrid bedsheets that were changed sometimes three times a day, the perpetual washing… and yet he never remembered hearing Rose utter one word of complaint.

Anna, who had had such a good, easy life; well, he shouldn't judge or condemn, but he couldn't understand this taking of a life. It was all the same, a pillow over the face or a bullet in the head… it was someone else's hand that killed you.

He saw the bedroom door open slowly and watched as the cat walked cautiously across to his shoe and rubbed her head up and down, marking him. He bent down and scooped her into his arms and heard her purring. Anna had so willingly paid the vet's bill. He buried his face in the warm soft fur.

"Jack." A face came round the door. "Are you okay?"

He wanted to tell Becky, to unburden himself. "Oh, it's just…" he started to say as Custard jumped on the bed.

"You're not gardening again for Mrs de Courtney, are you, ever?"

He shook his head. "We agreed to part."

"Mmmm."

He met her scepticism. "Look, it was getting heavy… she was relying on me too much, I felt it was easier. Any rate her family returns next week." He did not meet his sister's eyes.

"Something did happen, tell me?"

"Is that a woman's intuition?" He tried to laugh.

"I just know you, Jack; you're trying to make light of the situation but something happened, did she come on strong, is that it?"

He shook his head. "No, nothing like that, just a disagreement."

"A disagreement, is that all?"

"That's all, but I'm finishing with gardening now, getting ready for Mary to come back. Settling down!"

Becky reached across and kissed him. "I think there is more to it, but if it's finished and you're not seeing her again, then good."

As Becky left the room he called her back. "She gave me this…" he said holding the watch box out to her.

Becky opened the lid and started at the watch. "My God, it must be worth thousands!" she laughed, but it was not reciprocated.

"And this!" Jack held the card out to her.

After Becky had read the message, she raised he eyebrows and said, "you know what I would do, don't you?"

"Sell it!" Jack said.

"You bet," Becky replied.

Jack smiled before taking the box from Becky's hand and carefully placing it back in the bag. "It's insurance for a rainy day – and don't tell Mary."

Jack awoke to the sound of rain beating against the bedroom window. He opened his eyes; it was a dull miserable day. He struggled to sit up in bed and glance at the alarm clock and wished suddenly he could turn back time. Was it only a week ago that he'd been light-hearted and happy at the church barbecue? Anna and her love. Now he felt bereft, a hurt in his heart and a sense of betrayal. He still couldn't help wondering why she had felt the need to tell him. What had she expected his reaction to be? To merely say 'Anna that's all right, what shall we do tomorrow?'

He got out of bed lethargically and went into the bathroom to shave and then stand in the bath on the bath mat and draw the plastic curtain on the wobbly chrome frame round his naked body. To turn on the bath taps and try and adjust the trickle from the overhead rubber tube shower head that either came out too hot or ice cold; after a while it was just acceptably lukewarm. He soaped his body and washed his hair and closed his eyes for a moment and remembered how they had showered together in that extra-large cubicle.

"I've never made love in a shower before," she'd said as

he'd swung her up so she could wind her legs round his hips. He felt his tears mingle with the suds of shampoo. *I miss her, dear God; I miss her so much.*

He went into his bedroom to dress and stood at the window, watching the rain. He'd talked to Mary on the phone the previous night – it had been a long conversation. He had heard the underlying fear in her voice when she'd asked if he still loved her. He did, of course he did.

"I need you here, Mary." He'd heard the plea in his voice. She had started to answer in a bantering tone and stopped as if suddenly realising the underlying seriousness in his request. She had whispered words of endearment in her soft Irish voice and he had felt warmed by her love. He knew he was blessed, for he had love and now his life was beginning. He felt a sorrow for Anna who had nothing and he wondered how she would cope over the coming years with her guilt and her secrets.

He had decided his only course of action the night before. He was after all a Catholic. He would confess. But how much should he tell? He knew the confidentiality of the confessional box but still felt it a small betrayal of Anna's secret. He dismissed those thoughts – he had his own conscience to consider – and he cursed Anna's decision to confide. It wasn't as if he could talk to Rose; how could he tell her that her chairman of LATE, the caring and compassionate Anna, not only fostered an unwanted cat on to her, but had also killed her own mother when the going got too tough. Not the sort of conversation you bring up over dinner. Then there was Becky, who had proved to be a good listener, but he doubted whether she would understand the seriousness of how it had affected him. Gordon too; well, he couldn't trust Gordon with anything confidential... so there was only one place left to go and unburden himself.

Jack parked his car on the nearly deserted church car park. He had given a cursory glance round to see if the BMW was there and sighed with relief. He entered the Narthex, dabbled his fingertips in the Holy water and walked silently into the church, hearing the murmur of the women's voices as they recited the Rosary.

He saw the door of the confessional open and waited but no one entered so he shuffled along the pew and then slipped in, closing the wooden door quietly behind him. He hesitated over his option to kneel before the grill to confess or to walk into the room for a vis a vis with the priest.

He opted for the near anonymity of the old wooden box and knelt before the iron grill, seeing the outline of the priest who sat silently waiting.

"Forgive me, Father, for I have sinned…"

He heard the comforting reply and remembered one of the Fathers saying at a Reconciliation service. "Please, no shopping list; when you're in the confessional say what's on your mind."

"I have been having an affair with a married woman and have learned that…" He drew his breath in, conscious of the waiting priest behind the grill. Jack finally got his thoughts in order. "What do you do when you learn that someone has committed a serious crime?"

"How serious is the crime?" the priest replied.

"The taking of another person's life," Jack almost whispered the words. The priest remained silent and Jack had to continue. "It was supposedly an act of mercy, euthanasia some call it, but I find it difficult to accept the taking of life."

"What were the circumstances?" the priest asked

Slowly, awkwardly, Jack related what Anna had told him.

"This was told to you in confidence?" the priest asked.

"Yes, I think I am the only person who has been told," Jack replied.

There was a pause before he heard the priest's voice from

behind the grill. It was not his sin, it had been told to him in confidence. He could not break that confidence, neither could he judge the person who had committed the sin. Only God in his wisdom could judge, only God knew the reason why such an act had taken place. He could only persuade the person to confess. He could only show compassion. His sin was adultery and for that he had to make restitution.

He left the confessional and knelt down in the nearest pew for the best part of half-an-hour, reciting over and again the required *Hail Marys* and *Lord's Prayers*, and then more. Did his soul now feel clean? Had the confessing washed away the sin? No! He knew he would carry the knowledge – and the guilt – with him for a long time to come.

What Jack didn't see was the wooden door of the confessional opening the merest crack and Father Mathews, under the pretext of looking around, allowing his eyes to rest on Jack before sighing at the frailty of human nature.

CHAPTER FOURTEEN

The week after her final dinner with Jack had been painful; it became an extreme penance for Anna. It was not the first time she wished she had never attended Mass on that first Sunday. And why had he crossed the aisle to shake her hand? Why had she employed him as a gardener? So many questions pounded through her mind, yet there was no real answers, for she had had freedom of choice.

The first week Anna had been without Jack resembled a wake, for each morning spelt out just another day, a day without highs or lows. There seemed very little to hold on to in the fast sweeping river called rejection. She desperately missed their days out, the fun and his laughter. She also missed his lovemaking and the vanity of knowing she could bask in the knowledge that she was wanted passionately by a young, good-looking man.

If she had regretted attending Mass on that Sunday it had been overshadowed by her regret in having confessed her secret to him. She had assumed she knew him. Assumed that by his understanding of her life with Charles, his sympathy, he would be able to extend this to the death of her mother. Death of her mother that he called murder!

She could still hear the words and see the veiled horror in his eyes. She had been foolish, whispering secrets into his ears, placing her burden on his shoulders. Why did she expect him to understand? The ending, to what had been an enjoyable time together, had been brutal. Anna frequently felt ashamed and alone. Ashamed of her unleashed passion, her faithlessness to Charles, her guilt. And alone in the knowledge that love would not come again.

A tinge of bitterness had now clouded their time together for it was he who had the feet of clay, he who was in the end the hypocrite and the harsh moralist. When compassion had been sought he had condemned her without mercy. Had it been coincidence that the weather had broken so soon after their parting? Now the rain-soaked days added to her misery.

On the fourth day Anna decided to look at the more positive aspects of her affair. It was because of their time together and her revised attitude on life that she had driven into the city that morning. She had thought it out the previous night: change, this had to be the key word now. The family couldn't return to the same Anna they had left; time had moved on, it was important that they knew this. She had made the decision to change her image, to be the casual person Jack had almost moulded her into.

She parked the car in the multi-storey car-park and went over to the large well known department store. As she entered she caught sight of her reflection in the plate glass: linen skirt, over blouse, high-heeled court shoes, sun-glasses, large linen bag over her shoulder, hair neat in a single plait down her back. The typical respectable magistrate and chairwoman – an image she had created and was now about to shatter.

She remembered the one and only shopping expedition she had undertaken with Kate, who had paused at a window full of bright, very short inexpensive skirts for teenagers. "You're not shopping there, are you?" Her voice had taken on its condemning tone and Kate had sighed in a mixture of desperation and annoyance.

Now she too approached the boutique of today; the temple

of denim. Anna did not feel at home in a shop with no carpet, indecipherable music blaring from wall-mounted speakers, and wooden racks of clothes. Young, uninterested female assistants wandered aimlessly around, and the displays seemed to be nothing more than piles of clothes thrown together. She had stood knowing she felt and looked embarrassed, trying to appear dignified and knowledgeable as the casually dressed assistant sauntered by.

Anna had begun by telling the distinctly uninterested assistant she was looking for jeans for her daughter, but the bored look in her eyes made her realise that these were not like the fashionable boutiques she was used to, although there wasn't a great deal of difference in the price. Here, the assistants left it to you.

Surprisingly, this lack of interest gave her confidence to take handfuls of clothes into the sparse changing cubicle, where she found herself struggling into slim-fitting jeans. She couldn't help but smile to herself as she left the shop with her purchases of three pairs of denim jeans and an assortment of denim and cotton casual shirts. Her step was now more confident as she swept into the sportswear shop for training shoes; not any training shoes but those with a recognised brand name.

"Oh Mum, I wouldn't be seen dead in trainers from there…" Kate had exclaimed. Anna had not understood that the connotation of *there* was connected with the essential need to be seen wearing the *right* brand name.

In another shop she purchased knee-length shorts, new low-heeled, slip- on casual shoes, tee shirts, and a casual linen blazer. To complete the making of her new self Anna returned to the car and drove out of town to a factory outlet on the outskirts of the city where she purchased a short, close-fitting, zipper jacket of shiny, dark brown leather.

She returned home, unpacked her purchases and went downstairs to pour herself a glass of *Tio Pepe*. She was just about to take it into the conservatory when she turned on her heels and went back to the fridge and instead took out a can of *Budweiser* and ripped it open. It was cold and tasted good.

"Ladies don't drink beer!" she could hear herself saying as she sat back comfortably on the upholstered conservatory lounger.

It was late on the seventh evening before the weather had cleared and Anna was decidedly absolutely bored with being indoors. So to take advantage of the warm evening she sat alone outside on the lounger on the patio with a bottle of white wine in the cooler and a half-drunk glass of wine in her hand. She had contemplated a swim, but it seemed so pointless and it wasn't that hot anyway.

Instead she sat barefooted in her new shorts and casual shirt, watching the moon dancing on the shimmering pool. She tried to concentrate on the bleakness of her life, wondering if her voluntary work would sublimate the future years which stretched their celibate pathway to old age, and then death. The silence had been shattered by the ringing of the phone. As it broke through her reverie she had hesitated for a minute – would it be Jack? Secretly she wished it was. The ringing continued as she got up and glass in hand slowly walked into the kitchen. She stood staring at the wall phone before cautiously picking it up.

There was a thumping in her heart and she felt the sweat breaking out on her hands as she managed a strangled, "Hello?"

She heard Kate's voice and wondered why she felt a sudden disappointment. And then feeling guilty she had lightened her voice as she gripped the receiver tightly. She was glad to hear Kate reminding her she was not alone. Her affair was over, now nothing else mattered but the unity of her family. She closed her eyes in gratitude hearing her daughter say she and Steven were coming home earlier than anticipated and would it be all right?

"All right?" Anna exclaimed, knowing a week ago the conversation would have been strained; then it would not have been all right, but now it most certainly was.

Kate had given her details of the time of arrival of their flight from Bangkok at Heathrow and ended the conversation with, "Oh Mum, it'll be great seeing you again, I've got so much to tell you." The enthusiasm had taken Anna by surprise.

She had accepted that the bricks of her life would only be cemented together if she was strong enough, not riddled with guilt or indulged in self-pity. She was the mainstay, capable of allowing the family to disintegrate or to brace it up. She was not the same wife and mother they had left; so many old values had been replaced, so much she had deemed important had been cast aside.

Would they notice that she had changed? She had to gather the strands of family unity together now and weave it into something firm, or she would lose them forever. She would reassess her values, make her life positive and extend her boundaries. Would the family be stronger for her encounter with Jack? Yes, she was sure it would be.

She had returned to the patio and poured herself a second glass of wine. Their flight arrival was very early, but she had made a promise to meet them, even if it meant leaving home in the middle of the night.

Her gaze returned to the grass. The recent rain had helped but it was becoming scorched again and in need of watering, but now Steven could do it and Kate could trim the edges. Who needed a gardener?

Anna felt it necessary to make an immediate impact when she met Kate and Steven at the airport. It was important that they realise she had changed, not only in dress but in outlook. For indeed she had. She felt she was no longer that cold remote person with such rigid ideas. She had learned, well she hoped she had learned, to accept the other person's point of view, to be more flexible, to understand situations that previously would have been subjected to her uncompromising attitude. If Jack had taught her anything it was to live life to the full and that most situations could be dealt with through humour. No, she knew that wasn't true. Jack had taught her only one important lesson, and that was to never trust anyone. Mistrust, she thought bitterly, should be Jack's surname.

She had risen at three in the morning, showered and then without thinking started to dress in her usual skirt and top. Then she had glanced at herself in the mirror and almost heard Jack laughing at her choice. Swiftly she discarded the skirt and top and put on a pair of her new jeans with one of the denim shirts. On impulse she had loosened her hair and put on make-up.

She stood in front of the mirror, knowing that the only thing that was missing was a baseball cap! She turned sideways and found that the jeans did indeed fit well, especially around the hips. She seemed to have lost a little weight; at least there was some benefit in losing one's appetite! Her former prudish self might have thought such tight-fitting jeans more than a little racy, but now she looked forward with a buzz of anticipation at the thought of turning the odd male head or two.

Suddenly she wished Jack could see her, almost wanting him to come behind her and have his arms and his body pressing against her. She sighed; not long ago she would have grimaced at anyone who had been at the airport in jeans and trainers.

"Oh how common!" would have been her scathing remark. Now here was a middle-aged woman dressed like some American college kid – but did she care? No! A 'head-turner' is how Jack described her and she now liked the sensation, admiration and adulation.

The initial journey down to Heathrow was familiar in that only a few weeks ago Jack had travelled along the very same road with her on their day out in Oxford. She remembered how he had left the motorway to take a quiet secondary road but she didn't want to think of him now. Instinctively she switched on the car radio and listened to the soothing night music. She had missed the usual mad rush of traffic hold-ups and she was glad that their plane was arriving before the M25 became chock-a-block.

After attempting to decipher the apparently contradicting signs and directions for the numerous car parks, and uttering various creative but fortunately unheard curses at the impatient drivers behind her blaring their horns, she finally parked her car in a short-stay car park, with plenty of time in hand. Only, on walking the short distance to Terminal 3 she was confronted with the arrivals board indicating that their flight was half an hour late.

The airport seemed to be jam-packed to capacity with irate holiday- makers, screaming children and lost and forgotten old people wandering round. It was chaos. Anna silently cursed herself for agreeing to meet the flight; why couldn't they take the bus home, she thought, as a middle-aged man bumped into her.

She considered going up to the observation platform to watch the flight land, but with the usual cussedness of bureaucracy it was closed until eight o'clock. Anna yawned and walked across to the paper stand and then glancing round she saw the travellers' café. The paper cup of disgusting coffee made her grimace but soon the time had passed and she was standing outside the international arrivals gate, waiting for her children to appear.

Anna stood slightly to the side of the greeting crowds, her jacket slung carelessly over her shoulders, one hand in the pocket of her jeans. She saw them approaching intermingled with a group, laughing and talking, their eyes scanning the faces. Once she would have pushed forward, taken control and directed them in the midst of queries and questions. Now she did not wave or call their names and watched with amusement as they both walked past her, not recognising this stranger in jeans, long hair and trainers.

Kate and Steven were dressed in scruffy sawn-off jeans, boots, tee-shirts and torn worn denim jackets, dragging their rucksacks behind them. Steven had long shoulder-length hair that had bleached with the sun and a straggly moustache, and Kate a short close crop and a mass of earrings in her ears. Once Anna would have shuddered and been reluctant to acknowledge she even knew them. And hustling them out of sight. Now she smiled; they both looked young and healthy and she envied them their carefree lifestyle and lack of inhibition.

"Kate, Steven!"

They turned when she called, staring with marked embarrassment round at the crowd of faces, waiting for her to descend in her usual peremptory manner. Anna sauntered forward, feeling the power Jack had given her through his love, knowing she was attracting glances that once she would not even have noticed. Anna laughed at the incredulity on their faces, as they muttered goodbyes to the group who had also stared at her.

"Is that your mother?" Anna heard someone ask, and she smiled hearing the veiled compliment in the question as they nodded and walked towards her.

Then she sensed their disquiet, their uncertainty as to how to deal with the comparative stranger who in no way resembled the mother they had left behind. The three of them stood in awkward silence for a moment and she knew Steven and Kate were trying to assess the situation.

"Wow! You look great!" Kate managed to say and there was uncertainty in her voice.

"It's the new me!" Anna replied with a wide smile; she'd felt an inner glow of satisfaction as she'd seen the flicker of admiration in Kate's eyes as if she had suddenly realised Anna was an attractive person, not just her mother.

Steven stood back in a sulky silence. His blue eyes were veiled.

"Steven!" She held her arms out and embraced them both in a gesture that took them both unawares. Then Anna stepped back and she knew instinctively they were both waiting for her usual critical comment about Steven's long hair and scruffiness and Kate's sloppiness. Anna saw their watchful manner.

"Is Dad home yet?" Kate asked.

Anna smiled, "Tomorrow, but it's so good to have you both home safely," she said and Steven and Kate laughed in an uneasy way. She placed an arm round each of them and whispered that they looked at if they'd had a good time. They started to relax as they slowly made their way through the crowds.

"Are you hungry?" she asked, and saw the exchange of glances before Steven muttered, "I could do with a hamburger," as he looked in the direction of the fast food outlet. There was a pause, a waiting for the old Anna to sniff and turn away disdainfully. Now she smiled, dug into the pocket of her jeans and handed him a ten-pound note.

"You don't mind?" he stared at her.

"I don't mind, Steven," her eyes met his and he saw the change in their blue depths, for now there was laughter and warmth where once there had been a frown and coldness. He continued to stare as if seeing the change for the first time. Before, she would have been impatient, now she was relaxed, almost laid-back.

"You really don't mind?" he asked again.

"No, I don't mind. You must be hungry, perhaps Kate would like something as well!" hoping as she said it that Kate hadn't joined the throng of young girls and gone veggie. Kate and Steven raised their eyebrows and as Steven went off to get the food Kate and Anna exchanged small talk until he returned.

Anna listened to the shouts of goodbye and ribald comments from similarly dressed youths and saw the sadness on Kate and Steven's faces as they had waved the final goodbye. Once she would have commented about their friends' appearance, but now she could feel their sadness as a part of their life had ended and friends made would fade into the passage of time, remembered only in a photograph or a Christmas card. They too were going to have to re-adjust to normal living again. People came into your life, Anna realised, people like Jack, who spent such a brief time with you but who had the power to come and change your life forever.

"Goodbyes are always sad," Anna said quietly as she saw the unshed tears in Kate's eyes. She listened to their disjointed tales as they munched their burgers – Kate too, she was glad to see – and pushed the trolleys across to the car park. They had hung back upon reaching the car and Anna handed Steven the keys and watched as he ran the back of his hand over his moustache and then wiped the greasy palms down the side of his shirt. Once she would have snapped. "You're not getting into my car with greasy hands..." But now she told him to stow the rucksacks and parcels in the boot. He'd given her a furtive under the brow glance waiting for her usual comments and instructions.

She nodded as he'd closed the boot and held the keys out to her. "No," she shook her head. "Anyone that can travel far as you have is quite capable of driving me the short distance home. I'll sit in the back with Kate, we can talk," a gesture that had taken him completely off guard, she could see. He stared at her; only a few short months ago Anna would have wished to be in control and let no one else drive. She saw Kate raise her eyebrows in a quizzical manner.

"You've certainly changed, Mum," she commented as they got into the back seat. They had talked incessantly and laughed and impulsively she had reached across and taken Kate's hand

and squeezed it, a foreign gesture, for her, "I think the break has done us all good!"

"If I didn't know better, Mum, I'd say you've found a secret admirer!"

Anna just laughed softly to herself.

They talked without inhibition now, and she learned and appreciated how good it was to have them back. Sometimes, when their language had been crudely descriptive, from habit they had stopped and muttered sorry, waiting for her usual remark, "I really don't think that is nice..." but now she had accepted them without comment. They chatted to her as people, intelligent people who had opinions that really mattered, not her children who needed to be constantly chided. She knew it would not be long before the memory of Jack was replaced by the presence of her family; they too would benefit from her brief affair by her more flexible outlook.

"You've clocked up some miles," Steven said as he'd looked down at the odometer. "Where've you been?"

"Oh, here and there," and she laughed with a tinge of embarrassment and felt her face flush as she met the scrutiny as Kate's eyes flickered over her face.

The car momentarily came to a standstill in traffic and Anna watched as Steven took off his jacket, letting them see the tattoo on his arm – he had asked permission to have a tattoo before he'd left. "But they are so common," she had said disapprovingly. Now she saw his eyes meet hers in the driving mirror and knew he was making a statement.

"And where did you have that done?" Anna said as a noncommittal statement. It had been Kate who had replied in great detail; she'd opened the neck of her shirt and pulled it down to reveal a butterfly tattooed on her shoulder.

"Fisherman's Wharf, San Francisco," Kate replied, adding, "you're not shocked?"

"Should I be?" Anna asked.

Kate frowned, puzzled at this new woman sitting next to her; it was not her mother, but a complete stranger, but it didn't matter; she quite liked this new person and was suddenly glad to be home.

Their arrival back had not created the strained atmosphere that Kate and Steven had expected. Once Anna would have told them to take their bags to their rooms and start unpacking immediately. Now as they dropped the luggage onto the polished wooden floor of the hall, she'd shrugged; it was unimportant. They followed her into the kitchen and sprawled round after effulgently greeting Hector.

They had watched their mother cautiously as Steven fumbled with a packet of cigarettes, waiting for the reprimand and when none had come he'd asked her if she minded him smoking.

"I'll leave that to you, Steven," she had replied. He'd gulped and she'd watched as the cigarette packet had disappeared back into his pocket.

The rest of the afternoon Anna had spent alone whilst Steven and Kate had taken to their beds to sleep off the worst of the jet-lag. Anna had suggested a barbecue for the evening.

They had eaten outside and she had sat back and watched as Steven, naked to the waist, had prepared and cooked the steaks. More meticulous than Jack, but in the dusk, as he became outlined against the pool-side lights, she felt a moment's sadness, sighed and closed her eyes to blot out the pain that jabbed at her mind.

"Are you all right, Mum?" Kate asked quietly.

Anna opened her eyes and saw the concern on her daughter's face. "Yes," she lied.

"You can talk to me if you like...!" Kate said in an embarrassed but sincere manner and Anna wondered if Kate had been more astute than she had realised.

"Looks like you've had a few barbecues!" Steven had said, breaking through the conversation. "All the flares have gone!" Again she saw Kate's eyes on her as she nodded but offered no further comment.

The house and Hector had accepted them all again, and Anna had given thanks for their safe return. Charles's homecoming had been delayed; he had phoned two days later and Anna heard his dispirited voice on the end of the line. Hearing perhaps for the first time the echoes of his own loneliness, his tiredness and, beneath it all, his need of her.

His need would never be sexual, not that raw desire she had experienced with Jack, but a need for understanding and consideration. She heard her own usual abrupt replies to his questions take on a more caring tone as he told her he had not been well. She replaced the receiver. She had never discussed Charles's need to cross-dress; it was pushed aside, something she had learned to accept but never tried to understand. They had never talked about it, Charles's secret she had never wished to share. She had counselled so many people on such a variety of problems, but never Charles; she had given no time or thought to the turmoil he must go through. It had always been her needs, her wants.

Charles had arrived three days later. Anna had suggested that Steven go to the local airport and meet the shuttle from London. Kate had joined her as she took Seth for a walk in the field. It had been easy, with light-hearted conversation, and Kate had commented on the change in Anna's attitude. For a moment Anna had been tempted to tell her, "I've had a lover…" but, remembering the result of her last confession, held her tongue.

Anna stood in the porch dressed in the casual clothes she had come to enjoy wearing. She watched and waited as Charles got out of the car. It had to be different, she had to make it so.

Sometimes in the past she would not have been in to greet him. A meeting or a lecture or the court would have been more important. Sometimes she would have chided him for his late arrival, made his homecoming one of guilt. Swiftly and unkindly she now contrasted Charles with Jack, and then frowned. It was unnecessary, Jack had gone whilst Charles remained.

Charles stood on the gravel drive, stretching after his long journey. He then turned and seeing her hesitate before giving a tentative nod and a vague smile. She did not speak except to return his nod, seeing with surprise his tanned face – he usually returned as pale as he had gone away. Now she saw he was wearing designer gold-rimmed sunglasses, and he looked much thinner. But it was his hair that surprised her the most. Silvery grey; Charles had never wished to be grey or even silver. His hair had for years been discreetly dyed, or touched-up. Now it gleamed in the sunlight and she wondered if it had been blue-rinsed and then dismissed the uncharitable thought. He seemed taller than his five foot eleven. Gone also the dark, formidable double-breasted business attire, the white shirt and gold club tie; instead he was dressed in a casual lightweight suit in a thin grey and white stripe and a dark blue shirt open at the neck with a button-down collar and white shoes. Charles in white shoes? She had to blink to make sure it was not her imagination. But no, this was a distinguished looking Charles. He looked and was a man of substance. As Anna stared she tried to visualise him in the horrible garb of a woman, poor Charles. He looked up and their eyes had met as he too stared at her, seeing the loose hair, the jeans and overshirt. There was a pause, a re-assessment, and he smiled again.

"You look well," how stilted he sounded, and she hesitated before out-stretching her hands and moving to greet him.

"Charles." She took his hands in hers and then impulsively

leaned across and kissed him lightly on the mouth. "It's nice to have you back. You look… nice." She shrugged her shoulders.

He smiled warily.

"I mean it," Anna said as Kate came out of the house and ran and hugged Charles. As Steven took the luggage out of the car Charles had his arms linked by Anna and Kate as they walked into the house.

Anna made them all mugs of tea and they sat around in the kitchen. It was a babble of voices. Questions and answers were flying round, so answers had to be caught quickly. Charles, Kate and Steven exchanged news and suddenly there was forgotten laughter. Charles cast a wary glance in Anna's direction, waiting as Kate and Steven had waited for the remark that could cut the ground beneath them. But now Anna was relaxed, sitting with her head resting in the palms of her hands, elbows on the breakfast bar, her hair loose round her face. No yawns, no comments, just interest. As Charles was relating an incident, once she would have yawned, commented, lost interest… now she listened, hearing another of his humorous anecdotes, and she remembered how once she had laughed in genuine amusement.

She thought of Jack; he'd sat across the breakfast bar looking at her; she could still see his grin and more importantly the look of lust in his eyes. She could smell the sweat from his body she ran her tongue lightly over her lips.

"And you, Anna?" Charles stopped suddenly breaking through her thoughts, so she gave a startled jump, seeing Kate's eyes on her. "We've talked about ourselves, what have you been doing?" He stopped and they waited and she could feel the faint flush on her cheeks.

Once she would have snapped, "Oh, you've remembered I'm here." Once she would have reminded them she had been at committee meetings, looked after the dog, the house, Hector and the garden. Once she would have seen the veiled look slip across Charles's eyes as she subtly made him feel guilty for the moments he had enjoyed away from her.

"I've been waiting for you all to come home," she said and she smiled and reached across and placed one hand over Charles and the other over Kate's.

"No committees?" he asked and she shook her head.

"Mum's changed," Kate cut in, as if sensing Anna's discomfort. Then glancing at Charles added. "So have you... I like you hair," she grinned. "It's very..."

"Distinguished!" Anna said having regained her composure, and then laughed a companionable, understanding sound.

Charles had automatically taken his bag to the guest room and she had not suggested he did otherwise. She had watched through the kitchen window as Kate and Steven took Seth for the afternoon walk. Charles was unpacking and showering. It was as if they had never been away, except, well, faint regrets that the summer of Anna's life had passed.

Anna had prepared a family dinner. She had seen the immediate look of anticipation on their faces. Family dinners usually ended up in family rows.

Kate and Steven had sat down in a rather self-conscious manner. Anna saw too that Steven had shaved off his wispy beard and trimmed his moustache and tied back his long hair. Kate had put on a patterned skirt and sleeveless top. She looked young and beautiful.

Charles too was attempting to bridge a tentative link over their chasm, for he had also observed the changes in Anna. Now he had showered and changed into navy blue lightweight slacks and a blue-and-red striped short sleeved shirt. He had opened the wine and they had all toasted a successful homecoming.

They had laughed and Anna had listened, she had nothing to tell them, for her time had been Jack's time. She had seen

Kate's occasional glance in her direction but she had not commented or asked questions.

"You're quiet, Anna?" Charles had said.

"I'm listening," she'd replied quietly.

Then there had been presents. Charles had rather self-consciously handed her a slim package, and she had carefully removed the gift wrapping to stare down at the gold writing of the jewellers: *Tiffany & Co., Kowloon.* Slowly she had opened it up to see the gold and ruby pendant.

"Wow!" Kate said as she placed a hand on Anna's shoulder. "That's beautiful."

"Thank you, Charles," Anna said as she looked up and met his eyes. He always brought her gifts, but this, she felt, had been chosen with extra care. This time instead of closing the box she took the thin gold chain out and got up from the table and walked across to Charles and bent and kissed his forehead. "It really is beautiful, put it on for me!"

CHAPTER FIFTEEN

*I*t was after midnight when Anna lay in her bed alone watching the intricate pattern of light and shade that flickered over the ceiling. It resembled her life, she thought. Six weeks later her spring had now turned to summer and not so soon autumn would approach. Although the return of her family had sustained her following her rejection from Jack, she still had pangs of loneliness and a strange fear for the future. The family noticed a difference in her and the whole ambience of the house had changed, she felt much better. So much had happened since she last met with Jack. Anna had recently found it difficult sleeping and she would often lie awake reflecting on her family. Her nightmares over her mother had diminished but the guilt remained.

On this particular day Steven and Kate had spent the September afternoon at home talking to friends on the phone, then swimming and lounging by the pool. Somehow the weather had never reached the peak of perfection it had when Jack was with her. Charles had come home early and they had all relaxed and sat round the pool as a family. In the evening Charles and Steven had tended the barbecue and Kate had prepared the salad. Anna had lounged beside the pool; she gave no instructions, but lay relaxedly sipping a glass of white wine and felt the comfortable and friendly family atmosphere. Surprisingly, her relationship with Charles was friendlier and, in a way, easier than it had been in years. But they still occupied, through choice, separate bedrooms.

Now, Anna felt her eyelids close and instinctively stretched her hand out to the empty place beside her in the bed. She felt the tears flood into her eyes and the wanting in her body, for she was alone. Not for the first time she wondered what Jack was doing. Had he and Mary got married? Were they happy? Where were they living? Had Jack told Mary about her? She thought not.

Anna awoke to see the sun invading the room and to hear the birds clattering in joyful harmony. It was a Monday morning and Charles had left early for the train to London for a business meeting. He would be away for the night. He had sounded almost apologetic on the Sunday evening and she had placed her hand over his.

"You work too hard," she said in a conciliatory manner.

Once he would have walked away, but then, once she would not have noticed he looked weary through working too hard. Now he stared at her and nodded and murmured that perhaps she would like to go out for dinner that evening. She had seen the expected rejection in his eyes; how long had it been since they'd gone out together, except to business dinners? "That would be nice," she'd said quietly and he'd smiled and murmured that perhaps he would consider retiring, or reducing his workload, in six months' time.

Retirement meant Charles being home all day; that prospect caused her misgivings. They had so little to talk about. Could they survive their fragile relationship? But Anna knew that her predicament was not unique; many women viewed retirement with disquiet.

Did she really want to be one half of a retired couple? Suddenly the age difference between her and Charles no longer seemed unbridgeable. Ever since his return they seemed to have had a much better rapport and she wondered if her time with Jack had made her more tolerant of awkward situations? Or had Anna realised what she could have lost had their affair become known? Either way she was happier that the family as a whole were getting on much better. Their time away from each other had done them all good.

She glanced at the bedside clock and gasped with incredulity, she had overslept by an hour. Guiltily she struggled to sit up, but she felt unduly tired. She yawned and reached across to the bedside table for her *filo-fax*. Trying to engender some enthusiasm she saw the two committee meetings pencilled in for the morning, but she was conscious of a sudden feeling of nausea. She remembered how the previous morning she had been overcome by a bout of sickness, but had put that down to the prawn sandwich she'd eaten at lunchtime.

Still in bed, she now felt the sweat on her brow and the overwhelming need to rush into the bathroom, lift the toilet lid and vomit into the pan. With her head planted into the toilet, her hair cascading round the rim she felt a moment's disgust. She was never sick like this; everyone said she had a cast iron stomach and nothing would upset her, and she was always fussy what she ate.

She managed to stagger upright and fumble with the cold water tap, allowing a trickle to splash into the washbasin. She soaked her face cloth and dabbed it over her face noting as she did so her reflection in the mirror. She looked grey, her eyes deep set, her hair straggly. "Dear God," she whispered, "I look a mess!"

She sat down on the bathroom stool, still holding the cold damp sponge to her forehead. Eventually her malaise subsided, but then a sense of unease launched itself at her as she remembered the other two occasions in her life when she had been sick like this in the morning. Anna dismissed the thought.

Half an hour later, feeling drained, she showered and tried

to push away the horrible truth that was dawning in her mind. She stared at herself in the mirror and slowly her eyes went down to her waistline. If you looked hard enough she had to admit there was a slightly bloated look.

Tears suddenly flooded into her eyes as reality dawned. Was she pregnant? Would this be the ultimate penalty for her sins? She mumbled her morning prayers and rested her head in her hands and heard herself start to sob as the consequences mounted in her mind.

Anna sat down on the edge of the bed and gathered her thoughts together. There was no time to waste. She would not settle without knowing exactly what was happening. Should she go to a chemist and purchase a self-testing pregnancy kit? The thought embarrassed her. Say someone saw her? And how do you operate such a device and is it reliable? No, that was not for her. She picked the bedside phone and dialled Directory Enquires and jotted the number down on the pad. She stared down at the figures and then there was a faint noise outside the door before Kate entered the room.

"Hi, thought you'd overslept," Kate came rather self-consciously into the room barefooted and dressed in a towelling bathrobe and carrying a tray with a mug of coffee on it.

"You're not dressed!" she said as she stared at Anna before placing the mug of coffee down on the bedside table. "Are you all right?"

"I felt a bit off colour!" Anna managed a thin smile.

"Get back into bed... have a rest. Steven is going to mow the lawn."

Anna lowered her eyes, "I think I will have the morning in bed. I'll have to phone round and cancel my meetings."

Anna waited until Kate had left the room before she had lain back on the bed, once the aroma of the coffee would have made her pick the mug and take a sip, but now it only made her feel nauseous. Slowly she reached across and picked the phone up and placed it beside her on the bed then she punched in the number she had been given by Directory Enquiries.

The appointment at a private clinic on the outskirts of the city was made for the following afternoon at two. The wait would seem interminable and she wished she had the courage to go into the chemist and ask for the pregnancy testing kit. But it could only confirm what she already knew, her waistline had expanded and she had morning sickness.

But how could she have become pregnant? Jack had always used a condom and she had not engaged in any sexual activity since Charles had returned. A baby! Dear God! She couldn't cope, and Charles, how could she explain it? She lay back and stared at the ceiling, which offered her no answers. Although it had not been confirmed, she knew her own body. The thought terrified her.

Finally, at mid-morning Anna staggered down into the kitchen and noticed how clean and tidy it was; Kate was reading the paper at the table.

"You okay now?" Kate asked and there was concern in her eyes.

Anna gave a weak smile. "A little fragile," she replied.

Then in the background she heard the familiar sound of the lawnmower and walked to the window and sighed as she saw Steven, so brown with the glint of sweat on his bare chest and his long hair brushing his shoulders. For a moment she closed her eyes and could visualise Jack.

She bent down and scooped Hector into her arms. "You didn't come and see me this morning!" She buried her face into his soft fur, walked across to the utility room and placed him down before opening the back door.

A slight breeze was ruffling the water in the pool and she felt the first tinge of the passing summer. She walked to the patio, soon the pool would have to be covered over, the garden furniture stored away. Involuntarily she placed her hands across her stomach; perhaps she was wrong, perhaps this was all imagination!

Charles soon arrived home from London, saying his meeting was over earlier than anticipated. He had caught the mid-afternoon train and had booked dinner that evening at an exclusive French restaurant in a nearby village. Although there were other things on her mind she was determined to dress with care. A black outfit, a mourning for a loss, a row of pearls round her neck, her hair in a long single plait down her back. Anyhow, her digestion had settled down, and she could face the idea of eating again – if she didn't overdo it!

"You look great!" Kate had said approvingly in the hall before they left.

Charles had been conciliatory, kind and courteous. The original strain eased and Anna found herself talking to him as she had not done for years. She now put the new found relationship down to her own attitude and a recompense for the guilt she felt. They laughed and the sound took them both by surprise.

"We've grown apart," she said warmed by the wine and ambience of the discreet dining room. The restaurant had been a favourite with them years ago when they had celebrated their anniversaries. Suddenly she remembered her mother's seventy-fifth birthday. A happy occasion in this very room. Champagne and her mother's laughter and the glasses of nearby diners raised in celebration.

The evening had ended on a happy note, but once Anna had returned home and was alone in her bedroom the horrific task of the following day crowded in on her thoughts and she began to sob silently to herself.

Anna walked out of the clinic with tears behind her eyes. She was shell-shocked as she headed towards the car. Her hand shook as she opened the door and she sat in the driving seat trying to compose herself.

Suddenly she wished there was someone with her: her legs felt weak and her heart was thumping in her chest. No, that was wrong, she wished Jack was here with her, giving her a comforting arm on which to lean. She paused and took in deep breaths in an attempt to calm herself down. She now found herself in a ridiculous situation. Would Charles divorce her? Would the family walk out on her? Kate and Steven – would they be disgusted? A lover, twenty years her junior... it sounded dreadful!

Leaning back in the driving seat she recalled the events of the past hour.

She had walked up the steps to the clinic and the double glazed door slid back automatically; she went somewhat self consciously across the carpeted lobby to the reception desk.

"Mrs de Courtney," she had barely recognised her own voice. "I have an appointment with Doctor Freeman at two o' clock." The receptionist gave her a welcoming smile and indicated to the small well furnished, quiet waiting area.

The Gynaecologist introduced herself as Doctor Jane Freeman; she was middle-aged, and efficient as she proceeded with the examination. The urine test, blood test, blood pressure, weight, and physical assessment were all carried out with the utmost professionalism, with no questions being asked and no comment made. Anna sat down opposite Doctor Freeman, who glanced at her over the rim of her half moon spectacles.

"Well, Mrs de Courtney, you are certainly are." Anna stared at her; she had been praying it was a mistake, praying that the sickness and the extending waistline were her age. Her anxiety obviously showed on her face.

"I gather this was not a planned conception," the consultant asked.

"No," Anna sighed, "I feel I am little old for a second motherhood."

Doctor Freeman smiled. "There is obviously always more risk to the baby when the mother is nearing the change. But, a later child can be a joy."

Pills were prescribed for her morning sickness and another visit arranged for a scan and check up.

The consultation had taken less than half an hour and now Anna found herself still sitting in the driving seat of her BMW stared ahead at the red brick wall of the clinic. She had no plan of what to do. In a few weeks her slim figure would take on a different contour, it would be noticeable and was bound engender comments.

Anna didn't want him to enter her thoughts, but inevitably she had to think about Jack. Was he now married? She couldn't remember the exact date of their wedding and had deliberately not taken the weekly church newsletter for fear of seeing their announcement. Should she tell him he was the father? What would he say? Would he deny it? Knowing Jack, he probably would.

She sat for a long time, trying to make up her mind, until finally she decided she had no choice but to contact Jack and tell him of the situation. Knowing that both Steven and Kate would be out for the evening she proposed making the telephone call after dinner. But then she remembered she had torn Jack's telephone number up and thrown it away, never anticipating contacting him again. Not only that, she had never really known his address. That summed up her situation. She was having a baby and she didn't even know where the father of the child lived. There was only one course of action left for her and that was to ask Father Mathews.

She rummaged in her handbag to take out her mobile phone and punched in the Friary's pre-set number. She waited impatiently for an answer, only to learn Father Mathews was away for four days on retreat.

The journey back home was consumed with the problems of how to find Jack and communicate her news to him. But when she did tell him, what did she expect him to do? Comfort her? Support her? Or just share the problem. Anna doubted whether Jack would want Mary to know, but nevertheless she and Jack had to meet. He had to be told for they had produced the baby together and he had a responsibility.

Anna suddenly remembered the hours she had spent telling single women that the father of their child should not be able to walk away from what a night of lust had produced. Ironically, she felt quite strongly on the subject of single mothers.

Charles – his idea of retirement and travelling! A baby and the subsequent years would take up the rest of his life. She couldn't tell him, well not yet, Jack had to be the first to know. She sighed and felt the tears running freely down her cheek.

I am paying for my sins, but dear God, you are extracting a high price. But it was no use blaming the Lord for her own short-comings, and she wiped her eyes with the heel of her hand.

After what was a harrowing journey home, Anna turned the car into the drive, wondering why she always expected to see the orange Beetle sitting there. Perhaps it was a wish of her subconscious. The house was empty as well, as expected notes told her Steven would be out until late and Kate had gone to visit a friend and might be back by ten.

Anna kicked her shoes off and padded to the kitchen, glad of the quietness and the peace in which to think.

The following morning Anna awoke after a disturbed night's sleep. Tossing and turning with horrendous thoughts constantly plaguing her. The previous morning there had been hope, hope that the morning sickness was a virus; now hope had gone and reality had set in. She had a headache, an unusual occurrence, but she knew it was the result of the anti-sickness pills she'd taken the night before. She had expected to wake up free of the feeling of sickness, but as she sat up in bed and yawned and pushed her unruly hair from her face the churning inside started again and she realised the medication to stop morning sickness had not improved matters. She reached for the drawer in her bedside cabinet and brought the small brown bottle out and peered at the instructions. It was safe to take another pill in the morning, so she fumbled irritably with the child-proof cap and finally managed to get to the contents and spill one small round brown pill on to the palm of her hand. She reached to the bedside table and picked up the carafe of water and poured herself a glass. She took a small sip of the water in the hope it might help her. It didn't. She was forced out of bed to make an urgent dash to the bathroom.

I am going to loath this, she thought, as she repeated the procedure of the previous morning, only this time she went on retching and she felt mentally and physically strung out. The months that now stretched ahead filled her with uncertainty. She was too old for this. And Charles, well, he was definitely too old. How on earth would he react when she broke the news? How would any of them react?

A wave of depression engulfed her as she staggered back to her bed and flopped down wearily. Thoughts came in random fashion, nothing in her wardrobe was suitable, all her new lovely slim line jeans would be of no use. And her committees, all she had striven for over the years would now have to be cast aside. And what would people say? *A baby at your age!* The whole sorry mess was one long nightmare.

It had been hard enough all those years ago being a young mum, but to be an *old* mum was quite daunting. Her mind kept going back to Jack and she tried desperately to think of where he said he lived. But she couldn't.

Frantically she reached across for the bedside phone and picked up the receiver and looked at the pre-set numbers. She dialled the Friary and heard the familiar voice of one of the Brothers and hastily under the pretence of wanting more gardening work done asked for Jack Fearnley's telephone number. There was a long pause and she clenched the receiver and tried to calm her mind and body, eventually the Brother returned and she heard the now instantly recognisable telephone number.

There was no time to sit and contemplate what to do. She needed him to know; she needed to tell someone, have support and perhaps even a little concern.

Anna glanced at the clock. It was eight-thirty. Would Jack be still at home? Would Jack and Mary be living at his parent's home or had they got their own house? She had to take a chance. The action took her mind off the sickness as she sat up in bed listening to the ringing tone and she waited for the call to be answered.

Suddenly she heard a muffled, "Hello?"

"Is Jack there?" she could not disguise her voice but as she heard the faint Irish lilt she knew she had been speaking to Mary.

Jack had been abrupt when upon taking the receiver he heard her name and she knew he was tempted to cut her off. Her insistence of the urgency of her call had aroused his curiosity so he listened, not to her news, for the phone was not the place to divulge fatherhood. "I need to see you, Jack, believe me it gives me no pleasure to call," her voice was emotionless. "I cannot divulge my reason on the phone," she snapped as she named the time and the place which would fit in with his lunch time arrangements. "I am not interested in excuses, I will see you at one o' clock."

Anna felt a sense of satisfaction after she replaced the

receiver. She had worried him and now would rehearse what to say. He may wish to have access to the baby, adopt it, for she remembered his time in Romania, the hurt he'd felt at the orphanage. But then she also remembered his lack of courage.

She pushed aside thoughts of depression and a lack of energy and with determination showered and dressed. She could not face the idea of breakfast, even though she knew it was important to eat for two. Orange juice and vitamin pills would have to suffice; black coffee she knew was not recommended. She had hovered between casual wear and something formal and in the end to give her that edge she chose a more formal outfit. She pulled her hair back into a single plait.

At precisely five minutes to one o' clock, Anna parked her car in the large hotel car park and felt a twinge of nostalgia as she saw the battered orange Beetle carelessly parked and taking up two allocated spaces. She checked her appearance in the mirror and satisfied with what she saw, opened the door. She placed her white high-heeled sandalled feet on the ground before gathering her *Burberry* blazer from the passenger seat and casually draping it over the shoulders of her sleeveless blue linen summer dress. She adjusted her dark, gold-rimmed sunglasses firmly on the bridge of her nose and, locking the car, she walked with confidence towards the entrance of the hotel.

Jack was in the foyer reading the hotel notice board, his back to the entrance doors. His hair had been cut short and he was dressed in well pressed black trousers and a white shirt, sleeves rolled up to just below the elbows. He turned, conscious she was observing him. He was without the moustache, and he looked young and vulnerable as he came slowly towards her.

"Anna!" and she knew by the sound of his voice he was apprehensive at meeting her. She nodded to him and walked across the expanse of carpeting to a discreet corner table, gesturing to a waiter as she went.

"Would you like a beer?" she asked, and her voice sounded remote and businesslike. He nodded and she ordered, with a fresh orange juice for herself.

"You look well!" he muttered as he sat down and adjusted his tie. "What is it you want, Anna?" He was fidgeting and she could see he was not enjoying seeing her again.

"Are you married?" she asked her eyes going to his ringless fingers.

"Saturday week," he replied in a monosyllabic tone as he gazed down at his highly polished black shoes. Anna could see Mary was taking a hand in his appearance now. Curiously Anna looked at his left wrist: there was no *Cartier* watch. He saw her glance and interpreted the query in her raised eyebrows.

"It's all right, I won't sell it," he muttered.

The waiter reappeared with the drinks, making an elaborate play of putting down drip mats and placing a dish of peanuts and crisps on the table. Anna nodded and reached across to pick up the bill; she wished this fusspot would just leave them alone.... Jack took a sip of his beer.

"Have you told Mary?" Anna asked abruptly

"No. Have you told Charles?"

"Not yet..."

"Not yet?" he raised his eyebrows.

"Jack, I'm not going to waste time. I am pregnant." She waited to see some expression of sympathy or compassion; instead she saw only a complete lack of interest.

"So, you and Charles?"

She gasped at the incredulity of his statement. "Don't be ridiculous, you know about Charles... it is your child, Jack."

He stared at her and then shook his head. "But I took precautions, you know that, it can't be mine." His voice was defensive and she stared, not believing what she was hearing. Suddenly she knew that the meeting was not going to provide the support she hoped for. But now she had his attention and she could see the thin line of sweat on his forehead as he picked up the glass and drained it, signalling as he did so to the hovering waiter for a refill.

"I'll deny it." His eyes bore into hers with angry intent.

Anna gave a quiet laugh. "You'll deny it? How?" she asked simply.

He looked confused but did not answer.

"Jack," she said in a patronising manner. "DNA will prove it's yours; better accept the news gracefully."

Jack dug into the pocket of his shirt and produced a packet of cigarettes and without looking at her lit one and blew angry clouds of smoke into the air. "Are you deliberately trying to ruin my life?" he asked between puffs. "Is it revenge…?"

"Revenge? Good God, we're talking about a baby. It is fact. It has been confirmed. I am pregnant."

Jack sat shaking his head. "It can't be mine!"

Anna blinked: this wasn't the Jack she remembered, this harsh, uncaring man… but then perhaps he always had been uncaring and she had seen only what she had wished to see. "You disgust me," she snapped. "Talk like an adult and not like some ignorant teenager."

"Well, Anna, I don't want the baby, I don't want any part of it. You get rid of it– that's the best solution." She stared at him. "Oh come on, don't tell me that if you're really pregnant you haven't thought of an abortion… I mean well," and his lip curled into a faint sneer. "You got rid of your mother… so what's another life, eh!"

Anna felt the anger rising within her. She saw his complacent smile and instinctively she went to lash out with her hand. She wanted to hurt him. But Jack saw the blow coming and caught her wrist. He held it tightly.

"You've hit me twice, don't do it again."

"You bastard!" she said and with her left hand she picked her glass and threw the remainder of the contents over him. She walked out maintaining her composure, despite the curious stares from fellow guests.

Anna felt wrung out after the meeting and drove home in a state of disbelief. But what had she expected? He had failed her once, why had she imagined Jack had the strength of character to be supportive? He had fled from the challenge of Romania to the warm sybaritic life in America. For all his talk he could only sit on the fence. No, he could condemn too: mercilessly he had walked away from her when she had bared her soul. Now in a hypocritical stance he was prepared not only to walk away from his own child, but to ask her to murder it. A true conscience of convenience.

Back home Anna walked into the kitchen and placed two rounds of bread into the toaster and waited until they popped up, then she cut it into triangles. She would eat them dry, for her stomach was feeling queasy again. She poured herself a glass of warm water. Placing the glass and plate onto a tray she walked into the conservatory and sat down. The toast was unappetising and she could only nibble at it and sip the warm water.

She sighed, her life had gone full circle. Now she was in a worse position than when her mother was alive. An abortion? How tempting it sounded: an end to the problem and no one would know about her affair. A visit to a clinic and a life could be terminated. She could appreciate for the first time the conflict many young girls now faced, for on the surface it seemed such an easy answer to such a difficult situation. But psychologically she knew from the action she had taken with her mother, the consequences could never be wiped from her memory. Abortion and euthanasia were the two sides of the same coin.

Anna suddenly remembered all the horrific stories she had seen on the television depicting refugees, those homeless people grovelling for life, clinging onto it, wanting it, honouring it, whilst we in our comfortable environment viewed the life of someone else as worthless, something to be disposed off when and as required. Could she live with the image of the foetus being sucked out of her womb and cast aside? Yet, she could understand the fear of desperation of an unwanted pregnancy could bring. The church's teachings were also very strong in this respect.

"Are you okay, Mum?" Kate said as she came into the conservatory and saw Anna sitting with a bleak expression on her face. Anna gave a startled gasp and managed a wan smile as she nodded.

"You look…!" Kate peered down at her mother, seeing now the faint tracks of recent tear marks.

"I'm all right, it's been a busy day." Anna saw the concern on Kate's face and stood up, straightening her skirt. "I'll just have a shower before dinner."

Anna walked into the bedroom and slowly closed the door behind her. It would not be long before the family began to notice, her increased weight. Even now there was a veil of suspicion in Kate's eyes. She sensed something had happened during their absence. Anna realised she would have to confess to what she was sure would be a less compassionate earthly judge and jury than a heavenly one.

She showered and had started to dress when she felt her head start to spin and realised she had not eaten properly in days. The nausea had returned. She struggled into her housecoat and switched the fan on and then lay back on the bed.

"Mum!" She peeled her eyelids back and looked up seeing

the concern on Kate's face. "You look awful…"

"I think it's a virus," she managed, conscious of the weariness mingled with despair that she now felt. "I'll get up for dinner."

Kate pursed her lips before sitting down on the edge of the bed, her eyes travelling over Anna's face and then scanning her body. "Would you like to see the doctor?"

"No," Anna said vehemently, "There's nothing wrong," unconsciously she placed a hand over her stomach.

"Are you in pain?"

"No, I just feel sick."

"You were sick yesterday morning?" Kate pulled her face into a smile and tried to make her voice sound light as she said. "If I didn't know better I'd say you were pregnant!"

Anna stared at her and then closed her eyes and ran her tongue over dry lips. "You know all about pregnancy?" she tried to make it sound humorous.

"Oh a friend got knocked up… she was always being sick!" Kate said dismissively.

There was a pause and then Anna opened her eyes. She could feel the inner panic as her heart started to beat at an alarming rate. She felt breathless knowing now was the time to tell Kate. There was no easy way to say it, no matter how she could dress it up the consequences of the declaration would not change.

"Kate," she said softly, her eyes fixed on her daughter's face, "I wonder if you'll understand what I have to tell you…" she paused as Kate turned her eyes to met her mother's. "When you were all away…" she lowered her eyes frightened of the disgust and condemnation she felt sure would be there in her daughter's expression.

"When you were all away…" she started again, feeling now the sweat breaking out on her forehead, her heart pounding with fear.

245

"Mum, you had an affair… is that what you're trying to say?" Kate's voice was light and Anna opened her eyes and stared at her.

"You know!"

"Mum," Kate leaned across the bed and kissed Anna on the forehead and then gently stroked the dark hair back off the face, "you changed so much, there had to be a reason, and let's be honest most of the reasons for such a change are to do with men."

Anna reached forward and stroked her daughter's cheek. "I am so glad to be able to tell you… do you?" she stopped.

"No, Mum I don't condemn you. I'm glad because we could never have talked like this before," she stopped . "You're not…"

"What?" There was a sudden tension in Anna's voice.

"Leaving us, you're not going away with him?" there was naked fear in Kate's eyes as she stared down at Anna.

"Good heavens no," Anna said in surprise. "It was a dalliance, nothing more…" she stopped abruptly and then feeling the tears wanting to break through she closed her eyes. "There is more, of course. I am pregnant!"

Kate shook her head.

A silence engulfed them before Kate muttered. "You surely aren't that good a Catholic that you didn't you take precautions?"

"…Of course we did," Anna cut in and watched as Kate stood up with a moody expression on her face as she dug her hands into the pocket of her jeans and walked across to the window to stand with her back to Anna, gazing out.

"So who is he then?"

Anna picked a hint of condemnation in her daughter's voice before she answered.

"A young man, he came to do the garden!"

"God, Mum, a gardener…!" There was veiled hostility now in Kate's voice as she turned.

"I know, it couldn't sound worse..." Anna momentarily closed her eyes.

"Do you love him?"

"No." The answer was spat out.

"Then why... for God's sake why?"

Anna sat up on the bed and pushed a pillow behind her head. "The problems with your father... you know..." She struggled, seeing the indecipherable expression in Kate's eyes. "It was not planned."

"Is it ever?" Kate said abruptly and then her voice taking on a less harsh tone. "Do you miss him?"

"I did: you know I've never been carefree, drunk beer in a pub, worn jeans... it was different, another world and one I enjoyed it. I changed. I don't regret the affair."

"And this baby you're having, or are you? You could cast aside your religious beliefs and get an abortion, then nobody would ever know."

Anna shook her head. "I would know."

Kate stood beside the bed and Anna knew she was unable to take it all in. A mother, once thought to be the bedrock of society, a mother whose views were outspoken and condemning about all she was now confessing to have done. It was the shattering of an illusion. Her mother was flawed and suddenly that made her human. Anna waited, seeing the conflict on Kate's face, waited for her to slowly walk away.

"I am sorry, Kate," she whispered. "I am so sorry. You are my daughter. We've not always seen eye to eye, but I do love you and no one will ever replace that love. I want you to believe that."

Anna felt an imperceptible change in Kate's attitude.

"Oh Mum," Kate walked across and sat down again on the bed. "Have you told him, this gardener?"

"I have, and I can't have an abortion, Kate. I know I may end up alone, you may all walk away from me, and I couldn't blame you. I don't want the baby, but I will as time goes on; we have to be responsible for our own actions." she sighed. "I am so sorry, Kate…" Now the tears flowed freely down her cheek and then she felt Kate's hand on hers.

CHAPTER SIXTEEN

*A*nna had contemplated what Kate had said. Suddenly a great weight seemed to have been lifted from her shoulders. Although it did not make the future any easier to bear it did mean that she could talk to someone who perhaps understood her reason for her affair with Jack. She thought of Kate's suggestion. There was no option left but to tell Charles, and then Steven. With Kate preparing the evening meal it gave Anna time to think of the best way to tackle the problem. Now she had the plan in her mind's eye.

"Charles!" Anna said in a constricted tone after they had finished dinner. Steven had asked to be excused as he was meeting friends and Kate had given Anna a supportive pat on the shoulder and a warm, understanding smile. "Can we go into the conservatory with our coffee?"

Charles had returned home early evening, meeting her in the hall. As always he was dressed in business attire, a black three-piece suit, white shirt and a formal tie. As he placed his briefcase on the hall chair he glanced up. Anna was coming down the stairs after her confession to Kate. His expression indicated that he noticed her somewhat sloppy appearance, which for Anna was unusual. She was dressed in jeans and shirt, barefoot, her hair loosely tied back. Her eyes were bright through crying and she was totally without make-up.

"Anna!" he exclaimed, and she saw the surprise in his eyes at her appearance. "Are you all right?" There was genuine concern in his voice.

"Yes, of course. Dinner is almost ready."

"I'll change," he gave her a quick smile. "I like the casual wear, Anna, suits you."

She blinked, unsure as to whether it was a compliment.

Now dinner had ended. The conversation had been friendly and the family had talked about their day, with Charles giving an amusing account of his board meeting. Anna had listened and was again taken aback by his thumbnail sketches he so adroitly made of his fellow colleagues. Steven, dressed in a white T-shirt, lounged back and took part in the banter, whilst Kate's eye would flicker across to Anna and try and imagine what their lovemaking must have been like. Somehow it was difficult to imagine parents in a sexual content.

Charles dabbed his mouth with the linen napkin and gave Anna a brief but penetrating stare and then nodded before following her into the conservatory. He watched her place the tray of coffee down on the table and then turned and closed the glass doors behind her. He reached across to the table and picked up the coffee pot.

"Can I have mine white tonight?" she asked and met the query in his eyes, for she had always ridiculed people who had white coffee. "Might as well drink milk!" she would say as she would watch Charles mix his milky coffee. Now she watched as he mixed the hot milk with the coffee and then hand her the cup and saucer as she sat down opposite to him.

As she scanned his face she could see the lines of tension round his eyes and saw he looked worried and tired. He sat back and crossed one grey-flannel trouser leg over the other, but did not offer to open the conversation.

"Charles..." she made a tentative start; her body was shaking and she felt a dryness in her throat. Somehow her days of grace with Jack now seemed cheap and tawdry. A confession to her husband was the last thing on her mind during those passion-filled nights. Now like a gawky teenager she related her indiscretion. "There is no easy way to say this but I have to tell you." She lowered her gaze down to the ceramic tiled floor and sighed. "I suppose I'll have to start at the very beginning…." She felt compelled to raise her eyes and glance in his direction, but he had averted his and his attention seemed to be on the cup of coffee in his hand. Anna felt her hands grip the arms of the cane chair tightly as she tried to give an account of what had occurred. She gulped as she whispered the words she never thought she would say.

"I think you are trying to tell me you've had an affair, Anna?" his voice was remote and it was hard to determine his mood.

"Did Kate tell you?" she asked angrily.

Charles shook his head and sighed. "Anna, whatever else you may think of me, I am not a fool." He stared at her. "I return home from a business trip to find you are actually at home and not at a committee meeting. What is more I also find my usually bored and uninterested wife asks me questions about my health!" He raised his eyebrows expressively and she could only lower hers as she felt the embarrassment flush her cheeks.

"Then," Charles continued, "I find you are suddenly no longer that cold and remote person: gone is the efficient business executive, dressed to perfection, now you are in jeans and a loose shirt. An outfit you have condemned so many times. And our children, usually criticised and chided, are now treated as the human beings they are." Anna heard veiled sarcasm tinged with an overtone of criticism in Charles's voice. She looked up; his eyes were staring at her. There once would have been a time when she would have snapped back in a vitriolic manner, pushing her point of view forward and disregarding anyone else's. Now she took time to hear his assessment.

Anna realised that they had grown so far apart over the past years, that she hadn't bothered to know him. She had given him little or no credit or status in her life. He merely earned the money. Anna suddenly realised how hurtful her indifference to him had been. How lacking in understanding of his needs and how selfish she must have appeared to the family prior to meeting Jack.

But on the other hand Charles had hardly given her any consideration for his problem; he wouldn't discuss it or even seek help. It was compartmentalised into his life. She sighed inwardly; perhaps they were both to blame for their lack of co-operation in the marriage. What Anna didn't realise was that this was no time for self-justification or to minutely analyse the failure of her marriage; she needed Charles's understanding, but most of all she would need his support in the coming month and years. She had no alternative but to appeal to him. Even now she was unsure what his reaction would be.

"Oh Charles," she whispered contritely. "I must have been quite dreadful." She was not sure what answer she expected from him, but it was certainly not the one he gave her.

"Yes, Anna you were very uncompromising in many ways." His voice was firm and he glanced up and met her eyes and for the first time she felt fear. Fear that this man could walk away from her, that she had finally pushed him too far. And yet, since he had returned home from the east there had been moments of near empathy between them.

"Charles," she could barely whisper his name as she clasped her hands together. She felt ashamed, realising how curt and cruel she had been. "So you know I've had an affair?"

He did not answer immediately instead he reached across and refilled his cup with coffee and then milk. He gesticulated to her half empty cup, but she shook her head and repeated her question. He sat back in his chair and placed the cup of coffee back on the glass-topped table and then inter-laced his fingers across his chest. His gold watch glistened in the sunlight.

"Anna, you may not agree, but I know you very well. You are not the sort of woman to do anything without reason and the change was not to please me but to please someone other than yourself. A rarity if I may say so."

She stared at him angrily, still wanting to snap back in her old sniping fashion and subconsciously she knew he was waiting for the old Anna to reappear and to cut him down with one lash of her tongue, but she merely nodded and waited.

"I also think I can still recognise a woman who is sexually fulfilled," he went on, "in a way I have not been able to fulfil you. I realised then that my lack of sexual interest could have moulded you into the person I had come to..."

"Dislike?" she ventured.

He gave a faint smile. "I have never disliked you, Anna. I have often been irritated by your prosaic manner. So if this affair has made you more complete, more human, more understanding, then, Anna, I am really glad for you."

"You don't hate or condemn me?"

"We are neither of us without fault," his voice was low and his eyes lowered. "We have a strange marriage, I know that, but despite your..." he paused.

"...faults," she filled in.

"But I can see why someone wanted to be with you," he amended. "You can be very desirable," he gave a self-deprecatory shrug. "I don't know how serious this affair is... or if you are thinking of leaving me for..." He broke off and she saw beneath the surface of control he too was afraid.

"It was a summer dalliance, Charles... I wanted to be young again. I was flattered by a young man's sexual attraction."

"A young man?" he raised his eyebrows.

He listened as she faltering told him of her meeting with

Jack at the Church and how their relationship developed. She could see the regret in his eyes and wanted to go across and place her arms round his shoulders and tell him she would not leave him, but first she had to complete the story. Now she felt the apprehension for he may not want her to say. It was a double betrayal and she felt her hands shaking as she tried to bring the cup of milky coffee to her lips. She wished that was the end of her confession, wished it could all be forgiven and forgotten.

"There is more," her voice was low and he leaned forward a frown on his forehead. "Charles, I am pregnant!" the words seemed to shoot out of her mouth uncontrollably. She had wanted to say it quietly, to discuss it, to wait for his anger, but now she realised she was frightened, frightened of so many things. "I am so sorry, I don't know what to say." There was silence and for once Anna could not determine what Charles's next move would be. Suddenly, she felt quite ashamed.

"Pregnant?" There was incredulity in his voice.

"Yes."

Charles sat motionless in the chair and analysed what Anna had said.

"Have you told the prospective father?" his voice was cold.

"Yes," Anna said again.

"And?" Charles said impatiently.

"He didn't want to know."

"So what do you propose to do now?"

"I don't know, but I had to tell you."

"Correct me if I'm wrong, Anna, but you told Kate first," he said almost accusingly.

"Yes, I was upset."

"Did you not think about taking precautions when you were romping about with this young man?"

"I left that to him!"

"So much for your rigid Catholicism!" His eyes were sceptical.

"Don't you think I know that, don't you think it makes it so much worse. I've spent years telling people what to do and how to behave…"

"Don't lecture me on your good works – the family has lived with them for years. What do you propose to do now?" He sat staring across at her and she was unable to read anything from his body language.

"Do you want me to leave?" She stuttered. "Have I really bitched it all up for the family?" Slowly Anna lowered her head into her hands as she started to sob.

There was a silence. She could not raise her tear-stained face to look across at him. She heard the sound of movement and knew he was rising from his chair. She heard his footsteps. He is leaving, she felt an overwhelming sense of desolation and still she could not look up, could not plead and ask him to stay. Oh dear God, she heard the beginnings of an incoherent prayer on her lips and then she felt his hand lightly on her arm. "Anna," his voice was gentle. She managed to raise a tear-stained face.

"Are you going to leave me, Charles?" her voice was broken.

"Do you wish me to go?" he asked as he continued to stare down at her.

"Oh dear God no; I need you, I really need you to stay, to forgive me, to support me." He continued to stare down at her and she felt her heart pounding as she waited.

"Tell me what this young man said about your predicament?"

He listened impassively as she told him about her meeting that afternoon with Jack, his suggestion, his proposal that she should abort. She saw the flash of anger that swept over Charles's face at the mention of the word and suddenly contrasted the difference of the two men. One had professed to want and love her and the other had always been on the background supportive but saying little.

Then Charles, in a calm and controlled manner reassured her he would support her, and the baby. At no time did he use the word abortion, at no time did he suggest she did not carry the baby full-term.

"I don't deserve you, Charles," she managed to say between sobs.

"No!" he said simply. He got up and patted her shoulder; he was obviously emotionally affected. Anna realised silence was all there was left until he could assimilate the situation.

"You all right, Mum?" Kate came quietly into the conservatory. Anna gave a tearful sniff and nod.

It had probably been the most traumatic day of her life, Anna thought as she heard the bedroom door slam behind Steven.

He had not understood; Kate had warned her not to expect too much, but she hadn't been prepared for the fury that had swept over him. Anna had lain in her bed, going over the events of the day; she was tired and but thought about that brutal meeting with Jack. He was so lacking in compassion and so hurtful. How could she have had an affair with him? Yet, he had made all the running; she had been willing, but would she ever have instigated the affair herself? There had been a tenderness and an understanding between them; perhaps it had been her own way of telling him about her mother that was wrong. No, he was just a coward who now chose to ignore her. It was so unfair, but then that was life. Then Charles, angry at her deception, but forgiving, and Kate incredibly supportive.

Before Kate retired she had brought Anna a cup of camomile tea and murmured that Steven had just returned. She glanced up at the gentle knock on the bedroom door as it opened quietly. She saw Charles standing in his striped dressing gown. His silver hair was sleeked back still damp from the shower, his face smooth from a recent shave.

"Are you all right?" He walked to the end of her bed and stared down at her. It was a long time since he had been in her room at night.

"Yes," she said wearily.

"Kate told me what Steven said. I'll have a word with him in the morning."

Anna shook her head. "Leave it, Charles, it is the way he feels."

"No, you are his mother and I will not have him addressing you in that manner." His voice was firm and she smiled for this was a new assertive stance for Charles, who usually backed away from family problems. But then, Anna recalled, she usually got in there first and sorted it out.

"Thank you, Charles," she murmured.

"Good night, Anna," he walked towards the door.

"Good night, Charles," she whispered.

It was midmorning. Charles had gone to his office, taking with him Kate, who had something urgent to do, and a sulky Steven, who would be spending the day with him.

"A taste of work, we are a computer operator short!" Charles had smiled and winked at Anna and she had impulsively patted him on the arm.

"Thank you!" she said in gratitude.

Anna was just about to settle down and read through more committee work when the front doorbell chimed through the house.

"Yes?" She pulled the door open, annoyed she had forgotten to close the gates and gasped as she saw the huge bouquet of flowers that a smiling young woman was holding out to her.

She closed the door and carried the cellophane wrapped flowers into the kitchen and searched for the small envelope. Quickly extracting the card she recognised Charles's writing as she read:

'Dearest Anna, we all love and need you. You have all our support.'

She gulped back her tears as she saw they had all signed it individually. She knew Charles had deliberately taken them with him to the office; Charles and Kate must have talked to Steven and the flowers were a reassurance of their support.

CHAPTER SEVENTEEN

The re-adjustment of Anna's once organised life had been dramatic. Now she found little energy or enthusiasm to leave the house for committee work or for any other reason. Instead she had returned to attending a twice weekly morning mass and on one Saturday morning she had sat for some time in the pew, running the rosary through her fingers, trying to get her thoughts into some sort of order. She rose and left the pew and genuflected and then entered the Confessional. She opted now to kneel in front of the grill, to pretend anonymity existed as she whispered, "Father I have sinned."

Father Mathews sat behind the grill and adjusted his stole. He recognised the voice as he murmured the appropriate words and waited for the halting confession, knowing this would be no shopping list of minor indiscretions. He felt her pain now and closed his eyes and asked for guidance. Ironically, he felt a slight responsibility knowing that he had introduced Jack to Anna. He did not, could not and would not tell Anna that he had already listened to Jack's confession and now he was aware of the growing silence. He knew she was experiencing difficulty. "Just say what is in your heart, God understands, he is forgiving."

"Father, there is no easy way to say this," Anna gulped, "I have had an affair..." It was the confession he had expected and he frowned and listened as she related her infidelity.

"Has this relationship finished?" his voice was patient.

"Yes."

"Your family, do they know?"

"Yes, Father, I have told them."

She heard the faint sigh from behind the grill for she knew it was Father Mathews and that made it more difficult. He carried so many of the parishioners' secrets in his head and heart. His burden was greater than any of theirs, for he could talk only to God.

"Is there anything else you wish to confess?"

"I am bearing his child," she gave a sob now.

Father Mathews had heard it so many times before. He thought of the frailty of human nature, the unnecessary suffering that people inflicted upon themselves and their loved ones. He administered her the church's penance, but her true penance, Father Mathews knew, would be with her now for life. He gave her Absolution and waited as she rose and left.

Had a burden been lifted from her shoulders? Anna felt it hadn't; it had merely been shared. She returned to the pew and murmured the words of the *Lord's Prayer* and *Hail Mary*. She rose and walked towards the door, dabbled her fingers in the Holy water and then walked through the Narthex and out into the bright sunlight. She felt the warmth on her face, saw the brightness of the day.

Then not wishing to talk to any of her fellow-confessors she strolled across the pathway from the church entrance towards the rusty metal gate. She rested her hand on the latch and then pushed the gate open. It was quiet: only the dead, and the birds and the faint rustling from the trees, greeted her. She walked down the weed-strewn path, quietly passing the gravestones until she stood looking down at her mother's grave.

She bowed her head and read inscription again. "Oh Mum!" and she felt the tears coursing down her cheeks. "I wish you were here," she murmured as she accepted the irony of her situation. Had she traded one life for another? She felt she had been given a second chance. Not many had that. She now had a family. Once the people who occupied her house with her were just people. Charles had become just a name; now, dear God, he was her strength. Once, small things about Kate had irritated her; now she could only lean on her for support. And Steven, usually nervous and highly strung, was now becoming strong, reliable and caring.

Had Anna really traded one life for another, she asked herself again. A birth for a death? Was it recompense? Was life a lesson of learning your comeuppance?

Anna returned to the car park. The church was quiet. Tomorrow, Kate and Charles would accompany her for morning service. Perhaps one Sunday if Steven was home he too would join them. Father Mathews would see they were united – a real family.

She told Charles she had been to confession, and he had given her a comforting smile, placed an arm round her shoulders and hugged her. She had turned and stared up into his face; he had changed, he looked happier and fitter too. His dress was now casual, dark colours, nothing gaudy; he looked mature and almost good-looking.

Kate had been sympathetic to Anna's needs. She would not take a place in the Hall of Residence. Instead, Charles had said he would buy her a car so she could return home each evening, which would be a comfort to Anna. Her understanding attitude had surprised Anna and given her some much needed female companionship. Kate in turn had noticed how easy-going her mother had become. Gone was the strong dominant figure who had opinions on *everything*, and it its place was a person dependant on her family who required reassurance and love.

Not one night had passed when Anna hadn't thanked the Lord for having such an understanding family. She knew it would be long time before she stopped giving her thanks for that one blessing. Anna also knew that Charles had persuaded Kate and Steven not to enquire as to the name of her lover, although she was sure they knew his identity.

She had sustained the family. Her voluntary work had proved another hurdle to overcome. It was a hurdle that Anna was no longer sure she wanted to jump. The under-the-lid glances she had experienced on the occasional visits she made to LATE made her feel like a schoolgirl going through the trauma of having an under-age pregnancy.

Mavis, the Vice-Chair, had frowned and said, "Pregnant?" and raised her eyebrows in a semi-accusing manner. Later on she asked, "How's your gardener?" Anna could not help notice the faint smirk that had crept across Mavis's face.

Anna had shrugged it off, but the innuendo was not lost and it was at that moment she decided it was time to resign the Chair. The committee had given her a small party and a glass paperweight in recognition for all she had done. Anna knew that a chapter of her life had closed - forever. Surprisingly she found she did not miss the schedule of work nor had any regrets about her decision to quit LATE. She never returned to the bench and resigned her Magistracy soon after. It had been many years since she had enjoyed sitting and relaxing at home trying to get to know the real Anna once again.

Charles too had taken on the responsibility of making decisions and had early on booked an appointment for Anna in a private medical centre, twenty miles away on the outskirts of a small town. When Anna arrived there for her first appointment she was pleased with Charles's choice. The clinic was purpose-built and purely for private patients. It was spacious and overlooked a peaceful green park. The building had ample car parking spaces and gave off a sense of modernity, security and professionalism.

On entering the lobby Anna noticed there were plenty of fresh flowers, comfortable chairs, tables with up-to-date magazines and in one corner a large aquarium. The discreet reception desk and unobtrusive music were aimed at soothing away the tenseness of the waiting patients.

Anna checked in and was escorted to a small consulting room off one of the main corridors. Here she was introduced to a female gynaecologist, Doctor Patricia Cameron, around fifty years of age with steel grey hair and rimless spectacles behind which Anna saw intelligent, perceptive hazel eyes. Doctor Cameron wore very little make-up but when she turned to greet her, her face relaxed and Anna saw a gentle smile and perfect teeth. They shook hands and Anna was impressed by the firmness of the handshake.

Doctor Cameron had told Anna that her first visit to the clinic was just routine, recommending that, because of Anna's age, an ultrasound scan should be taken on a regular basis. After the check-up Doctor Cameron pronounced Anna and the baby both fine, and that she would book her in for her first ultrasound appointment.

Back home the three of them had talked about a nursery, realising the changes that were soon to take place in the house. Anna had refused to even consider taking over either Steven's or Kate's bedrooms.

"They were here first," she'd said and Charles had nodded his agreement. Then she had seen the conflict in his eyes and knew he was waiting for her to say that his private room would be a nursery.

"You need your space, Charles," she had given him an

understanding smile. "Initially the baby will sleep with me. Then we can see what happens!" He had not answered but merely place his hand lightly on her arm.

They had both walked from room to room, seeing the house her father and Charles had created: not a house for a baby. They stood in the dining room, and Anna knew she did not wish to change it, the furniture and paintings suited her and the house. The sitting room, lounge and conservatory were not baby orientated. And how would Hector react to something that demanded more attention than him?

"We need a comfortable day room," Charles said as they walked into the hall. "Your mother's room?"

"No," she said the word involuntarily and he walked across and took her hand. "I know, Anna, you always see your mother in there. But if you think about it, the room is ideal... it's a lovely room for a day nursery. Come on." He guided her across the hall, turned the handle and pushed the door open and Anna gasped as the ray of sunlight that swept over her as she stepped forward.

The room that had lain dormant and dull suddenly came alive. Charles was filled with an enthusiasm he had not shown when she had been pregnant with Kate and Steven. He seemed to feel a need to organise and take part in the decorating. It was as if he realised that without the baby, albeit not his, their marriage might well have floundered.

Once, Charles would have engaged decorators but now he was happy to come home from work and stand of an evening, dressed in overalls, paint roller in hand as he swished brightly coloured paint over the walls.

The night before Anna's first visit to the clinic for her ultrasound scan was tense.

"Are you sure you wouldn't you like me to come with you?" Kate asked.

"I am not a newcomer to pregnancy but thanks; it is just routine," Anna replied. Charles too had said he would now plan to be available for future visits to the clinic.

"You don't have to," Anna said.

"No, I don't, but I'd like to," he'd replied.

Anna's ultrasound was booked for ten o'clock in the morning. Dressed in maternity slacks with an elasticised waistband, and top, Anna knew the looseness of her clothes would help alleviate her frequent hot sweats. The extra few pounds she had put on had necessitated her purchasing one size up in clothes. She had even contemplated having her hair cut.

She did not have long to wait before she was shown into the small changing room to undress and don the pale blue paper gown, and then be helped on to the bed in the ultrascan room. The room consisted of a bed, a stand that held a computer monitor and various other items of equipment. It was spotless. A pull down white blind was closed over the window. The nurse had ensured that Anna was comfortable on the bed and then the Radiologist, a small dark man dressed in a white coat, came in and smiled down at her.

"I'm Doctor Patel," he said and went on to give a brief glance at her notes and then ask her a few questions before discreetly covering her with a blanket. He had asked the attending nurse to take the tube of clear jelly and smear it over her stomach. Then he had turned to the monitor and taking the small scanner head in his hand he slowly and methodically moved it across the surface of Anna's stomach.

"Is that it?" Anna asked as she tried to peer at the mass of dark and light shades on the screen. "I don't see anything!" Anna saw the nurse standing in the background, her eyes glued to the monitor. A frown momentarily flashed across her face.

"Oh, it's there all right," Doctor Patel said, but there was no reassuring smile and his eyes had a querying expression as he pursed his lips. "Do not worry, Mrs de Courtney, the baby will grow and you'll see it each time you have a scan." He leaned forward and peered more closely at the screen. Anna's first thought was that Doctor Patel was having difficulty focusing the equipment properly but deep down she knew he was searching for something.

Anna watched as the Doctor seemed to dwell for a long time on what looked like a white mass on the screen. She tried to peer at it, but it did not resemble anything she recognised.

"Is it all right?" she asked suddenly sensing concern in his attitude as he continued to move the scanner round and round in what now resembled a robotic fashion. Doctor Patel merely gave her a brief smile that did nothing to reassure her and left the room. Anna gazed up at the ceiling.

What had he seen? Her mind was in a turmoil going through endless possibilities before Doctor Patel and an older man appeared.

"My colleague, Doctor Mason." Doctor Patel switched the monitor round so that Doctor Mason could view it more easily and then slowly re-commenced the procedure of scanning.

"If there is something wrong, will you please tell me?" Anna blurted out, feeling the tension in her body and the thumping of her heart. She turned her head towards the monitor and noticed that both doctors seemed to be concentrating on a particular area. As they talked in subdued voices she heard the word spine. They refused to say anything and just kept looking at the image.

Anna attempted to peer at the monitor but could not make any sense of anything on the screen. Now as the scanner moved the definite outline of a head appeared. Anna had no idea what ultrasounds should look like but even to her the baby's head on the monitor seemed to lack some type of definition. It looked empty as if there was nothing there.

"Is that the head?"

"It is!" Doctor Patel replied.

"It looks almost empty!" Anna waited for them to reassure her, but Doctor Mason merely gave a faint sigh.

"Doctor Patel will explain everything to you, Mrs de Courtney." He gave her a nod and reassuringly touched her arm before leaving the room.

"What is it?" Anna could hear her voice rising and her heart went into wild palpitations.

Doctor Patel had switched the monitor off and was disconnecting the scanner, telling her to get dressed. With her whole body shaking, Anna went into the cubicle and with trembling hands tore off the disposable blue robe and threw it into the adjacent bin and then struggled with nervous energy back into her clothes.

Doctor Patel was washing and drying his hands as she reappeared. Then he pulled the small stool from beneath the bed and gesticulated for her to sit down on the chair beside him.

He hesitated before saying. "It's early days yet, Mrs de Courtney... but there appears to be a slight abnormality."

"Like what?"

"More tests need to be done, but indications show that the baby may have fluid on the brain, which is called Hydrocephalus." He stopped: he could see the naked fear mingled with horror in her eyes. He knew it was not the time to say what he really felt. Doctor Patel continued to explain that some babies develop Hydrocephalus due to a condition called neural tube defects but he could not be sure this was present in Anna's case.

"Spina bifida, that's what you're saying to me, isn't it?" Anna had been made aware of this condition when she had counselled for a charity organisation called LIFE.

"Mrs de Courtney," and there was sympathy in the Doctor's voice, "we cannot make a definite diagnosis at this stage. All I can say is that normally the spinal cord is protected inside a tube formed by the vertebrae of the spine. With spina bifida, in one part of the spine the vertebral bones do not fully enclose the spinal cord. This sometimes results in the coverings of the cord, the meninges, protruding from the hole. If they do, the nerves in the spinal cord can be damaged.

"So we are looking to see if there is any break in the continuity of the spine, which might suggest a menigocele, a protrusion of the cord, from the baby's spine. As you saw when we scanned your baby's spine, we had difficulty in locating this."

"Meaning?" Anna asked.

Doctor Patel repeated that it was too early to make a firm diagnosis and that more in-depth tests needed to be carried out.

Anna started to cry. Doctor Patel nodded to the nurse, who left and returned almost immediately with a cup of tea and whispered to her not to worry, that modern medicine could do wonders. Anna knew it was kindly meant but it did nothing to allay her fears.

Doctor Patel had become more business-like and told Anna he would make a referral to a private Foetal Doctor. "Do not worry, Mrs de Courtney, we will do all we can." But to Anna's ears his words seemed hollow.

Anna didn't remember leaving the clinic or the drive home. Charles had come home early and Kate, who had earlier seen her mother sitting in the conservatory with a distraught expression on her face had signalled to him. "I think she's upset, best leave it for her to tell us."

Dinner had been a subdued affair, Anna not surprisingly finding it difficult to eat. Her mind was on the baby she was carrying and instinctively she would feel her stomach with her hands; an action that was not lost on Kate.

Kate had left the table to bring in the pudding and Charles had stared across at Anna with growing concern in his eyes.

"Something is wrong, isn't it? Do say." He got up from his chair and stood beside her and then she burst into tears, unable to hold back any longer. Kate had returned to the dining room and sat down.

"Will you tell us, Anna, please?" he drew his chair up beside her, held her hand in his and pleaded with her.

Between sobs Anna related what she had been told that morning. She heard Kate gasp and felt Charles's hand tighten on hers.

"Possibly, spina bifida," Kate repeated the words. "Oh my God," and she too came to sit beside Anna.

Charles stood up and went back to his chair, analysing what Anna had said. "But it's not a firm diagnosis…" He wanted to reassure her but she replied between sobs that she had known deep-down something serious was wrong.

Charles stared down at his pudding and then reached across and picked up the half empty bottle of red wine and refilled his glass. "I don't know anything about spina bifida," he confessed. Briefly Anna outlined the little she knew. Kate was silent and Anna knew that an almighty black cloud had come over them. A disabled child had not been in their equation.

"We'll know more tomorrow," Anna managed to say between sobs.

"You won't be alone, Anna," Charles said with a bleak smile. "I'll come with you."

Anna had not slept that night, her mind was a mish-mash of confused and frightened thoughts. It wasn't the first time that Anna had wished she had never attended mass on that Sunday.

Charles had risen early and at eight-thirty he had telephoned the clinic to ascertain that Anna would be seen on time. Anna sat beside Charles in his Mercedes gliding comfortably along. She felt her body start to shake uncontrollably. Thoughts pounded her head. Without speaking Charles took his left hand off the steering wheel and placed it over her right hand. She closed her eyes to blot out the forthcoming nightmare.

Eventually they arrived at the clinic.

Charles ushered her into the reception area and without any delay they went through into the consulting room. "Good morning," Doctor Cameron rose to greet them and they sat down. They were joined by Doctor Patel who went into a lengthy explanation of the procedure for the morning.

Doctor Cameron went over the notes that Doctor Patel had written and explained what would be done. She ended with, "Mrs de Courtney, I know it is easy to say do not worry, but please believe me you are in good hands. I want you both to come with me to have a chat with the Genetic Counsellor."

Anna felt Charles's hand on her arm as he helped her up from the chair. She felt weak and she leaned heavily on his arm for support as they followed the doctor down a corridor to a smaller consulting room.

The Genetic Counsellor, Doctor Fiona Stewart, who was in her mid forties, gave them both a sympathetic smile as they sat down in front of her desk.

"Would you like a coffee?" Doctor Stewart asked. Anna and Charles shook their heads.

"Well, we'll get this under way. This is the difficult part," Doctor Stewart gave them a warm sympathetic smile. "We need a family history from both of you. Mrs de Courtney, perhaps you could fill in this form?" She slid the two-page document across her desk to Anna. "Will you complete this one Mr de Courtney?"

There was a pause and Anna glanced across at Charles.

"Is there a problem?" Doctor Stewart asked.

"I am not the father of the child," Charles said as he gently slid his form back across the desk and Anna was surprised that there was no sign of embarrassment on his voice.

"Oh, I see!"

Anna could sense that Doctor Stewart was quickly gathering her composure. In normal circumstances Anna knew she would have been tempted to laugh but it was obvious the doctor was unsure how to react to this information.

"Mrs de Courtney," Doctor Stewart had obviously decided to tackle it head on. "Do you know the history and background of the father's family?"

Anna shook her head. "No, I don't."

"Is there any possibility the father would come here, or could you get him to fill in this form?"

There was a silence. Anna rested her head in her hands feeling self-disgust. "Is it that essential?" she managed to ask without raising her eyes.

"Helpful!" the doctor said.

"You must decide, Anna," Charles said quietly.

"I would prefer to leave contacting him at the moment," Anna said decisively as she bent down and, taking the pen Charles held out to her, started to fill the form in.

Once it was completed Anna slid it back across the desk to the Doctor who gave it a cursory glance and then smiled. "There is no family history of spina bifida or any other chromosomal defect?"

Anna shook her head.

The doctor nodded, "We'll do the in-depth ultrasound scan."

Anna got up and looked at Charles for support.

"I'll have a coffee, don't worry."

"You can view the monitor with your wife if you wish, Mr de Courtney," the doctor said, uncertain now of their relationship.

"Oh please, Charles," Anna heard the words and was surprised at her own pleading.

Doctor Patel gave them a swift nod and it was obvious he

wished to get on with the procedure as soon as possible. A gowned Anna lay on the bed as the in-depth ultrasound commended; it lasted an hour. Anna could barely relax as tension built up and she tried to disassociate herself from the scan as Doctor Patel, Doctor Cameron and another doctor went painstakingly about their task. Anna turned to look at the scan and tentatively Charles stood at the foot of the bed.

"It looks so perfect," Anna whispered as the saw the outline of a living moving human. "I can see the hands," Anna cried. "Oh look, Charles, see the fingers moving." The scan showed each hand and foot, two eyes, a nose, a mouth, two legs and arms, two kidneys, two ears, an umbilical cord, and not only could they make out the heart, but to their amazement they could actually see it beating.

"The head?" Anna reached across and gripped Charles's hand.

Doctor Patel did not comment; the scan moved up and down the baby's spine.

"What are you looking for?" Charles asked.

"Just having a closer look at the spine," the radiologist replied.

"You can get up now Mrs de Courtney," he said a few minutes later. "You can get dressed and the nurse will take you for the amniocentesis."

Like a zombie Anna dressed and followed the nurse into a small side room where Doctor Cameron told then about things called NTDs, chromosomal abnormalities and what the amniocentesis test would confirm.

They returned to the Consultant's room, silent and depressed.

"It doesn't look good does it?" Charles said quietly as he sat down and clasped Anna's hands in his.

"No, I have to be honest with you both, it doesn't," Doctor Cameron glanced from one to the other. "The news I have is not as good as I would have liked: so I'll tell you what we think we have found, and while I'm telling you I must ask you to be prepared for what I have to say." This protracted preamble, although ominous, at least gave them a few moments to prepare themselves for the worst.

He gave the disturbing news that they would now have to wait ten days for a final result. "I must warn you that the baby might have a chromosomal abnormality, in addition to the hydrocephalus and spina bifida…" Doctor Cameron stopped and drew the fingers of her hands together. "You do, of course, have a choice."

"A choice!" Anna blinked, "what choice, Doctor?"

"You can terminate your pregnancy."

"Terminate!" she heard her voice rise and felt the pressure from Charles's hands on hers.

"Thank you, Doctor," Charles said, "obviously it is not a decision we can make without some discussion. But thank you, you have been very helpful."

CHAPTER EIGHTEEN

*T*heir drive home was made almost in silence. Anna's mind was in emotional turmoil. It had been confirmed: she was carrying a deformed child. She knew the consequences, and the tremendous burden such cases placed on families. The stresses and strains of the baby's needs. Were she and Charles too old to take on such a life-long burden? What would happen to the child when she and Charles were gone? Would if be fair to place the responsibility on Kate and Steven?

Anna's thoughts were interrupted with a start as she heard the crunch of the tyres on the gravel of their drive. "Come on, we need to sit down and talk," Charles urged as he helped her from the car and guided her into the hall.

Anna gave a weary nod, "I'll go up and change and have a shower first."

She made her way slowly up the stairs and into the bedroom, and flopped down on the bed. Her eyes suddenly focused on the crucifix and she heard herself whispering. "Oh Holy Mary, Mother of God, help me find the strength." She lay for some time, feeling the silence of the house, hearing only voices from her conscience. Again she asked, why had this happened to her? But then she had asked the same question when her mother had started to display the onset of her dementia.

Once she had been angry and resentful that her life was

being swallowed up as a carer; then she had made the difficult decision that it was up to her to alleviate the problem. Then she had taken a life. There would have been no Jack if her mother had been alive, and no Jack would mean no problem baby. It was a set of consequences she alone had set into motion. Now she alone had to make the decision to take another life or to take on the role she so resented last time around, that of a carer. To have a baby such as hers would mean sacrifice; a disabled child required unceasing care that would stretch unrelentingly year on year.

Now she had a decision to make. Life or death? Should she give the baby a chance or should she put a stop to the trauma before the emotional ties became too strong? Anna remembered counselling sessions where she listened to people in exactly the same position she was now in. Then, she had found it easy to secretly judge and condemn when women had agreed to abort, but now she realised the old saying of: *Never judge another person until you have walked a mile in their shoes.*

"Are you all right?" Charles asked as she joined him sometime later in the conservatory.

"Yes, thank you – I think so." She sat down in the chair opposite Charles and crossed one jeaned leg over the other: "Quite a day." She glanced at the plate of sandwiches and the glass of orange juice on the table.

"Thought you might be hungry," Charles said, a trifle self-consciously. She picked up a sandwich and bit into it. "I am, you have been very patient, Charles. I honestly do not know how I could have got through the morning without you."

He picked up his glass of beer and drank half before saying, "You've thought about what Doctor Cameron said?"

"I have been able to think of nothing else. And you, Charles?" She bowed her head.

"Anna, the decision is yours."

"But you must have an opinion."

"Of course I have an opinion – and we can talk it over – but the final decision is definitely yours," he said decisively. "I'll support you in whatever course of action you decide to take," he concluded.

"There is such a responsibility in having a disabled child," she murmured; "we are not young, you want to retire and travel, I would be inflicting a burden on the family." She looked up; he returned her gaze with an impassive stare.

"An abortion would put an end to the trauma..." he said cautiously. "...on the other hand... a Life is a Life."

Anna realised that Charles would not make the decision for her. Suddenly she thought of her mother and the feelings of guilt she experienced after her death. It seemed the right time to tell Charles about her mother's final days. "I have to tell you something – it may help you to understand that I cannot have another death on my conscience."

He raised his eyes and stared across at her.

Anna had promised herself that her mother's secret was to be just that and now she realised the gamble she was taking by telling Charles. Would he react as Jack had done? Would he walk away from her, leave her and the baby to cope alone? But Anna had no choice. She knew she had to pour out her guilt once more to Charles. First, her affair. Then the baby. And now her mother. How much could Charles take? And what type of person would it make her look to him?

Quietly she related the progress of her mother's illness, her descent from a pleasant, active, person into a mumbling, incompetent wreck; her own bitter dilemma, the destructing effects of her will and ability to choose by the almost total deprivation of sleep, her mother's death – liberating for them both... And finally the bitter truth: "I ended her life, Charles."

She found herself trembling and was conscious of tears

276

running freely down her cheeks. There was a period of silence that reminded Anna of the desperate atmosphere that lingered in the bedroom after she had told Jack the very same story.

"Anna, my dear," Charles said very quietly. "Don't distress yourself unnecessarily, I knew you helped your mother at the end... No," he held his hand up as she gasped, her eyes wide as she stared at him.

"You knew?" Anna was shocked. "How?"

"Your manner, your distress at the funeral, the circumstances of the death and because I know you!"

"You are saying I am a murderer?"

He shook his head gently. "No, I am saying you care and you couldn't see your mother living in such impoverished, degrading conditions."

She lowered her eyes and stared down at her hands before saying. "Then you know why I cannot have an abortion. I cannot have another death on my conscience."

Charles smiled inwardly; it had been the decision he knew she would make and he listened as she went on.

"The decision doesn't just involve me, it involves you, Charles." She shook her head. "You know if you want to walk away, travel, enjoy retirement, I will understand; this is my problem – I have to accept it."

"Anna! How could you imagine I'd walk away? This is one good reason now for remaining together." He smiled across at her. "It is a very hard decision, it would be so easy to have the abortion. The years ahead, you've thought, will be fraught with problems. I am older than you, you could be left with a disabled child. It is going to be a lifetime's commitment for the family."

As they chatted on they realised they both had to learn more about spina bifida. Charles had told Anna he would get all the information he could. He reassured her and some of the fear she felt dissipated.

It was Charles who told Steven, Charles who guided him into giving Anna an immediately compassionate response. Anna saw the flash of fear on Steven's face.

"Oh Mum," Steven said and there were tears in his eyes. "I am so sorry, we'll get through it." But there was little conviction in his voice. Charles gave Anna a brief nod, got up and followed Steven out of the conservatory, placing an arm round his shoulders as he caught him up. It was some time before Kate and Charles returned and it was obvious to Anna that there had been a family discussion. Anna sat reflecting sadly on the events; she had not expected such love and care from her family and silently she gave a prayer to the Mother of God.

The following fortnight had been fraught with tension for all the family. If Kate and Steven were annoyed that their once happy and easy life was going to be disrupted by a disabled child, then they did not say anything – at least to Anna's face.

The appointment to discuss the results of her tests had loomed large in Anna's diary. Now, on the appointed date, Charles accompanied her back to the clinic.

Once there Anna and Charles were ushered into Doctor Cameron's room and the question they had anticipated was asked the moment he had told them the clinical diagnosis.

"Do you propose to carry this baby to full term, Mrs de Courtney?" Doctor Cameron asked, in what seemed to Anna a matter of fact tone.

"Yes."

Doctor Cameron gave a warm understanding smile. "Perhaps it would help you if you knew the sex?"

Anna looked at Charles with a querying expression. Suddenly this information would personalise the baby. Anna nodded.

"You are carrying a daughter."

Anna started to cry. "Then I'll call her Jenna," she said

involuntarily, and Charles leant across and placed his hand over hers. She pondered over her sudden decision about the name: she hadn't given it a moment's thought before. Then she knew why the name had flashed into her mind, and she experienced a glow of satisfaction.

They left the consulting room and Anna went through the previous routine and lay back on the bed in the ultrascan room as Doctor Patel proceeded to scan her. They had discussed that it was best for Anna to try and identify and understand the area of Jenna's abnormality.

"You can see it," Doctor Patel said and pointed to an area of white and black.

Anna peered, "What should I see?"

"The hole in her spine. There is a gap in the upper sacral/lower lumbar region of the vertebrae," Doctor Patel explained. Seeing the querying expression in Charles's eyes he continued: "The sacral area is at the pelvis, lumbar is at waist level, thoracic is at chest level, and cervical is the neck area."

"Is that good or bad?" Charles asked.

Doctor Patel stated a low lesion was better. The lower the hole, the more function Jenna would have in her legs and bladder. Other information such as the size of the gap, and if there were any nerve endings protruding out of it, needed to be considered as well. Anna, he advised, still had a long time left and a lot could happen and that Jenna could still fall into a wide range of functionality.

On the journey home Charles had asked, why Jenna?

"My mother's middle name was Jennifer," Anna replied.

Charles gave a silent nod of agreement.

The confirmation that Anna was carrying a spina bifida baby had jogged Charles into action. He had spent hours in the library, returning home with as much information as he could lay his hands on. He had telephoned societies and searched out self-help groups.

With the help of Steven, Anna went on the Internet and looked up web sites containing information on spina bifida.

At one stage Anna waited self-consciously for a series of pictures to download. She had half expected the pictures to reveal children who looked sad and awful. But all she saw kept seeing was beautiful, joyful kids with *big* happy smiles

Anna was slowly coming to come to terms with the fact that Jenna was badly deformed. She had continued attending early morning mass and had smilingly acknowledged Father Mathews' enquiries of, "Are you keeping well, Anna?"

After a few weeks after the official diagnosis she had told him, "I am carrying a baby with spina bifida!" How bald; how uncaring she had made it sound! Father Mathews had just stared at her, hardly dumbstruck but totally reticent. But when she had told him of Charles's unyielding support and the family's incredible contribution, he had smiled sympathetically at her; he then placed a hand on her arm and gave it a decorous squeeze.

"God Bless you, Anna," he had said softly, and she saw the care and concern in his eyes.

For the next few months clinic visits were to become a regular occurrence. The family had seemed to accept that Jenna would be different and had planned their life accordingly. Charles had continued to surprise Anna; he had even taken her away on a weekend break to Bournemouth. It was relaxing at the time, but once home Anna still experienced attacks of self-doubt.

Although her family had accepted the dilemma, for Anna it was the total opposite. She was carrying Jenna and everything inside her felt different.

Some days she just wanted a break from carrying Jenna, a

time to think, ponder, but with the baby inside her, how could she? Anna wanted to desperately bond with Jenna, but was afraid too.

Anna would often remember with affection the precious moments after Steven and Kate were born. But this time was different. Jenna needed immediate surgery. Curiosity also consumed Anna's thoughts. Would Jenna have normal intelligence or be mentally delayed? Would she walk or have to use a wheel chair? Any other abnormalities? What about using the bathroom? But most importantly, would Jenna be happy? So many thoughts drove Anna mad at times. The unknown was the worst part. The family didn't care if Jenna was going to be totally non-verbal and non-responsive. They just wanted some concrete information.

So Anna kept on praying to the Lord for strength and peace of mind. She diverted her attention from the wondering by gathering even more information about spina bifida. She went frequently to the library and checked out the books they had and had joined many local self-help societies. It wasn't much, but it helped her gain some perspective of what was ahead. She also used this as a reference when the doctors gave her new information on Jenna's condition.

Life at home for Anna was one of continuous change. Some days she would feel happy, even contented; others she would spend most of the time lying on her bed looking at the ultrasound photographs of Jenna inside her given to her by Doctor Patel. Charles, not for the first time, had wondered if the whole traumatic affair was getting too much for her but on re-reading the books he had on spina bifida pregnancies realised that this was a quite normal reaction. He and Anna had kept in constant contact with the local support group and both of them found this to be a crutch in their time of need.

A turning point in their relationship came one Sunday afternoon. Anna was lying down in her bedroom when the phone rang. Thinking it was Steven she picked it up only to hear a man enquiring about a car for sale. She had called out to Charles and listened as he had picked up the receiver.

"Oh yes," Charles said, "it's a Morris Traveller…"

Anna stared at the phone as she replaced the receiver. Charles was actually selling 'that car', as she called it. He had not mentioned it to her and she tried to analyse his reasoning. He came into the room ten minutes later. "You're selling that car?" she said, surprise in her voice. A flash of embarrassment swept momentarily over his face and he gave a faint nod. "You're buying something else?" she asked as she fiddled with a paper tissue, avoiding his eyes.

"No, I'm not replacing it."

"Why not?"

He sat on the edge of the bed and leaned forward and took her hand in his. "I've suddenly found it's surplus to requirements." She stared at him for a moment and then he smiled.

In view of Jenna's condition, Doctor Cameron had said there was no option but to perform a C-section on Anna.

Charles, Kate and Anna had attended morning Mass the day before Anna went into the clinic. As Anna took the sacrament she gave a silent prayer for the safe delivery of Jenna. Father Mathews greeted them warmly as the walked into the Narthex.

"We will pray for you, Anna," he said, as he smiled from one to the other. "I look forward to baptising your daughter."

"Thank you, Father," Anna whispered softly and in that moment felt as if the burden of her sins had begun to be lifted.

In her bedroom the night before the operation Anna had quietly lain on her bed and thought about the traumatic months that had past. She didn't think of Jack with any bitterness now; their affair seemed such a long time ago. She wondered what he was doing. Did he ever think about her and his child? No, she didn't think he did. The possibility of dying came into Anna's thoughts. Would she die during the C-section? Would the baby? Again these were questions that had no answers.

Anna had her C-section on Wednesday 21st April, 1999 and Jenna was born at around lunch time. Ironically it was within a few calendar days of the day her mother died. Charles and Kate had spent the morning pacing up and down the hospital corridor. Steven had even travelled up to give his support.

The family came in to her private room and crowded round her bed when she returned from the operating theatre. The NICU nurse came into the room, a crying bundle in her arms. "Your daughter has good lungs."

Anna felt the tears coursing down her cheeks. It was over at last: this was the proof of all their decisions, their anguish. A howling yelling bundle!

"She is our beautiful daughter," Anna said, knowing now that she had seen the baby that whatever lay ahead they would all be able to cope with it.

EPILOGUE

*O*n the day after Jenna came home Anna had watched Charles from the bedroom window. He had risen early and put on a green gilet, old corduroy trousers and green wellington boots. He had stood in the garden and she could see from his stance he was happy. She watched as he painstakingly gathered together the leaves with the rake, and methodically built a bonfire.

Anna had gone down the stairs and into the kitchen and made two mugs of coffee and then putting on her anorak and boots she had gone out into the garden.

"Coffee?" He turned aside from the roaring flames he was poking with a metal bar as she handed him the mug.

He took it and gave a small self-conscious smile as she moved towards the fire, not believing what she saw as she peered down amongst the flames. A gust of wind caught one of the wigs and it sizzled at her feet. Anna watched as Charles emptied the contents of another bin bag containing a gaudy dress, tubes of make-up and an assortment of catalogues onto the fire. Charles raked over them until they were consumed to ashes.

"Charles!" she turned giving him a querying expression.

"I don't think I need this stuff any more," he said quietly. "We've all changed because of Jenna!" He stopped and she walked across to him and took his hand in hers.

Six months had now passed since Anna gave birth. Jenna was home after complicated surgery after the meningal sac had burst and needed to be closed to prevent infection. Then a shunt had to be inserted into the right ventricle of her brain and tunnelled beneath the skin to Jenna's stomach to drain away excess fluid. Anna and the family had been totally unprepared for the demands, care and time Jenna would require. No amount of books, talks, counselling sessions or helplines fully prepared them for the change in their lifestyle. There was little spare time to contemplate each day and far less on what the future held. The world now revolved round Jenna and her needs, and they were great and many.

The family continued to be Anna's rock. Their support, understanding and compassion had made them into a unit. Kate had changed from a frivolous teenager into a serious, compassionate person capable of attending to Jenna's needs so that Anna and Charles would have an evening out every week. Steven too, after an initial period of resentment and rebellion had found the changed atmosphere within the family incorporated his own needs. He previously could not talk to Anna or Charles but now found he could sit and they would listen to him. Anna watched his growing confidence. Even Hector had accepted Jenna and would often snooze on the chair next to her cot.

Anna still attended early morning mass to sit quietly in the pew, it was her time to put her thoughts in order. Sometimes she would give a surreptitious glance across the aisle and in her mind's eye see Jack striding across towards her. But it was a distant and fading memory. She would often think of her mother, knowing the demands she had made on Anna were infinitesimal compared to the demands made by Jenna.

"The mills of God grind slow, but grind exceeding sure..." she could hear her mother's voice for the first time in years. Her mother as the person she had been. Anna was not sure if she

remembered the quotation correctly, but she knew it was true. Through tragedy, infidelity, deceit and depression she had emerged a more rounded human being. She had drawn them to her, made them a family, made Charles a man again. Given him self-respect and, yes, love. Not the searing passion she and Jack had experienced, but a gentle, needful love.

Learning about spina bifida and Jenna had taken over their lives, drawing them together in a mutual bond. Charles had bought his own computer and with determination had struggled to grasp its intricacies. He had even set up a website and organised local support groups and meetings were held in their house. It had been Charles who had taken the burden onto his shoulders and Anna could not believe the dramatic change that had taken place. He had become so positive in outlook and so devoted to Jenna that at times Anna could feel the tears in her eyes as she watched him sitting beside the cot.

"There are no miracles," Anna had said to the family on one occasion and Charles had replied with a quiet smile.

"Sometimes God's miracles consist of not answering our prayers."

Anna had long since put Jack to the back of her mind. So his telephone call one afternoon, when Charles had been persuaded by her to go out for a long walk with Seth, brought her up short. What could he want? Jack had sounded unsure as he asked how she was. "The baby?" his voice had been tentative. "I heard about her. Mary and I live in Dublin now, I work for her father. Anna, can I come round?"

She hesitated; but then, because she wanted him to be aware of what the family had had to face, agreed to the following afternoon. That evening she told Charles of the proposed visit.

"Are you sure?" he had asked and she had heard the underlying concern in his voice.

"Yes, I want him to see Jenna," she said softly. "And I want him to know that you are formally adopting her."

The wait for Jack to arrive seemed to Anna like a flashback to another time. But on this occasion Jack arrived promptly. There was no battered orange Beetle but this time he drove up in a new red Fiesta. He got out of the car and noticed that Anna's BMW had now been replaced with a new Range Rover. He stood staring at the house, and Anna knew he was remembering. Jack was formally dressed in a dark suit, white shirt and striped tie. His hair had been cut and he was clean-shaven. He looked like an accountant, a married accountant at that. He was dressed as Charles had once dressed, she thought with a wry smile; she left the window and walked down the stairs to open the front door.

Jack stared at her, unsure what to expect. Motherhood seemed to have enhanced her beauty; it had softened her face, mellowing her features. Even the worry lines on her forehead seemed to add a new dimension to her attraction. Her hair was still luxuriously long, her eyes still ocean blue and her smile as captivating as before.

She was dressed casually in slacks and shirt and slip-on shoes.

"Anna!" He whispered her name, wanting to tell her she was as beautiful as the time he first saw her and he suddenly realised that he could easily fall for her all over again. She read his thoughts and gave a secret smile of contentment. He took her hand into his, seeing with surprise that the nails were no longer red talons, but cut short to a practical length. She saw his gaze.

"Long nails and babies don't go well together!" She said, faintly amused. "Come in, Jack." She held the door open and he could see she was in control of the situation.

"A teddy bear!" he said, indicating the package he was holding as he followed her into the hall.

"You know, of course, Jenna's condition?" she said in a

matter-of-fact voice. She had decided not to indulge in small talk and she walked across to the day nursery and opened the door. "This was my mother's room," she said, standing aside so he could enter the light bright room, with the carefully stimulating mobiles, pictures and toys. "Charles did all the decorating himself," he heard the pride in her voice as she walked across to where Jenna lay. He stood awkwardly by the cot and looked down at his daughter.

After a few seconds he looked at Anna and said, "She's beautiful," and there was a hint of a tear in his eyes as he stumbled on, "That last meeting with you… my attitude was unforgivable. I am so sorry," he said and Anna knew he meant every word.

"Sorry you suggested I should have an abortion?" she asked, her eyebrows raised in a querying manner. "Or sorry for the comments you made about my mother?"

"Both!" Jack said simply. "You'd had enough of my unjust condemnation. I behaved like a real bastard to you on the two occasions you needed me most. I was afraid… I was going to phone or write." He gave a self-deprecatory shrug. "Then the wedding and the move to Dublin." He paused and repeated again. "I am sorry, you deserved so much more from me than I gave you. Do you have any regrets about having…"

"Jenna? "She walked across and placed a hand lightly on the sleeve of his jacket. "No, Jack, I have no regrets at all."

"I am glad," he said simply.

He asked about the birth and she told him and although he tried to detect resentment or depression he had to admit he could not. Anna looked contented. He frowned, saying with surprise, "You seem happy, Anna."

"I am, Jack," she gave a laugh. "I really am!"

She could see he wanted to ask about her relationship with Charles, and was glad that he did not. She would have told him that yes, Charles had returned to her bedroom and bed. There were no great sexual highs or lows, just a reassuring need to give and to receive.

"You and Mary, are you happy?"

Anna saw the vague smile on his lips and instinctively knew he had become the person he least wished to become. A husband.

Jack sighed, not wishing to tell her he did not enjoy the constraints of his work, his life nor his responsibility. He missed the outdoor life, the freedom, but most of all he knew he missed Anna.

"Yes, I'm happy," he hesitated for a moment and added, "Mary is expecting…" He stopped.

"Oh Jack, I am pleased for you both."

"It's sooner than I expected, but…" He shrugged and there was a sadness in his voice, and Anna knew responsibility was lying heavy on his shoulders.

They talked generalities, neither mentioning the past, and after fifteen minutes Jack looked at his watch and murmured it was time he left.

"You don't wear I the watch I gave you?" Anna asked.

"No – but I'll always keep it." And there was a hint of a tear in his eye.

They stood together in the porch; it was a brief moment of remembrance for both of them; Jack leaned forward and kissed Anna lightly on the cheek. He walked to the car, steeling himself not to give a backward glance. He needn't have bothered: Anna had closed the front door, and wasn't there to see him drive away.